London Triptych

ARSENAL PULP PRESS VANCOUVER

London Triptych

Jonathan Kemp

First North American edition: 2013

Published originally in Great Britain by Myriad Editions

ARSENAL PULP PRESS
Suite 101 – 211 East Georgia St.
Vancouver, BC V6A 1Z6
Canada
arsenalpulp.com

Book design by Gerilee McBride
Cover image by Alex Dellow, Hulton Archive (Getty Images)

Printed and bound in Canada

Library and Archives Canada Cataloguing in Publication:
Kemp, Jonathan, 1967-
    London triptych / Jonathan Kemp.

Issued also in electronic format.
ISBN 978-1-55152-502-0

    I. Title.

PR6111.E526L66 2013   823'.92   C2012-906807-1

For George Cayford

A man's very highest moment is, I have no doubt at all, when he kneels in the dust, and beats his breast, and tells all the sins of his life.

—*Oscar Wilde, De Profundis*

1954

Another arrest reported in the papers this morning. Some poor sod caught in a public toilet. Hardly a week goes by without one. Now, I can't claim to know much about it, but it seems to me that when old men hang around public toilets while younger men are pissing, we aren't out for a glimpse of cock, or even a grope. No, in truth what roots us to the spot is the most profound feeling of envy because we can't piss like that any more. Respect, even. When you reach fifty, it trickles out.

He pisses like a horse. I can hear him through the whole house. A veritable Niagara. It's not a big house—he calls it "the doll's house," to my chagrin. Tall as he is, he's forever banging his head on my lampshades and doorjambs, as I totter behind him. He strides through my tiny rooms with such confidence and familiarity, as if it were a castle and he its prince, and I feel like the valet who can call nothing here my own.

He has so much life in him that it's made me realize for the first time that I am old. And it's not a feeling I'm happy with. Not at all. It's not something I ruminated on and came to a calm decision about. Not something I've been refusing to accept and can no longer hold in abeyance. I simply looked at my face in the mirror and said aloud, "You are old." It's not even the exterior that made me gasp with horror—the grey hair, the lined face, the tarnished eyes. These things I know. I see them every day. I can live with looking old, just about. Or at least I could, until recently. But I have met a boy whose youth makes me feel ancient to the very core, ossified and pointless. That's what made me smart.

When I first saw him, a month or so ago, I thought him quite the handsomest boy I'd seen in a long time. He wears his hair slicked into a quiff, and sports the general attire of what a newspaper last year nicknamed Teddy Boys. But when he removed his clothing I realized for the first time what I'd been missing in a model: someone who shines more when they are nude than when clothed. Skin with light trapped beneath it. Skin that looks complete, rather than exposed; that looks painted, full of colour and life, blood blue and flesh pink. Yellows, purples, whites. Tints I don't know I could ever reproduce. Strangely, he seems more relaxed when naked, more himself, more at home in his flesh than in his clothes. And because of that you don't really notice that he is naked.

His body is not exceptional, but he has tremendous definition, and a masculine grace that is best expressed by the word "noble," if that doesn't sound too grand. When he speaks, however, it is with the jagged edges of simplicity. And, while that is not without its charm, it is clear that the sophistication of his being is concentrated on the surface. All his grace lies there, beautiful and richly visible. Within is merely an embryonic soul, his speech suggesting nothing but the workings of a half-grown heart.

In the presence of such concentrated beauty, I feel inspired for the first time in eons: inspired to capture it in all its complexity and texture, all its pale beauty. I fill acres of paper with his crouched figure, his legs bent and twisted beyond recognition, his spine an abacus, a string of pearls arching impossibly as he nearly swallows himself like Ouroboros. The damp, dark caves of his armpits. The hairless plateau of his belly, tight and contoured. The planed edges of his muscular buttocks, carved to Hellenic perfection. If I placed my tongue there, I should expect them to be cold and hard as marble. The masculine sweep from his hairline to the right angle of his shoulder as fluid and mesmerising as any waterfall; the line of gravity that runs the length of his torso, from the hollow of his throat to the jewel of his navel, cruciformed by the stigmata of his nut-brown nipples blurred with hair; the pucker of his anus like a knot in a tree.

I can't help but wonder what it must feel like to be so exposed to the gaze of another, to know that you are being stared at and scrutinized. We seem to be obsessed with doing everything in our power to deny or avoid the thorny question of the body unclothed, except perhaps in art. All we have now is shame, and fig leaves, and sniggering like schoolgirls. All we have is prudery. How then does this young man feel, spread out before me? How can he not feel shame? I wonder.

After he left today, I walked into the bathroom and looked at myself in the mirror, and it was then that I muttered like an incantation the words *You are old*, the second-person address granting a distance that in no way diminished the painful truth. His presence diminishes me. And it is more than feeling too old to interest him sexually, and more than wanting my own youth back again: I am racked with envy that I am not him. They say desire and identification are almost indistinguishable, but I never understood it till I saw him in all his luminescence—a thing I have certainly never possessed. I removed my clothes and stood naked before the mirror, something I haven't done for at least forty years. It shocked me, suddenly, to reflect that at no point in my life, beyond that curiosity which adolescence precipitates, have I paid any attention to my body. I looked at my reflection, at my rounded, narrow shoulders with their tufts of grey hair, my rotund belly, my shrivelled privates, my stick-white legs, and I felt nothing but a deep, vertiginous sadness.

There comes a time in life when youth becomes just a word; a word whose meaning you almost feel impelled to look up in a dictionary, so strangely does it sit upon the tongue. I think it was Oscar Wilde—or was it George Bernard Shaw?—who said that youth is wasted on the young. And he was right. You look back on your own youth and view it with the eyes of another person, and it seems as foreign as another country, as distant as a star.

But sometimes, if you are lucky, you are allowed to view another's youth up close and scrutinize the glory and the invincibility of that infallible state. Perhaps that is why people have children. And, by the same token, that must be why childless old men like myself feel it all the more brutally, and crave it in others. I cannot now recall what it felt like to be young. I suppose that is because I was too busy *being* young to think about it. Or perhaps because my youth does not in truth warrant recollection. But I must have been a youth, at some stage in my life, all things considered! Must have been in some sense flawless and innocent—but again these are words whose definition evades me. Photographs must supply some clue. Almost another face entirely stares back at me though, from the few I do possess, never having liked to have my picture taken. I see in them a stranger, whose ways and wiles I no longer recollect; whose passions and fears are irretrievable now.

Christ, and I'm only fifty-four.

This young man has awoken me not to the value of my own youth, but to its tarnished loss and frivolous and unforgivable waste. He is a free spirit, as free a spirit as I have ever known, whereas I have never felt free. So, while his presence is a source of joy, it is also a source of incredible pain, throwing into stark relief the woeful inadequacies of my life.

1998

This night is the place from which I must move forward. I'm to be released tomorrow and resume my life, yet there are so many questions crowding my thoughts as I recall the events that led me here. When I walk out of here tomorrow morning, I would like to feel I'd left it all behind, but I brought it all in here with me, and I'll take it with me when I go. The past has a crushing substance. I'm on a tightrope, high above the ground, assailed by fear and panic, no safety net beneath me. I daren't look down and I daren't look back. I don't know what tomorrow looks like. But I need to try, at least, to understand. I need you, of all people, to understand me. It's because of you, after all, that I ended up in prison. But one of the many lessons I learnt in here is that things are what they are and will be what they will be.

This is for you, Jake. I never told you much about my past during the brief time I knew you. One of the great things about our time together is how in-the-moment it all was, how little we actually shared about our lives outside of the here and now of our bodies together. Not that we didn't speak, but somehow our childhoods, our pasts, never surfaced much as a topic of conversation. I've tried my best to erase mine, and not to have to speak of it to you was something I cherished. So this is for you, whether you read these words or not.

It's for me too, of course, though for completely different reasons.

As children, my elder brother and I, together with a group of other kids, would play on a nearby railway track, by a tunnel through which goods trains would occasionally pass—great rusting hulks of metal following one another in single file. We played chicken, standing on the tracks for as long as we dared as the train hurtled toward us. I always won, was always the last one standing there as the train rammed its way nearer. Every time, the others would flee to the sides of the track, leaving me alone, my heart racing. I can still remember watching the front of the train darken as it passed from sunlight into the black mouth of the tunnel. Only then would I run to the sidings. This wasn't an act of bravery. It took no courage on my part, because I didn't care that the train might pulverize me. I just wanted the rush that came from imagining my flesh spread across the front of that train. Even then, at that age, I used danger as a way of escaping boredom.

Growing up, I wanted for nothing. I had any toy I desired. I had affection, security, I never went hungry, my parents never missed a birthday, never neglected or beat me. In fact, they gave every sign of loving me—or if they didn't love me they certainly knew their duty and performed it well. They were good parents, and I was a good boy, an angel—never getting into trouble, never offending, always polite. Not because I wanted to be good, particularly, but because it was easier than doing anything else. Nothing existed for me—nothing real anyway. Fuelled by television, books and, most importantly, music, I constructed another place, a place I could value. In that tiny village I was cursed to endure, life was a thing with no value. The people around me seemed to live their lives like a person with one foot nailed to the floor, inscribing a perfect circle in the rotten earth and calling it home. Not only were the houses where we lived semi-detached, so were most of the lives. I longed to escape.

The lights have just been put out. I can hear my cellmate, Tony, beneath me, beginning to snore as he slides into sleep. Before long he'll be snoring louder than a sow in labour, and I envy him that sweet release into oblivion. He's from Hornchurch. In for stealing a car. He's not been here long, and no real friendship has developed between us. I've struggled to find some common ground, but every conversation gets beached by our differences and our inability to communicate. I'll probably never see him again. And I probably won't sleep tonight. Too many memories crowding in, vying for attention.

As if that ever did any good, raking over the past.

Because I'd spent my childhood doing more or less exactly as I was told, it was assumed that I would continue to do so. On the night before I had to confirm my O-level options, my father mapped out the entire geography of my future. I was told what I would do with the rest of my life. And the flatness of the terrain he described made me despair. He wanted me to have a secure future. He wanted me to become an accountant, or at least "in business" at some level. Something secure, something steady and lucrative. My father, who was a bank manager, not just by profession but also by nature, spoke to me that night as if he were turning me down for a loan. The subjects I loved—art and English literature—were not considered at all, while the subjects I hated—mathematics and economics, physics and chemistry—were attached to me like shackles. I nodded as he spoke, and the narrowness of my future oppressed me.

When my father was a baby, his mother taped his ears back onto his head while he slept in his cot in order to prevent them folding forward and sticking out permanently.

Sometimes, it seemed to me as if that tape had never been removed, and it prevented him from hearing anything I said. Each morning the same routine: he'd slice twenty discs of banana onto his cereal, and if, after twenty, he had a stump of fruit left, he would look up forlornly, unsure what to do with the excess. My mother would hold out her hand for him to drop it into her cupped palm. If he were ever to articulate what he feels about life, I'm certain he would claim that habit is the only route to happiness, or at least success.

My mother, in her own way, was equally taped down. Her overwhelming desire for an easy life rendered her incapable of contradicting anything he said. A more repressed human being I've yet to meet. She died three months after I was sent here. Cancer. I still haven't cried about it. I've cried about lots of things, myself mostly, but not her. I've had one visitor. An old client, now more of a friend—Gregory. Over the past year or so, he's come here regularly, almost like my confessor. I told him I hadn't kept in touch with my family at all, and he said I should write. I did, knowing they wouldn't have moved address since I left. The first letter from my father told me about my mother.

It didn't occur to me at the time that I had any other option than to accept—or at least to give the appearance of accepting—their terms. From that point until I completed my O-levels two years later, I began a life of duplicity in order to survive. Lies became my way of cheating boredom, the portal I would crawl through to reach a world in which I could breathe.

To the outside world—and, most importantly, to my parents—I was the perfect scholar. Although I hated the subjects they foisted upon me, I knew the secret to an easy life lay in doing well at school, for the time being at least. So I spent my days studying maths and economics, and I spent my nights with my friends—and they were not the sort of people of whom my parents would have approved.

A school friend of mine, Phil, was working at the time in a small bistro in a posh part of town, washing dishes from seven till midnight, seven nights a week. Under the pretext of working there, I was able to stay out every night till late. Dad liked the idea that I was willing to work. In reality, far from spending my time elbow-deep in boiling suds and grease, I cycled each night to the local golf course, to meet a crowd with whom I could smoke and drink myself into oblivion. There was Spike, with his skinhead and boxer's brawn, whose stepfather was forever in and out of prison and whose mother was too pissed to care what he got up to. Sometimes he would steal a car and drive us up to Saddleworth Moor. He was related to one of the victims of the murders that had taken place in the city in the mid-'60s, and he would take us to the spot he claimed the dead girl had been buried. Johnny, Spike's cousin, had long hair and wore AC/DC T-shirts. His elder brother was a dealer, and he always had what seemed like an endless supply of dope and acid. The lights of the city hummed the colour of radioactivity as we drove back home. Heather, Johnny's girlfriend, was all shaggy hair and denim. They both head-banged along to the loud rock music that was played in the car. But Julie was my favourite. Julie never head-banged. Julie looked like Marilyn Monroe, or so we thought. She confided in me once that she was actually trying her best to look like *Mike* Monroe, from Hanoi Rocks, but no one seemed to care much. She wore her hair impeccably bleached and her skirts explicitly short, and was known as the village bike because she let most boys do pretty much anything with her. Most of the time, though, she was Spike's girlfriend.

I thought that only drugs or music could supply me with the transgressive thrill I sought. I never gave sex much thought. I had had a lacklustre and lustless grope with Julie one night before she and Spike started what my grandmother would quaintly call "courting," but on the whole I knew even then that I preferred boys—knew that I would rather be kissing Spike. I hid this desire beneath a smog of drugs, claiming a cynical lack of interest in anything sexual, even though I imagined Spike naked and tied to my bed each time I masturbated. Spike and the others mockingly called me the Poet because books and the lyrics to songs—and the thoughts they inspired—were more important to me than trying to get laid. Whenever we got stoned, they would all sink into torpor around me while I grew more and more animated by my own fucked-up monologue, till one of them would shout, "Hey, Poet, fuckin' *can* it, will ya?"

Then I discovered whoring.

I wanted more than anything to leave this world behind, but

not in order to destroy myself; only in order to find another world, one in which bodies glowed and danced like flames. Such a world is not found, however, but must be created anew each time we want to live in it. I know that much at least.

1894

The name's Jack Rose, or Rosy Jack, as the gents like to call me, on account of that soft pink bud nestling between me rosy arse cheeks. I'm a Maryanne, see, and gentlemen pays me handsomely to do things I should likely enough do for free, though the cash definitely helps, make no mistake. Steamers, we call 'em, the gents what come around; or swells or swanks: moneyed geezers, well-mannered, classy, not like the lowlife I knew before I started in this game. But they all, to a man, love that arse of mine, love watching it pucker and pout, the filthy bastards—love to poke it, finger it, sniff it, lick it, fill it, fuck it. And I love them to do it, I'm not ashamed to admit. But I love too the gifts and cash what they show their appreciation of my little rosy star with—my asterisk of flesh, my puckered pal. This hole of mine has turned out to be a right little golden goose.

I don't suppose boys are any different from girls in liking to take presents from those what are fond of us. There isn't much wrong in gents showing their appreciation of the finer things in life with a trinket or a few shillings, is there now? I wasn't the first and I doubt very much I'll be the last, that much I do know. I know too that it is a harsh world, and harder still in this bloody shit hole city of London I was pushed into. Fuckin' impossible if the jaws of poverty hold you as they hold me ma and pa and the other seven miserable brats he sired. If that's your lot you'd do well to keep your eyes shut and crawl right back into the cunt you came from, if only that was an option. Instead we open our eyes and crawl forward, lambs to the slaughter every last one of us. A smack on the arse and you've no bloody choice is the truth of the matter. Every day a fuckin' battle. So if you can claw back a little happiness, a little pleasure, a little laughter and joy, it's no crime. It'll come as no surprise then when I confess that I feel like the king of the world when a coin is pressed into my palm after being pleasured. It's bleedin' hilarious to be making money so easily, isn't it? And this line of work takes me places I'd never have seen otherwise, that's for sure. When you have nothing to begin with you only stand to gain, and the way of life most rich gents take for granted seems to me to be the trappings of heaven itself. And the police are kind to me after their fashion. They shut their eyes for the most part—but then they've shut their eyes to worse than me and no mistake. The things I've seen in this town would make even old Queen Vic crack a smile.

Odd the way I fell into the whole business, really. By accident, you might say. I certainly never planned it, but then again I don't suppose anyone ever sets out to become a whore, do they? It was a bollock-numbing January in '93 and I was several months past my fifteenth birthday, though I looked much younger. Skinny as a runt and no trace of a beard as yet, though I had sprouted a soft dark down on my privates, which thrilled me. I was running telegrams. Fuckin' awful, it was. Perhaps you've known it yourself, that horror when you realize all your time is being given over to others, all your thoughts are about day-to-day survival. Perhaps like me you've felt yourself chained to a fate you detest. I don't know. Where I grew up, ugliness was the one and only reality; joy was unheard of except for the odd booze-up or street fight. I was working about fifteen hours a day running around in all weathers.

I was born and raised in Bethnal Green, a stinkin' hole of a place with a cesspit the size of a small lake down the road from our home that filled the air with the stench of shit the whole time. We shared the house with three other families. We had no running water, so going for a piss or a crap meant finding a space that hadn't already been used—in or outside the house. We were all of us permanently sick, and two of my sisters died before even learning to walk. My pa is a useless alcoholic crook. Never done a day's work in his life. Robs to get his beer money, and we never saw a penny of it. He's violent and spiteful, too, to all of us. One day I came home to find my two little sisters, Millie and Flossie, crying something awful and, when I could finally get some sense out of them, it seems Pa'd got them to pull on a piece of string threaded through a keyhole in the front door. "Pull it hard, girls," he'd said, so they did, eager to please their pa, not knowing that on the other side of the door the string was tied around the neck of a stray cat. He swung the door open to show them the poor strangled beast hanging there, dead by their own fair hands. That amused him no end. The cunt.

He beats Ma all the time. She always puts up a fight, but she always comes off worst, poor cow. He's a big fucker. I got good at cleaning her up afterward. We were scared shitless, the little ones crying and screaming every time he was around. I'll never understand why Ma married him in the first place. I asked her once and all she said was, "He used to treat me like gold." Sure, it's good to be treated like gold, but I can hardly believe that old bastard even knows how. She's deaf in one ear after he thought it a lark to smash two cupboard doors closed on her head one day.

It was all Ma could do to feed us proper once a week, let alone once a day. Then, at the age of fourteen, a stroke of luck landed me a job as a messenger for the Post Office in Charing Cross. True, I was delivering 'grams in storm and snow, frozen to the bone, miserable as sin, and tired as a dog. But being a thick bastard I considered myself fuckin' lucky. All my friends, my elder brothers too, had turned to crime, for where we lived it was steal or starve. I come from a fine line of criminals—though not very good ones. Pa was always behind bars. If we ever needed to find him, we knew he'd be in the pub or in the clink. But for some reason, I couldn't bring myself to do it. My one and only joy was handing my wages to Ma once a week and seeing her face light up from the glow of the coins, both of us knowing I'd earned them honestly. But I was soon to discover another much greater source of both money and pleasure, a way of life that would show me things beyond that narrow horizon of poverty and survival.

Strangely enough, I never thought it a crime, becoming a renter.

1954

He came over again today. I should stop saying "he." He has a name. But it is such a grotesque name that I fail to link it with him, with his beauty: Gregory. How can a parent burden a child with such a monstrous name? There's no nobility in it, no grace. It sounds like the death rattle of an ancient bullfrog. He told me some of his friends call him Gore, and, since this is the name of a novelist whose books I enjoy, I feel happier calling him that.

Gore's not shy at all and strips off as soon as he's in the studio without having to be asked. Just stands there and disrobes. I usually offer models the use of a bathrobe and get them to undress in the bedroom before coming into the studio, but he'll have none of that. It's as if he can't wait to be naked, as if wearing clothes is an encumbrance he escapes at the first opportunity. We start off with a few short poses to warm up and then move to longer ones. He's very good and doesn't fidget like some of the models I've had.

We often chat as I sketch, and he is pleasant enough company, at ease talking about his life. His parents are gypsies—or, as he prefers to call them, travelling people. His mother is French and his father Italian, and he's fluent in both languages, as well as English. He was born outside Brighton, but they moved all over the country while he was growing up, never settling anywhere more than a couple of months, always being moved on, made unwelcome, and sometimes hounded out. Since he left his parents at the age of sixteen, he has been travelling all over the world, mainly on merchant ships, doing all sorts of jobs, working in circuses, working on building sites, gardening, occasionally whoring. Dodged national service by going abroad, spent most of the war years wandering across Europe, often ending up imprisoned for vagrancy. Seemingly immune to the social imperatives to forge a career, to settle down, he has lived off his wits, working with bands of actors or street performers, doing mime, juggling, fire-eating and the like, or, when that dried up or bored him, selling his body. He has studied yoga and meditation in Tibet, rope work in North Africa, and Noh theatre in Japan, picked grapes in Italy, smuggled drugs in and out of just about everywhere. It seems incredible that he could have done so much in his twenty-nine years. I have never met anyone quite like him before in my entire life.

He told me a rather fascinating story about spending an evening with a group of young Arab boys in the middle of a desert somewhere outside Morocco, conversing through the only youth who spoke French. Having chatted underneath a star-flecked sky on myriad topics, smoking hashish and drinking wine with them all evening, he was told that they were all about to indulge in a homosexual orgy, and he was welcome to stay or be taken to the nearest town. He chose to stay. He described in detail the combinations of bodies and pleasures he enjoyed that night.

His stories provoke such profound inadequacies in me, just as his presence works such magic on my art. The drawings I produce disturb and excite me, as I try to capture not just his likeness but his energy, his charge. I feel this peculiar mixture of desire and regret, and these feelings seem to spill into the images that appear when I draw, images that both disgust and fascinate me. Even as he makes me recognize the narrowness of my life, I still feel freer than I have felt for years—perhaps ever. There's an urgency in the way I am working now that there has never been before, a tension that expresses itself in the most ambiguous and intriguing ways. These new sketches look like nothing I've ever seen before.

He has only been back in London eight months, lodging in a house in Islington. It's the longest he's ever spent anywhere, he told me. I've never been any further from London than Hampshire, and I find this lifestyle almost incomprehensible, though fascinating. I responded to the revelation that he is a renter with a worldly nod, as if I meet them every day, though inside I was rather shocked and excited. I wanted to bombard him with questions, but underneath his apparent openness he is remarkably guarded so I restrained myself, saying only, "And do you find your work interesting?" What a pompous bore I must have appeared. Or perhaps am.

He said, "Whoring isn't a job, it's a world view. It's an art form, even a kind of philosophy. It contours the way you see everything. Nothing is important. Except money. And the only way you can get money is by whoring. So you end up on a treadmill that formulates your entire outlook. What makes a whore anyway? I sell my time. My labour. My body. Whether I get my cock sucked or whether I work at a job I hate for a pittance, it amounts to the same thing. I let my boss suck me off, that's all. It takes less time to earn the same money. Prostitution is the apotheosis of capitalism. But with the added advantage that, finding I rather like it, it keeps me free."

Of course he didn't say that.

But his whole life said it. His whole body said it. What he actually said was that it was an easy job that gave him plenty of money and sex and saved him from having to work.

What could I say, who have bartered my life away for a respectability that now mocks my timidity? Haven't I survived (don't we all, in some sense, survive) through a more subtle form of prostitution? We may think that prostitution is something that only prostitutes do—that it names only the selling of one's body—but what of the selling of one's soul, or one's freedom, one's individual spirit? Doesn't one's life also have a price? How much am I worth? How much is he worth? I wonder. I daren't ask. Not yet.

He seems to know exactly what he's doing, and why; and I for one cannot stand in judgement. I am, however, plagued with questions, having had so little physical pleasure and placed so little value on it in my own life. I want to know what it is like to give and take pleasure in that way, to live outside normal society so gleefully and shamelessly. When he told me, I asked none of those questions that rose so urgently within me, however, but simply continued to draw in silence.

"Most of the models who pose for the group do it," he said at last, and I knew that I was expected to pick this up as a topic of conversation.

"And does it pay well?" I asked.

"I made ten bob from one fella last week."

"Good lord. He must have been well off."

"He's a don from Cambridge. You know what he wanted me to do?"

"What?"

"He wanted me to sit down on his face."

I looked up at him. He was grinning.

"Clothed or unclothed?" I asked. I could hardly believe the conversation was for real. I had never spoken of such things with another human being in my life.

He looked at me as if the question were preposterous, which I suppose it probably was.

"Unclothed! He wanted me to rub my arse in his face while he played with my cock. And the whole time he's trying to speak, but his words are being muffled as I crush down further onto his mouth. Then I spilt onto his fat belly."

I was looking at him by now, my hand stilled, struck dumb by this image he had conjured. I was not at all certain what I might say at this point. I am utterly ill-equipped for this. He, of course, was grinning like the Cheshire cat, amused by my discomfort.

"It was all over in ten minutes and he hands me the bread."

"The bread?"

"The money! That's the most I ever had."

"And will you see him again?" I asked, sounding like a maiden aunt discussing courtship prospects.

"I fuckin' 'ope so," he said with a smile that seemed to invite something I could barely recognize. I pulled myself together and continued to sketch, but still, long after he has gone, I continue to be plagued by the image of him crushing his behind into a man's face—and find myself imagining what it must feel like to have Gore do that.

I cannot sleep for imagining it.

1998

One night, I left Spike and the others on the golf course and went to meet Phil at the bistro where I'd told my parents I was working. It was New Year's Eve, the full stop to 1985. I was fifteen. As I arrived at the kitchen door at the back of the bistro, Phil was just finishing. We went through to the bar, where the rest of the kitchen staff and the owners, plus some regulars, were gathered, celebrating. Phil and I got chatting to one of the regular customers, a musician in his late twenties who talked fast and intensely. He announced at one point that he was off to the toilets to do some coke, and did we want some? I'd never tried cocaine before, Johnny's brother didn't deal in it, so of course I was curious. Cocaine represented wealth, glamour, debauchery, decadence, rock'n'roll. I knew this much already, knew that there were other worlds. Phil declined, but I agreed. I followed this man up the spiral staircase that led to the toilets and into a cubicle in the gents'. I watched him unwrap the little pouch of paper and tip the white powder onto the flat ceramic surface of the cistern. Every move he made was observed and recorded.

The chopping of the powder and scraping it into two fat white lines with a credit card, the licking of the card's powdery edge, the rolling of the crisp ten-pound note, the finger closing off one nostril while the other one hoovered up the trail of white grains, the tipping back of the head. Then the furious sniffing, the licking of the finger to gather up the loose granules from the cistern, the squeaking of the dusted fingertip against the gums. I took it all in, like an actor preparing for his role. He handed me the note like a gauntlet while he continued to hold one nostril closed and sniff hard with the other. I bent over, the note up my nose, and chased the length of my line with the sort of enthusiasm I had not applied to anything for a long time. I looked at him. He was beaming, and the rush I felt expressed itself in a return of that smile. "Good, huh?" he said. I nodded. Another vista opened up before me, glistening with possibilities.

As Phil and I were leaving that night we ran into a local eccentric who used to come and hang around the kitchen. We'd nicknamed him the Count because he looked like Bela Lugosi. No one who worked there liked him, or even knew him, and I'm not really sure why he used to come in. There were rumours that he was a paedophile, a pervert. He was certainly sinister, dressed in black, his dark hair Brylcreemed back across his scalp, a widow's peak pointing down toward his gaunt face. He would usually engage us in mindless chitchat, his voice reedy and slow. His nails were long and grubby and turned my stomach.

By this time, I'd had several trips to the toilet with the cokehead and was feeling pretty wired. The Count began asking us questions that soon moved from the inane ("Where do you live?") to the obscene ("What kind of sex do you like?"). He asked us what we would be prepared to do for money. Would we, for example, have sex with a fat, ugly woman, or an old woman, or a man, even an animal? I knew that, like me, Phil was a virgin. He'd confessed to me once that he used binoculars to spy on a teenage girl in a house opposite his, watching her undressing, or parading around with a handbag. Throughout the Count's interrogation, Phil laughed like an embarrassed child, clearly terrified, but I was fascinated. Here was someone totally unlike anyone I had ever met before. Someone strange and dangerous.

We reached Phil's house, and he went indoors. I remember he gave me this look of victory, that he'd escaped while I was still held prisoner by this weirdo. There was still some way to go before we reached my home. The Count and I continued to walk, and he continued his questioning. I was pretty much saying yes to everything—yes I would do that, why not, if I was being paid. My heart was racing. My cock was hard. He asked if I had ever had sex with a man, and I said no. He said, would you let someone—a man, for example—suck your dick for twenty pounds? I said, sure, why not? We were by now walking by the golf course, and he suggested we go into some bushes. I held my hand out for the money, and he took out a fat wad of notes from the inside pocket of his grimy suit jacket and peeled off a twenty and placed it in my hand. I screwed it up and thrust it in my pocket as I followed him.

Perhaps I can return to that moment and find in it something that makes sense of my life. Perhaps, like Phil, I could have retreated from the situation—what if my house had been first on that journey home that night, and I had left Phil with the Count? But the encounter thrilled me, and then sickened me, and that was a pattern with which I was to become only too familiar. I had several more encounters with the Count, and over the next few months he introduced me to some of his friends. First, he took me around to meet an enormously fat man whose large front room was always curtained, and whose pet budgie would fly around in a frenzy of feathers and noise, shitting everywhere. I made him cage it when I was there, wary of its erratic flight. He wanted me to fuck him. He called it rooting. "I want you to root me," he'd say as he lay on his side, this mound of white flesh that pooled against the mattress. I learned to function somewhere beyond desire.

Later, he took me to this tiny, skeletally thin man who had a pinball machine in his front room and would get me to stand and play pinball in a pair of tight green shorts while he crept underneath and pulled my cock out. He lived in a cul-de-sac in a quiet middle-class suburb, and his house stood out from the rest because it was so dishevelled, his front garden manically overgrown, a rusting bike upturned in the long grass like a giant insect caught on its back. The paint puckered and peeled on the front door. I had heard from Mr Root that Mr Pinball had served time for molesting young boys, and once when I was there, a car pulled up outside and a huge slab of paving came crashing through the front window, scaring the shit out of both of us.

One of the Count's friends lived in a flat that was cluttered with piles of old newspapers and stacks of empty champagne boxes. His pale, loose flesh, revealed by an unbuttoned shirt, stank of stale sweat, and his dentures clicked and whistled as he spoke. Judging from his accent, he was clearly educated, though I have no idea about his profession (even if he had one). He seemed far from destitute, while somehow at the same time appearing utterly penniless. He offered to take me on a cruise around the Mediterranean as I stood there masturbating in a pair of Lycra knickers he'd provided. Every time I went there he would say the same thing, make the same promise, but a year went by and the cruise had still not materialized. Not that I wanted to go. I had other plans, for I'd saved up those £20 notes and now had enough to get away. On the day after sitting my last O-level exam I left home and came to London. I told my parents I was going with Phil for a weekend. Instead I went on my own and I never returned home. I'd acquired a taste for adoration and the power it gave me. I wanted imposture, anonymity, and lies, and prostitution provided all three. Most of my clients wanted to believe I was straight, wanted to believe I had girlfriends (and many of the rent boys I met did, though even that may have been a reluctance to drop the act). Clients wanted to imagine that we only did what we did for the money. I was only too happy to act the part. Distance is my tendency.

After arriving in London, I wrote to my parents telling them that I would not be coming home and not to worry about me, but I never gave a contact address. Being a dutiful son wasn't part of my plan. I was beginning to formulate a way of life radically at odds with what was expected of me.

1894

There was this other older lad who also worked the 'grams; Terence Thickbroom was his name. Handsome as they come and charming as the devil with it. He was always larking about and we soon became good friends and then one day he took me to the water closet in the Post Office on the Strand to show me how nice it is to have yourself touched by another's hand and though I knew well enough already, truth be told, having shared a bed with three older brothers, still I quite liked the look of him and was curious besides to see what his yard looked like so I pretended not to know and let him show me anyhow. And he wasn't called Thickbroom for nothing, either.

We met frequently after that and I looked forward to it, I'm not ashamed to admit. And then one day he told me about the money I could make if I were to go to bed with a man.

I said no.

He said, "You'll get four shillings."

So I said yes.

That very afternoon he introduced me to this older fellow named

Taylor who runs a boyhouse in Fitzroy Street in Bloomsbury. It was nothing compared to some houses I've seen since, but on my first visit there I thought it was a palace. The carpets in the hallway weren't exactly new but at least he had them—gaslights too. And a bog out the back. Luxury.

He's a fuckin' odd little bugger, is Taylor. I'd never seen the like. Thin as a rail with sunken cheeks and no eyebrows and, I swear on my life, face powder. Pinched little lips, beaky nose and restless eyes, his gaze never quite meeting your own. But he was friendly enough, giving me a big toothsome grin when Thickbroom introduced me, his eyes roving up and down my self in a look of exaggerated delight. "'Ello, 'andsome," he chirped.

He was dressed in turquoise silk pyjamas underneath a red silk kimono covered with silver birds, and a pair of jewelled golden slippers on his feet. I was mesmerised and horrified in equal measure. He ushered me into the parlour before turning to Thickbroom and saying, "Make yerself scarce, ducky, and well done."

Despite it being bright daylight outside, the thick dirty gold velvet curtains were drawn and the room was dimly lit by gas lamps. The flames were encased in red glass bulbs, which made the whole place blush. Perfume clouded out from brass burners and filled the room with a vicious musky scent that did nothing to cover the stench of burnt onions. Despite the poor light, I could make out a few old armchairs and a long, battered and stained divan which Taylor gestured at for me to sit on. He immediately squeezed himself down right next to me, practically foaming at the mouth. He said, "Terence said you was good-looking, and he wasn't wrong. You know, you could make lots of money if you cared to."

I said that I did. "If any old gentleman with money takes a fancy to me," I said, "I shan't mind. I'm terribly hard up."

At this, he arched an eyebrow.

"The extra money will be most welcome, Mister Taylor, sir," I explained further.

"*Extra* money?" he said. "No, dearie, you misunderstand me. You'll live here and work here with me and the girls. No more running the 'grams for you, my fine Ganymede. You're far too good for that."

Well, I'd never considered I had any particular value, so this was news to me, and so, while I knew it would break Ma's heart to see me leave (though she'd be grateful for one less mouth to fill), all the same I also knew that I'd be able to earn much more working for Taylor than I would running 'grams. I'd have much more fun, too. The situation with my father had made living at home hell and so it didn't take much reflection before I agreed. Besides, having worked the West End enough times to know it felt like the centre of the universe, I liked the idea of living near there. Liked it a lot.

Taylor pushed ever so close to me and said in that hissy way of speaking he has, "Young man, whoring is a calling, a talent, an art of the highest order. There's a fine tradition to be upheld in the giving of pleasure for money. A fine tradition. It's not called the oldest profession for nothing." And he licked his lips and grinned before continuing. "Thankfully this knowledge has been passed down from cock to mouth for generations. But only the chosen few have been bestowed with the knowledge of this esoteric and erotic art. These keepers of the flame are amongst the most talented givers of pleasure the world has ever known, the most gifted of whores. In this house, this *temple*, you shall in time join their number and become one of the anointed. You shall know that power. You shall know it well."

He suddenly clutched together the folds of his kimono, which had fallen open to reveal his pale white chest where the pyjamas were unbuttoned underneath. I could hear laughter coming from the kitchen, where Terence and the other boys were.

"Yet forget this at your peril," he said, tapping a bony fingertip on my sternum. "There are those in this world who'll condemn you, condemn you as fiercely as they condemn their own bodies, for what you do. There are those'll tell you that pleasure is *bad* and that giving it for money is the work of the devil himself. But know that they are *fools*. And no sane man listens to a fool. There are those who believe that only pain can give pleasure— and indeed, aren't a good deal of 'em the very swells you'll be servicing, giving 'em a fair crack of the whip for the pure hell of it?—but sure they are worse than the fools, they are hypocrites and you'll come to recognize them soon enough. For aren't they running the country, the most of 'em? And doesn't each and every one of them pass through that door, or one as like it as to make no difference, at some time or other in their miserable, Janus-faced lives?"

He stared at me with eyes wide, and I was unsure for a minute whether or not he was waiting for me to answer. But he had only paused to inhale enough breath to fuel the next onslaught. I had never known anyone talk so much; not even Pa in his cups went on so.

"These fools preach not what they practice," he said, "and they must be held by each and every whore in the greatest contempt.

For the fools and the hypocrites know *nothing* of joy and would have you know nothing of it too. They have the body for a dirty thing, an animal thing, and place it second to the soul or mind or whatever else they call it."

His finger pointed at the window, as if those he spoke of were stood behind the closed curtains.

"They find the body ugly and its parts despicable," he said. "They curse the body and wish it dead. For only in death, or so they claim, can the spirit live in all its purity. What bollocks! And they spread this ignorance of theirs wherever they can. And they will try all they can to spread it upon you, young man, and make no mistake. But don't you listen to a word they say, for whatever they say, they are doing the opposite themselves. You know they are. You know it better than most. You know that they are not to be listened to, only laughed at, exposed and ignored. The Establishment—for it is they I talk of—will use us, will use *you*, as often as it suits them, but it is for no one to know but themselves."

He placed a hand on my knee.

"A whore's life is no easy thing and is not to be embarked upon lightly." He moved in closer, narrowing his eyes to slits like a sly cat, and said, "But they are all wrong, see. They are all so wrong. And their mistake is your reward."

He rubbed his hand against my thigh.

"Because pleasure is the greatest gift God gave you, so it is. Pleasure is divine. To give pleasure is to spread joy, and to spread joy is godly, isn't that the truth? Now aren't we doing God's work right here, aren't we spreading joy? I think you'll find we are. Just look at the smiles on the faces of those that leave."

He grinned, revealing yellow, crooked teeth.

"In 'ere you'll learn the ancient knowledge of whorecraft: the art of giving pleasure will be yours. Didn't the Whore of Babylon alone leave enough volumes to keep you busy in your studies for years? Not to mention Nell Gwynn or Lucrezia Borgia? And that Emma Hamilton passed on a trick or two. The boys may be less famous, but they are there if you care to look. Sporus, the beautiful slave boy who was castrated and dressed as a woman in order to marry Nero. What he didn't know about sucking cock isn't worth knowing, believe you me. Why do you think Nero wanted to marry him so desperately that he chopped off the poor boy's knackers to make him resemble a girl? And those lovely boys that serviced King James I—they have passed on their wisdom, too. How to make a man feel like a king, or even like a queen if needs must. And it can be yours, that knowledge, all yours."

He then took hold of my chin and turned my face toward a pool of red light, examining my face with screwed-up eyes. "What did you say your name was, dollface?" he asked, running his calloused thumb across my lips.

"Jack, sir," I replied.

He let his hand drop into my lap, his gaze scanning the room as if he was suddenly not sure where he was.

"Yes," he said at last, "it can all be yours, Jack, this wisdom. You will learn the secrets of your body; you will scale its heights and move beyond its limits. You'll experience new pleasures, *forbidden* pleasures—pleasures beyond anything else you've known. You'll understand completely what it means to be taken into another dimension. All the distinctions you've so far relied upon to give the world meaning will be destroyed and replaced by new ones.

A new world will begin to emerge before your eyes. A world of brighter colours and fresher smells, a world of joy and perfection. All the things that aren't usually allowed to make sense will *make sense*, finally and joyously. You are a chosen child, my boy, one of the blessed."

He moved his hand further up my leg and continued, "There are things about the human body only a few people are allowed to comprehend, secrets the body keeps locked deep within. Things about its limits and how to move beyond them, things about the edges of pleasure and how to transgress their boundaries. You'll understand every organ and orifice and surface of your flesh so much more than you do now, in ways you are currently incapable of even imagining. You'll unearth an entire archaeology of pleasure as yet buried beneath the shifting sands of philistine opinion. A palace lies beneath those sands, Jack, a beautiful glittering palace."

He emitted a faint gasp as if this palace had erected itself right there in his front room. He held a hand out as if to touch it, then turned to me and laid his clammy palm across my cheek.

"The perfection of its structure will leave you breathless, lad, but you'll not be able to resist entering and exploring every room, every corridor, every crevice of its domain. You'll be a slave to its spaces, its rhythms, its commands. You'll shiver as you perform every exploration. You may even on occasion suffer most profoundly. But over time, if you succeed, you'll learn your way around its labyrinthine interior, room by room, secret by secret. And when you know all there is to know about the vagaries and potencies of pleasure, well then, Jack, my lad, you'll be the master of that palace, lord of all you survey!

"Are you game?"

And with that he grabbed my privates and moved his face so close to mine that I could smell his hellish breath. Stifling a response to retch, I nodded most eagerly, looked him straight in the eye, and said with a smile, "Aye, sir, aye, I'm game."

For didn't I want to know everything? Who doesn't dream of knowing everything?

"Come on then, handsome, show us what you're made of. What can you do with this?" And he whipped out a stand that gave off a stink like a latrine, and then he leaned back with his hands behind his head. I knew this was a test and that I had to pass it—I had to impress the bastard. The smell was making my eyes sting. I don't think he'd washed the damned thing since the day his mother stopped doing it for him.

I slid onto my knees and turned toward him—toward it—trying to look as pleased to be doing so as I could. By the time my mouth had reached it, bile had risen and a watery mouthful spilled out onto his cock. I rubbed it in and he sighed. I spat some more and rubbed some more and washed the bugger down in my own spittle before letting it anywhere near my mouth. My ingenuity paid off, for he groaned all the while and I slipped the whole thing into my mouth now that it smelled slightly sweeter, or at least of myself, and the cheesy muck had for the most part been washed clean away. He only once barked at me the word "*Teeth!*," clipping the side of my head as he did so. It was a job well done, and he said I could work for him.

I moved in there and then.

1954

I should explain how I came to meet Gore, for I'm afraid that the impression I have given of my life is one of self-imposed exile, which is not far from the truth, but is not the absolute truth either. Once a month on a Friday afternoon for the past six months, I've been attending a life-drawing group run by Miss Wilkes, a large, exuberant woman with the kind of scatter-brain so characteristic of those members of the aristocracy who have fallen foul of the arts, or "living *la vie de Bohème*," as she puts it. She's a retired art teacher from one of the private girls' schools in the Home Counties. And it shows. She treats us like schoolgirls. There are five of us, all middle-aged men or older, and all, I imagine, of the same persuasion as myself. Maurice calls everybody "dear," and I'm convinced he wears rouge. Kenneth is a retired navigator from the Royal Navy, though how he ever navigated a ship is anyone's guess. He's late every single week, having got lost walking from the station to Miss Wilkes' house, even though it's less than a minute's journey. He stands incredibly close to the male models during the tea break, cornering them so they can't get away and then boring them with stories about his life at sea, poor things. (He completely loses interest when it's a female model.) Malcolm is the most verbally explicit. He has a code for rating the standard of the male models' backsides. The ones he likes best he calls Harrods. He does tiny, cramped watercolours—two squashed onto each page of his small sketchbook—and has a nasty habit of sucking on his paintbrush, which makes a repulsive sound and leaves him with a black tongue. Peter is like me, hardly says a word. We've chatted alone on occasion—though, as is the way with two shy people, it's a bit like pulling teeth.

Every first Friday of the month, come hell or high water, the six of us gather in Miss Wilkes' large cluttered house in Mortlake. Many of the surrounding houses were bombed during the war, but Miss Wilkes' house, much like Miss Wilkes herself, stands defiantly upright amidst the rubble. We congregate in the spacious sitting room to draw from a live model. We have male and female models, though the male models are never completely naked, their genitals always tucked into white posing pouches. It might be art, but we don't want to scandalise the community. I met Gore when he came to model for the group last month and, chatting alone with him during the tea break, I found myself arranging for him to model for me privately. I have done this occasionally with models from the group, though none ever came more than once or twice. They can be terribly unreliable—sometimes not showing up at all. But Gore has been three times now and is always spot on time. I do hope he continues to come, because I find that the drawings he inspires are far superior to any others I have ever done. I feel I am on a journey with this—with him—and I like the look of where it's going. Perhaps it would be more accurate to say I like where it's been. I like the journey so far. I don't know yet where, if anywhere, it is going. But if he were suddenly to stop coming I know I should be most annoyed. He has awoken something in me, something that, whilst unsettling in the extreme, is not entirely unpleasant.

I've been trying this past week, without success, to recall who it is that Gore reminds me of. For there is something familiar about him I cannot quite place. In the way that people sometimes do, he brings to mind another face, another person. And it finally came to me today, as I was drawing. Rather disconcertingly, Gore is the spitting image of a young man I met once thirty years ago, under the following circumstances. Since leaving art school at twenty-one, I had been working for three years at an advertising studio in Regent Street run by an acquaintance of my father's—a man called Frank Symonds. On this particular occasion, I had been assigned a job that involved drawing the male figure. I think it was a catalogue of some description, a men's clothing catalogue, as I recall. During the briefing, Symonds told me he thought I should brush up on my figure drawing. That afternoon he asked me to stay behind after work, and once everyone had gone, he explained that he had arranged for a model to come round whom I was to draw for a couple of hours while he did some paperwork. As he finished explaining this, the bell rang and he went to answer the door, coming back with a beautiful young man, whom he introduced as Trevor. Tall, broad-shouldered, with black hair and green, cheerful eyes. Symonds took us down to a store-room in the basement, where he'd set up some anglepoise lamps and some cushions, a white sheet thrown over them rather maladroitly. There was no heating, and the subterranean room was cold, but all the same my heart raced at the prospect of this boy disrobing before me. I felt no concern for his possible discomfort, I must admit. Symonds and the lad were clearly familiar, and they joked while Trevor removed his clothes. "I'll try and locate a heater," Symonds said, "otherwise your shivering will be most distracting." Symonds looked at me and said, "Don't worry, it gets bigger," and gave a wink before leaving. It was a side of him I had never seen before, slightly effeminate, slightly repulsive, in thrall to this boy in a way that I was too, I'll admit, though I'd never have dared let another human being know what thoughts assailed me. Never.

Trevor stepped out of his undershorts and appeared before me in all his glory. I'd only ever seen the life models at art school, in their coy little posing pouches, like a handkerchief tied to a runaway's stick. He didn't seem at all shy about his body but stood there proudly, hands by his sides.

"Where do you want me, mister?"

I found my mouth dry and had to swallow before replying. "Just stand over there to begin with," I muttered, pointing vaguely to a pool of light between the two lamps.

He stepped over to the spot and stood stock still, arms behind his back, legs slightly apart, feet firmly set on the floor, looking into the far left-hand corner behind me.

"This do?"

"Perfect," I said, sitting down and grabbing my paper and pencils with sweaty hands. Symonds came back, carrying a three-bar electric fire, which he plugged into a socket and aimed in Trevor's direction. "This'll ensure it doesn't shrink to nothing, eh, lad?" he chuckled, before turning to me. "Fine figure of a man, isn't he?

Such stature, such masculine grace. He should be cast in bronze, don't you think?" That wink again. The penny suddenly dropped that he knew all about me, could see right through whatever disguise I thought I wore, right down to the deepest recesses of my dampened desire. I felt myself blushing.

"Yes," I said, looking down at the blank sheet on my knee, "perfect."

"Mmm, he most certainly is," Symonds drooled, staring openly at the young man's genitals. "Anyway," he chirped, dragging his gaze away reluctantly, "you've got him for two hours, so make the most of him. I'll be upstairs should you need me. Be good." Then he was gone.

I don't know whether those first drawings were any good. I'm sure they weren't. I seem to remember spending long stretches of time just drinking in that body, my hand making random marks on the paper that bore little resemblance to the vision before me. I couldn't take my eyes off him.

At one point he got an erection and laughed an apology.

"No, no, it's fine, don't worry about it," I said breathlessly, trying desperately to capture its likeness on paper.

After the two hours, he climbed back into his clothes and we walked silently upstairs. The three of us left the building and Symonds hailed a taxi into which he and Trevor clambered, and my imagination has reconstructed many times in the intervening years what they went off to do that night, always with the same mixture of jealousy and admiration. I went home and pored over the sketches I had made, my heart racing.

Every evening after work for the next two weeks Symonds would present me with a different boy, but it is Trevor's ash-white body and crow-black hair, Trevor's pale tan nipples and pale green eyes, that remain for me the indelible memory of that time. I never saw him again. I drew ten different young men in as many days, and yet only that first one registers with me now. The others, beautiful as they were, have faded in my memory, so that Trevor's has become the face and body I attribute to each of them. He has, I suppose, delineated my desire.

Symonds never made any reference to these boys, never told me how or where he found them, nor disclosed the precise nature of his relationship with them, yet he drooled after each and every one in my presence, and always disappeared with them afterward into the shadowed interior of a black cab and off into the foggy darkness of a London night. And, far from reassuring me that there were others like me, instead the knowledge of Symonds' true nature made me more resolute than ever to quell this thirst, not quench it; to stamp out this fire, not feed it.

There began my pact with solitude.

There began my road to hell.

Looking at Gore this morning, it was like looking back across the years and seeing Trevor once more, the same green eyes and boxer's nose, the same angle of the shoulders, even the same pucker to the foreskin.

I think about all those men arrested and imprisoned for doing what I dare not bring myself to do, and in some strange way I envy them. If I myself actually had the courage to do it, I tell myself I shouldn't at all mind a spell in prison, though I know in truth that my fear of the place is precisely what stops me.

1998

I wanted to live in a city big enough to lose myself in, big enough to keep boredom at bay. I wanted to live in the spaces between buildings, to disappear. You can't really do that, though, because each disappearance is also an appearance. No absence goes unnoticed for long. Not if you know where to look. I can't now recall what it was I thought I had come to London to find, but I knew what I had left behind. Anything else had to be better than that, I told myself.

As I stepped off the train at Euston one night in June 1986, I entered a city in which I knew nobody and nobody knew me, and I could taste the anonymity like aluminium on my tongue. I licked myself clean. I had nowhere to stay. I was unutterably terrified. I sparked up a spliff and began walking down Euston Road, toward King's Cross. With each step my shadow got lighter. I made my way to the Bell, which I had read about in a copy of *Gay Times* I'd bought at the station before getting on the train that afternoon, and had read furtively from cover to cover during the journey. I walked past the bar several times on the opposite side of the street, my stomach churning. I looked at the Thameslink station next to the Bell, and thought of that game on the train tracks as a child, of that stupid, willful determination not to run away like the others.

I crossed the road and pushed open the door.

I hadn't really considered what the place might look like inside, but I hadn't for a minute expected it to look like any other pub. I was expecting decadence, I think, and I got a shock. Young men and women stood around drinking. Music played. The only difference from any pub I had been in at home was that the people knew how to dress and the music was palatable. The Buzzcocks' "Ever Fallen in Love" played as I sat there with a pint of lager, smoking a cigarette, withdrawing behind the clouds of smoke I was exhaling, and scanning the room. I watched their faces, the men and women who were there, while keeping a regular eye on the door for newcomers. I wanted to take in everything. I wanted to be somebody else, so I was. Where I grew up, it wasn't possible to do this.

I sat alone, armed with the eye of an anthropologist and the heart of a beggar. I knew there must be someone who would take me home and give me a bed for the night. It was simply a process of discovering that person. I looked at each boy in turn. Already I knew what I could achieve. Still, it was new. A test. In those days, everything was a test to see how far this new me would go. I had only ever had sex with men I found repulsive in exchange for money. I didn't know anything else. I was hungry to learn.

Only one person approached me all night. After I had been sitting there for hours, what can only be described as a flaming creature came over and sat next to me, blue hair spiking above a bizarrely made-up face. He wore a black lamé jacket over a tight yellow T-shirt, a tartan mini-skirt, and orange tights, his feet wrapped in purple platform boots with a silver ankle-star. He looked like something from another planet.

"Hello, what's your name?" he asked, offering me a Consulate. "David," I said, taking one. That isn't my name. It's my brother's name. I don't know why my own name seemed so inadequate at that moment, or what I was trying to hide. Or who I was trying to become.

"I'm Edward," he said, holding out a lighter in his bejewelled hand. I leant forward till the cigarette's tip hit the flame, and inhaled, noticing that his black-varnished fingernails were chipped.

He launched into a monologue the majority of which I can no longer recall. He was an artist and a musician, and he organized clubs and gigs. He sang in a band called Hollywood Knee, who played hard-edged, cross-dressed covers of songs by '60s girl groups. He proceeded to bombard me with questions. What music did I like? Did I like this, did I like that? Who were my favourite artists? What films had I seen, what books had I read? Initially I was barely able to string two words together, so shocked was I that such a person existed, but so glad that he was talking to me, this being who seemed to speak the same language as me. One of my own species. As a consequence of that shock, however, I responded with such monosyllabic answers that at one point he stopped, looking perplexed, and asked, "Were you a test tube baby?"

"Why?"

"I have friends who were some of the earliest test tube babies.

You remind me of them. They never say a word."

"I was grown on a wet flannel," I said. "Besides, I can't get a word in edgeways."

He looked at me. He pulled on his cigarette, not taking his eyes off me. "This place is closing now, dear. Fancy going somewhere else?"

I guessed I had my bed for the night. "Sure."

Throughout the conversation I had been staring over Edward's shoulder at a handsome man farther off, near the bar, who had caught my eye. Our eyes had met, but I had not known how to extricate myself from Edward, and didn't really want to, and Handsome had eventually left with someone else, taking my gaze with him. I tried to imagine myself having sex with him, but my thoughts were diverted by Edward standing up quickly and saying, "Come on, then, heartface, let's go."

He led me to some den in Shoreditch, where transsexual prostitutes played pool and rent boys in tracksuits and baseball caps sat around smoking joints. One boy, in a leopard-print baseball cap worn back-to-front above eyes lit with mischief, was repeatedly shouting at one of the trannies, "How much, girlfriend?" to which Girlfriend's increasingly annoyed response was, "Too much." He continued to repeat the question until she threatened him with a pool cue. We walked past two middle-aged would-be gangsters playing cards in a fug of blue cigar smoke, up to the bar where a beer-bellied cabbie was sucking the face off one of the lady-boys. We were soon deep in conversation, and I told Edward things about my life I'd never told anyone before, stories of my escapades that I had kept locked inside. There's nothing like a bent ear to dispel shyness. Stories erupted like smoke from my mouth and the trail they formed led straight to his flat in a council estate in Hackney.

In his hallway, one wall was lined with framed covers of old movie magazines—Joan Crawford, Marilyn Monroe, Jayne Mansfield, and Bette Davis all stared down at us as we entered the front door—while the other wall was filled with the framed covers of pornographic gay magazines. *Inches. Honcho. Drummer.* We stepped into this corridor of tanned men and glamour girls and he led me to the lounge, where fun-fur rugs of every colour covered the floor like some Muppet-culling. The walls were furnished with silver moulded plastic, like the inside of Barbarella's spaceship, which reflected the light emitting from the sleek '60s lamp that hung from the ceiling. A white leather sofa rested against the far wall. Dominating the room, though, in front of the window, was a large Art Deco display case, inhabited by dozens of Barbie dolls, most still in their boxes. An army of smiling, vacant faces, like pretty corpses in glass coffins.

I assumed sex was almost inevitable. And though I didn't want it, I was still disappointed when Edward said, "I don't wanna fuck you, David. You're not my type. But you can stay here. For a while. Till you find somewhere, find your feet."

"Thanks."

"Let me show you around."

Above the kitchen door, right at the back of the hall and pinned back to form a curtain leading into it, hung two brightly sequinned dresses, one green, the other red. The light in the kitchen was already on, creating the effect of an empty stage. Once we stepped through the sequinned dresses curtaining the doorway, it was fairly plain and functional. The fridge and cupboard doors were completely collaged with postcards and pictures from magazines.

Edward's bathroom was done out like a Vatican shipwreck. Statues of the Virgin Mary and cherubs holding seashell fonts fought for space with plastic lobsters and starfish. Above the sink was a golden bathroom cabinet with a ceramic fish perched on top. Above the toilet, a Tom of Finland drawing of a merman. From the top of the toilet seat an enormous cut-out goldfish with its mouth open stared up at you.

The bedroom was the dullest room in the entire flat, like a Whitby B&B circa 1962, complete with twin beds. I must have looked confused, because Edward said, "Oh, I can't be doing with all that sharing-a-bed malarkey. Even when I do have someone stop over, which isn't often, I always make them sleep on their own." He kicked off his platform boots and collapsed onto the nearest bed with a dramatic sigh. "I can't bear anyone close to me like that, clinging on," he shuddered, "it's abnormal."

So I was here, in London.

Sharing a room with a fruitcake, but at least I was here.

1894

On my first morning Taylor explained that, to begin with, I'd just practice with him or the other boys every morning, then rest for an hour or so to get my strength back, and then spend the night entertaining the gentlemen who visited. He said they always did it that way when a new boy arrived. I didn't much like the idea of having to suck him again, nor did I imagine there to be much more to it than what I already knew, but I couldn't have been more wrong. Taylor has all sorts of implements and lotions for giving and receiving pleasure, and over the next few weeks he taught me how to use them all with absolute expertise. He made good whores of us, Taylor did. He calls it studying, what we did in the mornings. Well, I say mornings—we were never up much before midday, truth be told.

I never knew there was so much to learn about the art of love. Taylor taught me every trick of the trade in the weeks after I arrived. He has a series of brass cocks of bigger and bigger sizes. We started on the smallest and worked our way up to the largest, which he has nicknamed Moby-Dick. It's the size of a blacksmith's forearm, but it didn't take long before I was able to wriggle my way onto its oiled girth without so much as wincing. As for taking it in the mouth, though, I never got beyond the ten inches of solid brass he called Priapus. Taylor brags about one boy he tutored who managed to swallow Moby-Dick all the way to the base, though none of us believes him. Taylor dabs his eye as he tells us the story, swearing it's no word of a lie.

"And then the ungrateful little cunt ran off with a priest!"

You could say he takes his work too seriously. "Knowing how to suck cock properly, may I remind you," he always says, "is a very useful skill to have. It's gotten me out of many a fuckin' scrape, that's for sure."

Taylor hasn't just taught me the pleasurable but the practical too, like how to milk a man's cock to see if he's got the glim before you let it anywhere near you, though that's hardly fail-safe. When Ackerboy came down with it recently, Taylor made him drink some rank-smelling concoction made out of gin and chicory and God alone knows what else three times a day for five days on the trot, and demoted him to strictly non-sexual duties for the duration. Taylor told us that some people claimed fucking a virgin would cure you, though he's never seen proof of it and besides, as he said, slurping on his gin, "Where the fuck would you find a virgin in this city?" He showed me how to wash out my arse with a funnel and a bucket of water so I'm clean and shitless and ready to be fucked. He says he wants us to provide something the gents can get nowhere else.

"You're the élite, you are," he tells us every evening before we start work. "You are the crown jewels of Christendom. Those syphilitic she-skirts down the Dilly don't know a dog's arse about giving pleasure, not like you boys. Never forget, my dears, that you are angels dressed as handsome devils. Now bugger off and earn your keep!"

And I found that it wasn't so bad. Despite the stench of them, they aren't bad men, on the whole. Just hardened and nervous and often very grateful for the little pleasure we give them.

I spent yesterday morning with a young French aristocrat who visits us every time he's in London. He only ever wants to sit and masturbate while watching two rats tear each other to pieces in front of him. He sends a telegram in advance so we can catch the rats, though there's never any shortage of them in this city. And we have to keep them separate and starving until his arrival so that they are hungry enough to tear each other's throats out when thrown together. This Frog gets so excited he squeals like a pig as he comes. And it goes everywhere.

Then, in the afternoon, I met a regular swell on a certain platform at St Pancras station, and together we boarded a train. It's the same every time. We have to have a carriage all to ourselves, and I am not to speak at all during the journey. All he wants me to do is to sit opposite him and, at a certain point in the journey, I have to lean across and draw a line on his cheek with the piece of blue chalk he handed to me before we boarded the train. At this point he ejaculates with a slight gasp and twitch, and then we continue in silence until the next stop. I get out and leave him in the carriage and hop on the next train back to London.

When I got back I hardly had time to rest before another regular turned up. This gent likes to take me out to Epping Forest by horse-drawn carriage and once we've found a secluded patch I strip down to my birthday suit and just run around as he watches me. After he has spent I get dressed and we climb back into the carriage and return to the city. One of my most regular visitors—a peer of the realm, no less—arrives every night at the stroke of seven without fail, barring Christmas Day. All he wants me to do is to stand naked before him with my backside a foot away from his face. It was a bit strange at first, but I'm used to it now.

"I want to breathe you," he whispers, frigging away. "How I love the smell of you." He never lays a finger on me. He simply kneels there making little sniffing sounds, followed by tiny gasps, as if he can only breathe this way, gasping those words over and over. "I love the smell of you. I love the smell of you." I let slip a fart once by mistake (I couldn't help it), and I thought he would be cross. But instead he came straight away, most violently across the backs of my legs, making more noise than ever. So that became a regular occurrence, the farting. I was learning.

I made the mistake recently of saying that he could touch me if it pleased him to, and he was most offended. He said, "Good lord, no. I am far too ugly ever to touch such a thing of beauty." He said that he would be certain to adulterate my beauty immediately should his hand touch my flesh and that he was worried lest even his breath got too close to the perfection of me and threatened to sully it.

I've been here eighteen months now and, believe me, I reckon I've just about seen it all.

The other boys who live here are all a year or two older than me and all beautiful and corrupt as pirates. There's Charlie Carter, alias Lottie. He hails from the East End, like myself, Stepney or somewhere like that, though I think from his voice that he's had some schooling. He's blond and pink, a rosy glow to his white,

white skin that gets pinker with shame—though he never truly shows any, if I'm honest with you. His hair is white as an angel's, his body hairless as marble; and the end of his cock is as red as his nipples.

And there's Sidney Acker, alias Ackerboy, a South London lad with raven-black hair and eyes like jet, the left one a touch lazy, giving him the most charming squint. He has the biggest and most impressive yard out of all of us. I took a shine to him straight away, bewitched by his sleepy black eyes and their impossibly long lashes. He's known as Ackerboy on account of him being the most popular with the swells and making Taylor the most ackers.

Then there's Walter Flowers, alias Princess Pea, who is from up north, Manchester way, and who always makes us laugh with the way he talks and the phrases he has. It's like another language at times, blunt and crude and fuckin' funny. I never knew him to take anything seriously, always laughing and cracking jokes and making us roar.

Finally, there's John Maynard, alias Johnnycakes, a tall, blond-haired, blue-eyed Yank, with a face like the sun and a voice like buttered sunbeams. He tells us such stories of New York that I have a dream to visit the place some day.

Taylor himself likes the men well enough and will trawl Hyde Park at nightfall in search of cock. He's spent many a night in the cells in Marble Arch after being caught in the bushes sucking some guardsman. He is partial to a bit of uniform, the guards especially. He claims to have spent his youth in the Royal Fusiliers, but it's hard to believe, him being so womanly. He also claims his father was a rich cocoa manufacturer who died when he was twelve and left him a fortune that he frittered away. He spends hours hanging round Albert Gate, or will tramp across town to a particular barracks, his favourite being South Kensington. He'll travel miles, for sure, and will on occasion drag them back—all the Queen's men. And then he gets them to thrash nine bells out of him. His particular taste is for pain, which is foreign to me, though I can do it for a price.

I never go in for that malarkey unless I have to, preferring a quick frig or maybe a suck, but most of the gents do insist on putting it in me, either their fingers or their tongues or their pricks. And we get all sorts of pricks in here—bankers, peers, lords, members of parliament, members of the National Liberal Club. They all of them pay us frequent visits. Royalty, once or twice, even. We're popular, we are, and no mistake. It's the life of Riley compared to what I was used to. I consider myself truly lucky—one of the blessed, as Taylor himself promised.

And Taylor makes a small fortune out of us here. We work long hours, though truth be told it never really feels like work. It's just like one long party. The sex is mostly boring after doing it for this long, but I fuckin' love the rides in Hyde Park, high tea at the Ritz, champagne at the Café Royal. I take my ma the flowers that gents offer me, and the little trinkets and gifts, and she loves them. Once a week I go back home to hand over my wages. I'm able to give her much more now, lying about more and more promotions at the Post Office. She's so proud of me I haven't the heart to tell her the truth. What good would it do, anyhow? Things at home are still the same. Pa's drinking more than ever. It breaks my heart to leave. Making my way back to Taylor's always feels like travelling into another country.

Taylor was in a right flap when I got back from visiting Ma this afternoon, telling me to make sure I looked my best, saying that we were going somewhere special to meet someone special. "Make yourself pretty," he said. "Mr Wilde likes nice clean boys." I had no idea who he was going on about, but I must've done something right 'cos since I came downstairs after a scrub and decked out in my best suit, hair brushed and parted, he hasn't stopped beaming and pinching my cheeks, his pupils the size of guineas. "Beautiful," he keeps saying as we climb into the cab, me and him and Charlie, "bloomin' beautiful! Mr Wilde's gonna fuckin' *love* you!"

I've never seen him so excited.

1954

I am a man of few friends. Until recently, I worked as a commercial artist for a moderately successful advertising company. I left six months ago, to become an artist. Or at least, to find out if I am one, if I can become one, if I have anything to say. I remember sitting in my father's library as a small boy and poring over volumes of Hellenic statuary. Their eroticism was potent to me. I had seen men naked at swim, and relished the furtive sight, but the poetry of the marble was electric. I first masturbated over a photograph of a sculpture of Hercules and Antaeus. Looking at art has always, for me, been a source of profound pleasure. Now, of course, you can buy these wonderful *Physique* magazines full of delightful photographs of young men, but I still prefer the paintings and sketches that first awakened lust within me.

One day, when I was about five, I took a sheet of paper and a pencil and I tried copying a sketch by Leonardo. I produced an appalling scribble, of course. But I started again, and over time, over many weeks, something emerged. I did it till I could copy images without looking at the original, by simply concentrating on a point of light that seemed to shine like a star on the tip of the pencil, a spark created by its contact with the paper. I began to spend all my free time sketching, or looking at art books from the library—and, when I was old enough, visiting galleries and museums. It felt like living in another world, looking at art, and it still does, sometimes, though I have stopped going quite so often, as I travel to the West End far less frequently now that I don't work there.

But the life that art creates is not the same as the life that creates art. As I continued to draw more and more, I began to see the world around me in a completely different way. Home for the summer holidays, I would go for a walk in the streets where we lived and see billowing sheets of bright light hanging out like God's laundry from the sky. There would be colours that danced in the treetops like angels on fire. Above my head, a cupola of birds flocked across my field of vision like a veil and was gone. Rainbows snaked their way out of houses and chased each other down the road like otters playing in the shallows of a sunlit stream.

I am still not sure if such a confession makes me an artist or a madman, or whether this question itself might indeed be the answer I seek. How can you ask other people if they see the world the way you do? For how can you risk their saying no? We all accept without question—on faith—that the way we see the world is the way it is, the way other people see it, a truth or a fact that need not be corroborated. As Pascal said of religious faith, "Kneel down, move your lips in prayer, and you will believe."

My parents died in quick succession last year. My mother was one of those women who should never really have had a family but, given the limited social horizons for single women at the time, undoubtedly felt it her duty to marry and breed. I didn't perceive bitterness so much, because she did, after all, achieve a great deal with her public life, but I experienced her distance and exhaustion a great deal of the time. She was, for the first part of her career, a Justice of the Peace, later to become Mayoress of the Borough of Camden. We lived on Camden Road, in the house in which I was born and raised. She did, to her credit, refuse to hand me over to a nanny, and insisted on balancing her busy public life with her duties as a mother—when I was home from boarding school, that is. Many a time I would see her clambering out of the Rolls-Royce that had driven her to and from some council meeting, laden down with shopping she had stopped off to buy, having made the chauffeur wait outside the local grocer's. It never occurred to her that the neighbours might view this as an act of ostentation, as showing off. It only struck me when I was much older and I overheard some gossip in the very shop at which she would stop in her "fancy may-oress's car." She was completely indifferent to the trappings of social status, a true socialist at heart. On her return from a dinner party at Buckingham Palace her only comment was, "The food does come up cold on those gold plates." She was, by any stan-dards, a remarkable woman, and it is one of my deepest regrets that I never really knew her. She came from a family of staunch republicans. I remember one Christmas party when Uncle Bruno spat into the fire while declaiming against the King. Since he had just taken a swig of the whisky he'd been supping for hours, the flames flared up in a sudden heated rush, lifting the row of Christmas cards that hung on a string above, like laundry in a swift breeze. My mother had an unshakeable and stoic work ethic and, while she accepted my artistic bent, she nevertheless insisted it be channelled into a professional capacity. Not for her son the bohemian life of the artist: I would have a trade and graft for a living.

Father is more difficult to conjure. Like a phantom, he defies contour, wavering between being and becoming. A man in outline only. He was a placid, almost invisible man, who went along with his life without complaint. Mother and he spent little time together. He was a tailor by trade, running the family business as his father had before him, and his grandfather before that. He did very well though he wasn't quite Savile Row. As a child I was always immaculately dressed in suits that he, or more likely one of his underlings, had made. He was a man devoid of energy, a man from whom all enthusiasm or sign of life had been removed, drained gradually, over years, in slow and steady drips. Nothing seemed to cheer him, nothing ever amused him. I don't think I ever heard him laugh. He would sit and read the newspaper for hours on end, tutting to himself intermittently like a clock slowly ticking. If he had dreams or interests, I've no idea what they were. He had no hobbies that I was aware of, unless you can call criticising everyone and everything you come across a hobby. I suppose it passed the time for him.

I can recall only two occasions when the topic of our conversation was at all intimate, though I use the term with vast reservations, as you shall see. The first time was the occasion on which he imparted to me the facts of life. I was ten or eleven, and it must have been one of the school holidays, during which I would return home to that silent and cheerless place in which my parents lived. On this particular occasion, Father was watching out of the drawing room window, which gave out onto our modest lawn. I was sitting reading, or most probably drawing. He called me over, by name, and I ran to his side, pleased to be receiving his attention. It was rare indeed for him to acknowledge my presence at all. He pointed out of the window and I followed the direction of his finger. On the lawn outside were two of our dogs copulating, though at the time I hardly knew what they were doing, and the scene merely struck me as humorous and shameful. I was immediately disturbed, wanting desperately to laugh, though sensing I shouldn't. "If you do that to a woman, you'll get her pregnant and have to marry her. You would do well to remember that," he said, in a tone that conveyed unequivocally that that was to be his one comment on the subject and the lesson was over. I returned to my chair, not knowing whether I wanted to laugh or to cry. I knew already that I had no desire whatsoever to "do that to a woman," though I had already begun to fantasise about what it must be like to be a woman succumbing to intercourse.

The second occasion was nearly twenty years later, when I was approaching my thirtieth birthday. I was still living at home and had never once courted a woman. One morning over breakfast, from behind his newspaper, Father said, "Colin, your mother and I think it's time you were married."

I dutifully found a woman quiet and compliant enough to be my bride. Joan was one of the secretaries at the commercial agency where I then worked, and we'd been friends, sort of, for two years before I asked her to marry me. We had been to the cinema together, sometimes as much as once a week, and often discussed novels over lunch, exchanging books we'd particularly enjoyed. She was a handsome woman, with large, soft brown eyes and a generous smile, and she smiled often. (She said, "It costs nothing to smile.") Not overly talkative, but intelligent and well-read, with an irreverent sense of humour I admired. I didn't know if she had ever considered what we were doing to be some kind of courtship, but I knew that I never had. Until my father suggested I marry, I had regarded it as no more than a simple friendship: we never approached discussing our private lives. But I realized I had never known her to go out with any other man during that period.

She agreed to marry me with a tender glee. In our own way, we were happy. We knew that we enjoyed each other's company, and she seemed relieved by my reluctance on our nights out to impose upon her any physical contact. Joan herself was fast approaching thirty, and when I think about her now I know that there must have been some unspoken acknowledgement which passed between us, a tacit agreement that our life together was to be little more than a convenience for which we were both truly grateful.

Our marriage had about it the air of two people stranded on a desert island who, just at the point of accepting that they would never be rescued, spot a sail on the horizon. That isn't to say it was devoid of love. Love and gratitude are not so far apart. It's hard to underestimate the happiness that someone can bring to you when they do exactly what you need them to do. My parents were content, and pleasing them was really all I cared about in those days.

No children, of course. We tried sexual intercourse only once, on our wedding night, but a barely veiled disgust on Joan's part and a distinct lack of enthusiasm on mine left us reluctant to try again. It was a massive relief for both of us, I think, to discover that life was much easier that way. I'm fairly certain that Joan herself had certain lesbian tendencies. Over the years of our marriage there were one or two very close friendships with women. She would see an awful lot of one particular woman for a while and then it would end abruptly, without much explanation. I, for my part, masturbated occasionally, swiftly and guiltily, as if undergoing an unpleasant though necessary bodily function. Visions of men fuelled these sessions, images I had taken in the street and preserved like photographs in my memory: a coal delivery man stripped to the waist, blackened and shining in the sunlight; a bus conductor's handsome smile; the bulge in the trousers of our office boy; the outline of a cock in the swimming trunks of a bather down by the Serpentine; the tanned and dark-haired forearms of a road-sweeper. I would roam the city, picking up these faces and crotches and limbs and storing them like treasure. Then I would spread them out before my mind's eye, imagining all the terrible things I longed to do with these men. I was always assaulted afterward by a horrible sense of shame. I thought myself a monster and yet could not do otherwise. It was my nature, that much I accepted. I had to learn to rise above it, that was all; had to discipline myself to channel my desires into these harmless pursuits. I had read too many newspaper accounts of men whose lives had been ruined by this inclination ever to risk being foolish enough to act upon my desires, to solicit from another man the acts to which I gave my imagination free rein in order that I might quench its appetite. I even prided myself on my restraint, like a fool who thinks himself virtuous for permanent fasting. Permanent fasting brings only death. I suppose I let my desire die.

Joan was killed in June 1944, in an air raid. While I was posted to Hampshire, she had stayed in London, working as a secretary for British Intelligence. From her letters it was clear she loved the work. In losing her I lost the best friend I ever had. She and I would spend our evenings basking in the glow of each other's company, listening to the radio or reading. It was the closest I ever came to finding whatever it is I am looking for. She had few friends; I had none apart from her. After her death I became extremely lonely extremely quickly. I tried to make friends at work, but found it impossible. It was too late: I had been cast, or had cast myself, in the role of someone friendless and unapproachable and, once a role has been cast, it's difficult to play another part.

I wish I'd been able to tell Joan that I loved her. But it was just something that we never said. Silly, really, but even during the brief period we were apart, once I had been conscripted and was working in Hampshire, the almost daily letters we exchanged were always signed off with "Yours," or "Sincerely yours." There was always this peculiar formality that kept our emotions in check. Or maybe it was just me, and she simply conformed to what she perceived to be my wishes.

I know my coldness all too well. I can sense it with Gore. I can feel myself stiffen in his presence, policing my every word and every gesture lest I give myself away. The result is a stand-offishness I cannot seem to shake off. It's as if there's a glass wall between us, constructed by myself. I noticed it this morning when he was over here. He was joking about my not having any friends, and never going out, and said he would take me out if I liked. I paused, unsure what to say, and I could tell from the expression on his face that he was slightly insulted. He snapped, "Don't do me any favours!" and went into a bit of a sulk. I said that I'd love to go out with him but the damage was done: he had retreated, and my loneliness had scored another victory. After he left, I took a stroll down by the river, watching the boats going by, each one representing a world that was going on without me. I have always felt that life was something other people do. I noticed, for the first time, as I strolled along the towpath, solitary men loitering. Since meeting Gore, I see the world differently, see it full of sexual possibility. I considered trying to engage one of the men in conversation, to see where it would lead, but lacked the courage.

As I turned to return home, a pea-souper was gathering and descending, as thick and grey and heavy as my heart. I never used to mind spending so much time alone, but now, since Gore, I dread the long, empty hours between his visits. Especially at night, I find myself feeling increasingly restless. I pour myself a gin and tonic and listen to the radio, or read a book, but I can't shake off this feeling that time is running out and I haven't done anything with my life. This rage and frustration mounts, and it doesn't go away until I have drunk enough gin to send me to sleep. Often I nod off in my chair, waking in the early hours cramped and aching, making my way upstairs and falling onto the bed still fully dressed. This is my life now.

1998

Edward Wayward was a kind of post-punk shaman, an Aleister Crowley for the club scene. His art, like his personality, was loud and colourful. The morning after I first met him, he dragged me out of bed screaming, "I didn't show you the studio!" He used the second bedroom as a studio, and I stood at its centre blinking as he spun me around and pointed at his work, clutching a sky-blue satin kimono around his skinny frame. Huge, garish canvases clashed and smashed their way into my consciousness like broad daylight. I thought they were dreadful but hadn't the heart to tell him, so I said they were brilliant.

As I got to know him, I discovered that he'd contradict almost everything anyone ever said to him, not necessarily because he thought the opposite, but because he hated to be seen to be agreeing with someone. He lived to be contrary. He had to be the one with the different view, the different take on life. It was all a pose, of course, but then he wasn't the only one posing. There were plenty of us doing that. He used to say, "If you aren't going to cause a stir when you enter a room, don't bother. Stay at home and bore the cat."

He told me that a few weeks before he was born his mother dreamt she gave birth to a rabbit. When he arrived a month later, covered in a pelt of thick black hair from head to toe, she screamed till he was removed from her sight. She refused to have anything to do with this vile freak she'd produced, even when her mother-in-law assured her that his father had been just the same, and that the hair would moult within a fortnight, which it did. For those two weeks she couldn't even be in the same house as Edward. He knew that he was a freak, but he grew to wear his monstrosity with pride. A very regal freak, he was.

His father was a vicar, his mother a vicar's wife, and he grew up in the remote suburbs of London, dressing up in skirts and frocks at every opportunity and lip-syncing to David Bowie, dreaming of escape. His one and only friend was a fat girl, Yvonne, who had stones and insults thrown at her every time she left the house because of the outrageous way she dressed. They would sit in her bedroom smoking Consulates, listening to Patti Smith's *Horses* over and over, talking about London and the day they would live there.

On the day he finished school for good, he came home to find a packed suitcase in the hall and his parents standing there looking more morosely stern than ever. They'd had enough of him going out dressed up like someone from another planet and coming home late and wired, if at all. His father explained that now he was of legal age to leave home they expected him to do so, that afternoon. His mother wouldn't meet his gaze, but gave him a hug with tears streaming down her face. They gave him an envelope stuffed with banknotes. He told me that he felt as if he'd been handed the keys to the city, and practically ran to the train station before they changed their minds, calling in on Yvonne to say goodbye. She hurriedly packed a case and left with him. So he knew all about finding your feet in the big smoke. They spent their first few nights sleeping rough. That, he said, was why he had let me stay. That was five years ago. (As for Yvonne, she returned home about a year after their arrival, after they fell out about something and nothing.)

I had moved to London hungry for one thing, striving toward one goal: to be stronger, more wicked, and more profound. With curiosity as my only map, I moved across the surface of this occluded world searching for a way in.

I traced around its borders with a torch, sniffing out a hole in the fence. The heartbeat I detected when I moved here was faint, but I followed its call and found those dark chambers, thanks to Edward. We found it in the clubs where the freaks hung out. All those others who were also desperate to escape the daylight. The drag queens, the druggies, the prostitutes, the good-time girls of either gender. Although escaping isn't quite right. For in their flight they picked up the nearest objects, some of them quite everyday—cosmetics, for example, or clothes—and brandished them like weapons against anyone barring their way. In their midst I could breathe for the first time, speak for the first time, and share in a lust for all things rotten. When I found myself in a council flat in Belsize Park with a cocaine dealer known as Timmy Toots, snorting the white lines as quickly as he could cut them, and for free, I felt at home. When he proudly showed me his collection of guns, I smiled as if admiring family snapshots.

When he showed me a photograph of his fourteen-year-old son and suggested I might like him, I began to fear for my life. For years, my desires were a question mark whose dark curve I followed, never knowing what I would find at the end. I certainly didn't expect prison. Although in truth, even now—especially now—the inevitability is complete.

After spending nearly two hours in the bathroom that first afternoon, Edward swanned out wearing a white suit printed with enormous red roses, a leopard-print fez, full slap and Chanel No. 5. Lots of it. We spent the afternoon going around his favourite fabric shops in Soho where he bought yards of cheap garish fabrics. Everywhere we went people stared at him, open-mouthed, perplexed. He took me into a church off Leicester Square to show me a mural painted by Jean Cocteau. He took me for a drink in the Golden Lion and chatted to some rent boys who were friends of his. Toward the end of the day we called in on his friend Lilli, who worked in a sex shop on Old Compton Street. She was near the end of her shift so she bunked off early and the three of us went off to Pâtisserie Valerie for a coffee.

Lilli was Jayne Mansfield with tattoos. Platinum curls, cherry-red lips, with roses growing down the trellis of her arms. She wore a loose-fitting leopard-print vest top and a powder-blue pencil skirt with black fishnets and Westwood rocking horse shoes, her hair crowned with a black beret. She had a gold front tooth when nobody had gold front teeth. As well as working in the sex shop, she did porn movies and whoring and a bit of life modelling. She told us about posing for a camera club the previous evening, where they employed a bouncer to make sure nothing too risqué went on, but every time the bouncer went for a piss she would offer to give the photographers a "flash of pink" if they chucked her some extra money.

Lilli was Edie Sedgwick to Wayward's Warhol. Fucked-up sexy rich girl. Her parents owned a castle somewhere. Lord and Lady Something-or-other. She was beautiful and sweet most of the time, but if she had too much to drink or too many drugs she would mutate into a psychopath, running across the tops of parked cars and jumping up and down on the roofs and bonnets in her massive Westwoods, screaming incomprehensibly at invisible demons. She was always getting into slanging matches, punching people, or worse. I saw her hurl a glass ashtray at a man in a club once because he said something she didn't like. The ashtray cut his head open, and Edward and I had to get her out through the back door because the bouncers were after her blood.

She was hopelessly hooked on speed, and she regularly had horrendous come-downs. Countless times we had to talk her out of killing herself. She was a bizarre mix of absolute ferocity with absolute fragility. But given the right amount of drugs and alcohol she would shine, almost every night, from the chaos within. When she was dressed up in all her finery she was always being mistaken for a drag queen, always getting her tits or snatch out to prove her authentic womanhood. We met every evening in Valerie's, recounting our days and planning our nights. Like the woman in the nursery rhyme, I shall have music wherever I go, for our laughter on those lost evenings chimes like bells on my fingers and toes. Even now.

One semi-regular at our coffee evenings was Alan Baker, or Alana as he liked to be known (or Ma Baker as he was known in his absence). When I was introduced to him he looked me up and down ostentatiously before turning to Edward and saying, "Well, someone's certainly been answering *your* prayers!"

"Oh, God, no, nothing like that—God, no." Edward screwed his face up in disgust and waved his hand as if to dispel a bad smell. I must have looked hurt, because he stroked my face and added, "Adorable though he is." (Edward only liked them straight—and preferably rough as a dog's dick, I was soon to discover. He had a changeable harem of builders and truckers and cab drivers who would come round occasionally, and I would be ushered out of the flat and told to stay away till evening so he could make as much noise as he wanted.)

Edward's response made Alana think he stood a chance, and he wouldn't take his eyes off me. I could decode that look all too well. Edward began reading out the personal ads in the gay press in silly voices, and Alana said, "Read the escorts."

I asked, "What's an escort?"

Alana looked at me pitifully, then said to Edward, "Oh, dear. H-B-D."

Lilli turned to me to explain that H-B-D stood for Handsome But Dim.

"Child, how long have you been in the wicked city?" Alana asked.

"Less than twenty-four hours," Edward replied for me, managing to make me feel even more infantile.

Alana took his cue. "So much to learn. Listen to Mother, little one, and start learning. An escort is a hooker. Rent-a-cock. Male for sale." He made a sound like a mule. "He-whore, to use the vernacular." He paused, before adding, with a salacious wink,

"And what I wouldn't give to find your number in there."

I had already told Edward stories about my whoring back home, and he said to Alana straight away, "Well, you won't have to wait too long, darling, I'm sure."

I looked startled enough for Edward to say, "You've gotta earn your keep somehow, sweetheart. You're eating me out of house and fucking home."

It was inevitable, really, that I would pick up where I had left off. I didn't want to get a job, and the dole could never provide enough money to live on. There was always a new club or a private viewing or a party or an opening to go to. And Edward was always broke. Pretty soon I was earning what to me seemed vast amounts of money—500 pounds a week, sometimes—which I was spending as rapidly as it appeared—on clothes, drugs, and going out every single night and partying till sunrise. I wrapped myself inside the moods and colours of this city. I licked it as if it were the white-powdered edge of a credit card. I learnt to move through it by following men. And by doing outcalls. There was one man who owned a lock-up in the arches on Pancras Road and who paid me to go around and whip him with chains as he lay face-down, naked, on a thin bare mattress on the floor. In the house of a dwarfish old queen in North Finchley, all scalloped curtains and violent clashing florals, I waited while he took his yapping pooch outside to lock it in the car. When he returned he informed me in a high-pitched clip that he wanted to watch me cum across a photograph of his father. In Willesden Green an old man of seventy-five would enquire after experiences of canings at school, and I would invent stories of having my buttocks exposed in front of the entire school and being whipped senseless. When he was sufficiently frenzied he would remove a slipper from his briefcase and use it to redden my behind. In a flat in Pimlico, a man wanted to be chased around the room whilst wearing fishnet stockings and whooping like a banshee. Every now and then I would have to rugby-tackle him to the floor (which made him shriek even louder) and then I would let him wriggle free and start the whole thing again. I regularly visited a man in Hammersmith whose flat was piled floor to ceiling with books, and who simply wanted me to do his ironing naked whilst he sat in another room doing paperwork; on one occasion, he got me to clean out the thick crust of limescale from his bath with spirit of salts, wearing nothing but a pair of pink marigolds. In a flat in Earl's Court, I was fucking a client when his boyfriend walked in, having come back earlier than expected. He had a bottle of wine in his hand, which he immediately smashed against the doorjamb, running toward us with the jagged bottle neck raised above his head, shouting, "You fucking cunt!" We moved in time to avoid the glass, which tore into the pillow on which our heads had been lying. Feathers everywhere. I didn't stick around to be paid. Another time, a man booked me to be his boyfriend's birthday present. I had to go to a pub in Camberwell and pretend to pick him up, and then the three of us would go back to their flat for a threesome. The birthday boy was very drunk and very effeminate and disappeared into the bedroom the minute we arrived back at the house, whilst the other chopped out lines of coke on the Conran coffee table. After we had taken a line each he picked up a camcorder and handed it to me. He pulled a rubber sheet from underneath the sofa and unfolded it, laying it out flat and standing on it. Then he took his small and brutally circumcised cock out of his fly, spat into his hand, and started wanking furiously. At this point, the birthday boy glided back in, naked but for a square of chiffon, which he wafted around like Isadora Duncan with her scarf as he danced, lost to his own imaginings, lost in being someone else entirely. I saw all this in monochrome, through the viewfinder of the camcorder. Isadora swanned out again and I swung the camera around to catch the boyfriend coming in rapid jets that sprayed across the rubber sheet.

There's no such thing as human nature. Nothing is hidden. It's all on the surface, if you can be bothered to look.

1894

Last night Taylor and Charlie and me went by omnibus to Soho and met this Mr Wilde in Kettner's on Romilly Street. A supernatural glow came from the pink lampshades that sat like blushing angels at the centre of each white-winged table.

We dined upstairs in one of the private rooms, and with us not being used to such grandeur, Taylor showed me and Charlie what cutlery to use, and I never spoke unless spoken to. I was introduced to Mr Wilde and his friend, who's a real lord, apparently. And it was like meeting royalty at first, I was that nervous. That is, until I discovered Lord Muck is as rough as a navvy's ball sack beneath that hoity-toity exterior. I smiled my biggest smile, put at ease by the desire in their eyes. By now I'd learnt to read the signs of hunger and bask in their heat.

"Our little lad has pleasing manners," Mr Wilde said with a smile, holding my gaze till I broke it, spitefully. I was seated next to him, and throughout the meal he would pull my ear or chuck me under the chin whenever I said something that made him laugh. I didn't mind.

Mr Wilde and Taylor and Lord Muck did most of the talking and they talked so fast it was the devil's own job to keep up. And they talked about such peculiar things. At one point Taylor started to recount stories about who'd been to the house recently and at the mention of one name Mr Wilde arched an eyebrow and said, *"He's* always in pursuit of the hirsute, that one; he couldn't care less about the hairless."

"Although I hear he does no more than suck their yards," said Lord Muck before turning to call the waiter to order more champagne.

"Whereas with you, dear Bosie," said Mr Wilde, "the onus is always on the anus."

"Now, now, Oscar," said the young lord, "judge not, lest ye be judged."

"Oh, I know I should be more Christian, but my tastes are far too catholic."

And on they went like that for hours.

I'd never heard such talk before, all manner of things I'd never heard of. The usual punters talk, don't get me wrong, Christ, some of them never shut up, but what bores they suddenly seemed in comparison. Mr Wilde talked of art and music, of passionate love and the stupidity of the ruling classes, and it was like another language. And yet, all through the meal, all I could think about was how fat and ugly he was and how I hoped, even though this young lord was stupid, that he was the one I had to do it with. He was slim and pretty, at least. I've got used to feigning joy in the presence of some of the ugliest bastards you're ever likely to meet, don't get me wrong, but still, if there's the possibility of a nice face, I know what I prefer.

I focused on the way Mr Wilde's chin shone with saliva and I told myself he was nothing but a fruity old sodomite and I've met plenty of them. Nothing special about this one, just thinks he's clever is all, thinks he's better than the rest of us, and he's only a paddy, after all. He said, "I love London as Joan of Arc loved the pyre that canonised her; it will be the death and thus the making of me, at one and the same time."

"Saint Oscar," laughed Lord Muck.

"The paradox made flesh."

"And you've got that in abundance," the lord said, pinching Paddy's waist.

He said, "Don't you think London is like a drying pool of vomit at which pigeons are mindlessly pecking with no hope of nourishment? Coprophagy would be preferable—feeding straight from the rank fundament of the City. Each pallid citizen is just one more pigeon staking its claim on a morsel of bile, heedlessly shuttling from one side of this barnyard to the other."

The others laughed, Taylor and Lord Muck—even Charlie. All laughing, pissed as newts. But I didn't find it funny at all, and I didn't want to fawn all over him the way they were. It made me sick, especially the way he lapped it up.

I found myself warming to the thought of sex as we got to the end of the meal. The champagne hadn't stopped coming and my head was woozy, but my prick was standing and I knew from experience that Charlie was always up for it, and good at it too.

After the meal, we all took a hansom to the Savoy where Taylor waited in the bar downstairs while the four of us went upstairs to Mr Wilde's room. All inhibitions were by now dissolved. Mr Wilde kept his clothes on while Charlie and me and the arrogant lord stripped off and got down to it. Christ, he's a foul-mouthed bugger, that Bosie—swears like a costermonger and has the manners of a farmer. Fuckin' this and fuckin' that. Worse than Pa. He got us both to suck on his member, and a big fucker it was too for such a skinny runt. While we sucked he played with our arses, pushing the neck of an empty champagne bottle as far up each of us as it would go, ramming it in till we squealed and gasped. Then we stood up on the bed while he sucked both of our members at the same time. Mr Wilde sat and watched from a chair by the window, his breeches undone, frigging himself at the sight of our debaucheries, making funny little noises all the while. We finished off with a human sandwich. Lottie was the filling, I was the bottom slice, and Lord Muck was the top slice. We moved in perfect rhythm. like those clockwork toys you see in the windows at Whiteleys.

As we were dressing, Mr Wilde dropped a coin in each of our breast pockets and said, "Thank you, my cherubim," opening the door for us and dropping a curtsy like some chambermaid. Taylor was the cash-carrier and we didn't normally see much of it, to be honest, till we got paid once a week. We knew it was no good telling him we'd been given no coin, for he'd only shake us by the ankles till the pennies dropped out if we didn't hand them over.

1954

Mother died first, in January 1953, and in her absence my father expressed a grief far surpassing any love I'd seen him express toward her while she was alive. It unnerved me to see this usually taciturn and stoical man crumble into a pile of ash without her and hear him howling with grief. You don't really know a person till you have seen how they grieve, till you have witnessed how they deal with loss. Or don't deal with it, in my father's case. He faded away as if the air that had sustained him had finally run out. As if he had relied on my mother to wind him up each morning and without her he simply unwound, stopped ticking like the grandfather clock in the nursery rhyme. It was a difficult time. He and I had never been close, but despite this distance between us I thought that at least I knew him, his foibles, his habits, his character: understood how he worked. I had predicted the usual stiff-upper-lipped response to Mother's death. When he crawled inside that grief, when I found him prostrate on their bed eating her face powder, I was totally unprepared. I no longer recognized him as my father, and any attempt at communication was swiftly curtailed. He began talking nothing but gibberish. He attempted to take his own life more than once. On the family doctor's advice, I checked him into a private asylum in Roehampton. I visited him a couple of times, but he no longer recognized me, and on one occasion attacked me, so I kept away. He was more of a stranger to me now than ever before. I was more alone than ever before. I realized that, however estranged we had been, my parents had provided something akin to structure in my life. Since Joan's death I had visited more frequently and, though our conversation was awkward and rather stilted, it was a bond of sorts. In my own way, I miss them.

Within six months of Mother's death, Father gave up the ghost too. He died of a broken heart, I suppose. So he really did have a heart, after all. That was the biggest shock, that hint of a passionate love beyond anything I might have expected of them. I was financially solvent without having to work. So I gave up my job, sold the house in Camden in which I'd been living since my parents retired, and moved into their house in Barnes in order to paint. But that isn't it. That isn't really why I gave up work. In my heart, I knew even before Mother died that this was what I would do. What their death did was to focus my dissatisfaction and spur me into action.

Sometimes, don't you look at the world and wonder what kind of madhouse you're living in? Have you ever felt, deep down, somewhere so hidden that you overlook it time and again, a pulse that taps out faint coded messages of distress? Don't you hear a tiny, desperate voice pleading for salvation, for mercy, air to breathe, freedom, space to move? That's all I did. I found somewhere quiet. Somewhere so quiet I could hear the SOS. I sat in a corner of Highgate Cemetery after my father's funeral and I listened to the absence of sound, listened to it as it became punctured by birdsong. I sat down and let myself *become* that absence of sound, and be punctured in a similar manner. I swept aside all the voices and the clutter inside my head. The birdsong that punctuated that silence passed through me like light through dust, showing up all my crazy thoughts.

I imagined myself outside the world, imagined the world without me, the teeming threads of life that encircled me, the sorrows and joys of millions of other people, unknown stories, unknowable lives, all buzzing gently in the air around me. I pictured it all as if I had never existed, and nothing seemed different without me. The feeling of monumental insignificance that assaulted me at that moment was both horrifying and liberating. It made me realize that nothing really matters until you decide it does. I'd never allowed anything to matter to me, and I felt the loss enormously. I can't say I felt any grief at my parents' passing. As I said, they were virtually unknown to me. Having very few friends themselves, my parents knew almost nothing about friendship, other than sensing in it the danger of responsibility, perhaps. This sense of danger they passed on to me in the form of a knowledge I don't think I ever truly questioned. My parents taught me how to absent myself. I've trawled my memory in search of something approaching a treasured memory of them, something that might prove their existence as other than ghostly apparitions. I can vaguely recall the smell of the perfume my mother wore and the sound of my father's hacking cough. Or perhaps the time he taught me to shave, after years of watching him doing it at the same sink, performing the task with a curious tenderness and attention to detail that softened my heart with its vanity. But I didn't feel any great sense of loss after they died. Not like with Joan. Not the loss of a person, more the loss of possibility. I knew what they wanted of me, and beyond that I knew nothing. I did what I was told to do, and with each acquiescence I lopped off another limb, until I had completely disappeared.

After I left art school, father secured me the job with Frank Symonds' firm, and my life fell into a pattern that provided a structure the way the bars of a prison provide a structure. Before long I got used to the fact that I'd never get out of it—resigned myself, I should say. Resigned from life. I have always been shy by nature, so I got on with my job as invisibly as I had got on with my studies. I had no friends; people thought I was strange because I was so distant. I found it impossible to get close to anyone. I rarely went out. Until I married Joan, I remained living at home. And I strung my life between the two poles of work and home, wearing tracks in the ground as I shuttled between them, like a shire horse ploughing a field. I never registered my own desires, but concentrated solely on fulfilling theirs. I denied myself, and a feeling of complete and utter grief overwhelms me when I think of the waste.

Gore was meant to come over today, but he rang just now to say he couldn't make it. He has to visit his Cambridge don again. I never knew such jealousy before. It shames me.

1998

Edward knew everybody, it seemed. Wherever we went, people flocked around him. Amongst his friends were plenty of artists, and I soon began to model for many of them. My world was changing and I with it. I knew nothing of restraint and let my desire lead me where it would. Within a couple of months of my arriving in London, Edward took me to a party in an old missionary chapel in Angel. August 1986.

As Lilli, Edward, and I arrived at the door, the air was static with all the frenzy and glamour of the Oscars. Lilli was decked out like a Las Vegas showgirl, a powder-pink feather boa wrapped around her like the ghost of a snake. A tiara bit its way through her platinum beehive like an angel's dentures tackling candyfloss. Edward was dressed like Dolly Levi, complete with a stuffed bird spraying tail feathers from his massive black-and-white hat. In my black leather chaps and waistcoat and black sequin-covered Stetson, I was fit to ride in the devil's rodeo.

As we entered, the first thing I saw was the DJ, dressed in a black lamé jacket, a studded leather dog collar around his neck, and huge red prosthetic devil's horns rising from his temples. He was leading the crowd in waving their arms to "Jesus Christ Superstar." Behind him, two enormous stained glass windows, depicting biblical scenes, spread out like angels' wings. He supplied an endless flow of '60s soundtracks and psychedelia, giving the entire proceedings the ultra-glamorous air of a film set, as did the larval lightshow dripping down the walls around us, amoeboid colour-forms coagulating above the throng like glass candle grenades popping. Silver lamé curtains ran the entire length of one of the walls, reflecting the lights like oil on a puddle. We made our way to the bar, which was constructed from scaffolding poles stretched out across another wall, covered in zebra-striped fabric; a crowd had gathered like lions around a fresh kill. Huge abstract paintings, the offspring of Wayward's drug-addled imagination, adorned the walls. Everyone was dressed up, desperate to be seen. Some weren't even dressed at all. One woman, naked as Eve, carried a shiny green apple with her all night, out of which one bite had been taken. A green-sequinned merkin gave her an iridescent fig leaf. A gigantic man in platform boots appeared, his powdered cleavage bursting out of the bodice of a red velvet crinoline dress, his bald white head strapped with an illuminated light bulb above each ear. An exaggerated red mouth took up half his face, split in the biggest slice-of-watermelon grin I'd ever seen, his manic eyes black as bruises and big as dinner plates. He danced like a drunken dervish, clumsily knocking into everyone, collapsing in a heap in an act of pure drama before picking himself up to continue the assault in another direction. One woman, dressed like a Brassaï tart—black beret, fishnets, tatty fox fur curled across her shoulder like a sleeping pet—sipped red wine as she sashayed to the music. A man was lying on his back in the middle of this dancing throng, kicking his legs in the air and waving his arms, his feet, encased in three-inch brothel-creepers, busy kicking anyone who got too close. He was wearing a pinstriped jacket inside out, with the word "Gucci" stitched in large white sequins down one arm, "Chanel" down the other. His vampire-white face with its enormous fuchsia eyes stared up at me as I leant over him and he roared with laughter. I roared back.

Cybele, an elegantly tall strawberry-blonde transsexual, glided past, wearing a transparent black dress and nothing else, clutching a small black PVC handbag with one hand and the arm of the handsomest man I had ever seen with the other. Tall, broad, dark, and chisel-featured, he was sporting a tuxedo and shone like a film star. Their glamour was enough to take your breath away. Claudia, a pre-operative black transsexual, wearing buggy blue contact lenses, had wrapped a white fun-fur stole around her naked body and was teetering her way through the crowd on monumentally high Westwood heels. She was so well tucked you would swear she was a real woman, each step a painful reminder of the shameful biology fate had flung her way. Or maybe it was the shoes. The first time we'd met Claudia, she had come running up to us in a club yelling at Lilli, "Girl, you're well tucked tonight." Refusing to believe Lilli was a real woman, Claudia had proceeded to bombard Lilli with questions about the operation until Lilli had to get her pussy out to prove she wasn't a trannie. Even then, Claudia just sucked her teeth and said, "Miss Thing, they sure make them motherfuckas look *real* nowadays!" Ma Baker had come dressed like a woman from a painting by Otto Dix, complete with an empty picture frame that he carried around in front of him all night. His best friend was decked out in a seventeenth-century hoop-skirted ballgown made completely out of Tesco carrier bags.

I left Edward and Lilli and wandered off in search of adventure. In one room a four-foot television screen flickered with '70s gay porn movies, while in another, black-and-white Super-8s projected chiaroscuro images of men and women fucking from some distant age earlier this century. They could have been my grandparents, or great-grandparents, linked to me by blood, by the chains of DNA. The fact that they weren't made my connection with them more powerful, rooted as it was in the desire to fuck in front of a camera. In the cellar, a labyrinth of rooms: damp, brick-powdered walls, bare earth underfoot, the chill of a grave. In one room, a bunch of stoners sat around a campfire. One of them, wearing a purple wizard's tunic, his bald head painted blue, cast some powder onto the flames, making them flare up in blue sparkling tongues as he recited an incantation: "In the beginning there was *fire!*" He was grandly shamanistic, and a little absurd. I'd wandered down there with a handsome American we'd met in the pub beforehand whose boyfriend we'd lost sight of upstairs. We moved on. One room was dark, the only entryway a wide hole gaping in the wall. As I poked my head through the darkened, blasted hole, the American said to me, "Climb in there, I'll give you a blow job."

Inside the room, there was a patch of light bleeding through the hole, and by its barren glow we discerned a thin, narrow mattress on the floor. I lay back as he unfastened my trousers and began to suck my dick, and all I remember now is that the pleasure derived almost completely from the situation itself, the location, the anonymity, the betrayal of the boyfriend upstairs. Selfishly, I came, his trousers still unzipped, his body untouched. He said he'd like to watch me suck off his boyfriend. The boyfriend didn't appeal to me. I was more interested in the boyfriend never knowing or, if he did find out, being annoyed at being left out, rejected. Even then, I knew all about the power of betrayal.

As I was climbing out of the room, Edward appeared from nowhere. "There you are, duckie, we've been looking all over for you." Behind him was a buxom woman with bright red ringlets, wrapped in a dress made of loosely coiled telephone cord and nothing else, and carrying a bright copper kettle, which served as a handbag. Clocking the guy behind me, Edward arched an eyebrow. He held up a packet of white powder and grinned at me. "Want some sweeties, little boy?" he said in a creepy voice. I nodded and followed, leaving the American to his own devices. I had never known such happiness. Sometimes I thought I might explode with the intensity of it.

It's strange to recount all this, to tell all this to you, knowing that you will never hear it. There hasn't been a single day in here that I haven't thought about you, wondered what you're doing, and if you ever think of me.

Just now, Tony got up to take a piss, and when he'd finished and turned around he had your face.

1894

Today began as regular as any other day. Taylor woke us up
prompt at half-eleven with a raucous rendition of some bawdy
song. He knows loads. "Morgan Rattler" is his favourite, and it
was that one he screeched out this morning: "First he niggled her
then he tiggled her, then with his two balls he began for to batter
her, at every thrust I thought she'd burst with the terrible size of
his Morgan Rattler."

That shrill banshee voice of his, like some poor beast with its
head stuck, dragged us out of our sleep by the hair and shook us
awake. He went about the whole fuckin' house caterwauling till
we emerged from our beds cursing him. Worse for wear from the
cheap gin we drank last night, and from general lack of sleep, we
pleaded with him to stash it. It's rare for us to tumble into bed
much before sunrise and last night was no exception. Taylor has
his own room, but we have to dab it up in one large room with
dark blue walls and no carpet. There are two dilapidated double
beds, their filthy mattresses spewing straw through various rips
and holes, and we usually sleep two to one bed and three to the

other, though we have to change partners from night to night so as not to encourage any alliances, though, of course, they form anyway. Once up, we washed together, each standing in a small tub of cold water and soaping his neighbour. Walter thought it hilarious to piss on us all as we stood there and rinse us down with his very own hot water. I gave him a sharp cuff round the ear, and he stopped that lark. A quick dry-off and then off downstairs to the kitchen.

Taylor was standing there, of course, by the door as usual, leaning slightly forward with his cheek turned out, waiting for us to plant a kiss on it as we entered and say, each in turn, "Morning, Mother."

He loves that.

Even at that early hour he was already on the gin.

Only in the bitter winter months do we bother to dress for breakfast; in fine weather like today Taylor likes to watch us eating our porridge as naked as babes as he sits there smoking and babbling on and on about this swell and that, who was coming later, who's been involved in what scandal or betrayal. It's an entire one-man show every morning, better than anything you'll see at the music halls, with a cast of thousands wandering in and out as he puts on voices and gestures and runs riot. It's hysterical. We're always telling him he should go on the stage. This morning, though, I was too addled to pay much attention.

After the dishes were done and the house cleaned up from last night, we wandered back upstairs and dressed. Then we gathered as usual in the parlour, ready for trade to commence.

By dusk I had already seen six swells. Taylor was raking it in.

The way it works is that Taylor lets them in and ushers them into the parlour, where Johnnycakes, if he's free, asks them if he can get them a drink. Taylor thinks his American accent adds a certain exoticism to the place and it's true, his deep purr makes you wanna fuck him just to hear him speak. The drink isn't free, it's all included in the thicker they give Taylor when they leave. Anyway, while they're having a drink (if they have one, that is; some just take any boy available as soon as they walk in the door), they decide which boy they want out of those that are free, or if they want a lad already working then they will wait their turn. In that respect, it works much like a barber's shop. The chat flows free on all manner of topics, though mostly here the gents like to talk about what we get up to. They like to talk filth. And we're more than happy to oblige, regaling them with tales of our antics.

So today was much like any other until come midnight we get raided, don't we? Pandemonium spreads through the house like a fire. I'm upstairs sucking a certain high official of the Church of England and he's taking a fuckin' age to spend and I'm getting bored and irritated when there's a storm of banging on the bedroom door and next thing I know there are two crushers in the room and the churchman starts to spend and then like a shot he is hoisting up his trousers and I'm sitting on the bed laughing as he hops around the room with one leg caught in his strides and his jiss flying all over the place. The bluebottles just stand there, not sure what to do. They tell me we've been busted and they wait for me to dress and then escort me downstairs, where everyone else is gathered. There are about a dozen crushers all grinning like bedlamites. All the swells, of course, are allowed to go back to their homes and their wives. It's only us they want. So we're all loaded into their growler and driven to Holborn salt box. It seems that although I wanted to avoid a life of crime I've ended up inside anyway. Ah well, sod's law always gets you in the end, ain't that the truth?

Taylor was at his fiercest and foul-mouthed best as they bundled him into the van. It was worth it to watch the air turn blue around them. They're a bunch of vicious, humourless bastards, though, who'd cosh you without a thought. In that sense they're no different from the men I grew up with, only this lot think they're better than the rest on account of that fuckin' uniform they wear and the authority it brings. I hate the law.

We were all thrown in the holding cell, and it was already packed. It stank worse than a stable, with piss-soaked straw on the floor and the odd turd trodden in for good measure.

Add to that half a dozen unwashed, inebriated men. God knows how long they plan to keep us locked up. I'm due to see Mr Wilde later tonight, so I just hope we're not in here long.

1954

I've been following in the newspaper with great interest the case of Lord Montagu of Beaulieu. He and his cousin, Michael Pitt-Rivers, and some journalist called Wildeblood, are being charged for conspiring to incite or commit acts of gross indecency. As I ate my toast this morning, I read with utter fascination about their dalliances with RAF men. It seems England is scandalized by men of different classes having any sort of contact whatsoever. Just as in Oscar Wilde's time. I remember this Montagu fellow being arrested last October and being tried for indecency with Boy Scouts, but he managed to escape conviction then. Now they've got him in connection with two RAF chaps, who are giving Queen's evidence. Poor sod doesn't stand a chance. The papers, of course, are having a field day, calling the men involved "Corrupters of Youth." I wonder what they would make of my relationship with Gore. Would they call me a corrupter of youth? Gore is far more corrupt than I. If anything, he is more likely to corrupt me. Dear God, I wish he would. I want desperately to ask him what it's like, being beautiful. How does it feel to look in the mirror and like what you see, not hone in on the flaws and the imperfections that can burden a face, nor turn away in shame or, worse, recoil in horror? What emotion is provoked by the desire you must encounter in every pair of eyes into which you gaze? What must it be like to possess that power, that gift? Even when I was young I was ugly or, if not ugly, plain; I knew early on that I was fated to be looked over and promptly overlooked, with my narrow, rounded shoulders and my shortness and my frizzy hair. Even at boarding school I was invisible. I wanted desperately to be initiated into those things about which there were rumours, notes exchanged, suspensions, expulsions, suicides, scandal.

Could I ever tell him? I wonder. Tell him how much I look forward to our Wednesday afternoons? I'm sure to him it's just the day he has to trek over to Barnes. Or if he does look forward to it, it's because he'll be financially better off at the end of it. I can't imagine he feels toward it the way I do. I find myself waking up earlier than usual, with a feeling of great expectation. Christ, I even whistle as I shave. My heart is buoyant, my energy high, and as the hour of his arrival approaches I suck on my own anticipation, my hands twitching, unable to lie still. To my shame, I act just like an expectant lover.

And it's not just the prospect of seeing that body again, though I still find myself staring at it each time as if it were the first time. And it's not simply the company, though I find myself getting lonely out here these days, in a way I never used to when I worked. It's as if he supplies a different air, richer in oxygen, and I feel myself getting high in his presence, and I become more animated as I talk, and I find myself thinking all morning of things we could talk about, and I suppose it's like a youth drug or something. It's as if I'm a young man again. As if I'm in love. Christ, my hand won't stop shaking.

I've decided to stop going to the drawing group. It seems I have become the object of malicious gossip. Peter, in whom I had stupidly confided about Gore's visits when we were chatting last week, has gone and told the rest of the fishwives. It isn't that I deliberately kept it from them, it's just that I am by nature a very taciturn and private man. It's none of their business, I told myself. I don't really know why I told Peter. I regretted it immediately. On the way home, after I'd let it slip, I berated myself for my stupidity, for my ridiculous vanity, showing off what? My wealth? My devotion to art? Or was I showing off Gore, my trophy? Bragging about the fact that he visits me regularly, in private? The trouble is, I find it so damned hard thinking of things to say to Peter, and I mentioned, without thinking, during one of those awful lulls in our conversation, that I was thinking of painting in oils again after years, doing sketches in preparation. He asked who was modelling for me, and before I could think to say I was working from the sketches made at the group, I blurted out Gore's name.

"Gore?" he said. "Who's Gore?"

And before I could think to say vaguely, "Just someone I know," I said. "You know, Gregory—he's modelled for the group a few times."

"And you call him Gore?" He moved in closer, his eyes betraying his fascination. I regretted ever opening my mouth. But I stumbled on, getting deeper in the mire.

"Well, he said that's what his friends call him."

"So you and he have become quite pally, then, have you?"

God, it was excruciating. Luckily Miss Wilkes clapped her hands loudly, announcing the end of the break in her usual manner.

"Chop, chop. Next pose."

I was released.

After a couple of days, I had reassured myself that Peter could be trusted—that he was so shy he was unlikely to divulge the information to the others. Then, this week, the chatter in the room fell silent the moment I entered. They all looked up and smiled a greeting, which made me instantly suspicious, as they don't usually do that. I looked at Peter and he looked away, and I knew. A sense of panic gripped me. I don't know why, it's not as if I'm doing anything criminal, but I felt such a sense of shame, I'm sure I blushed like a guilty schoolboy. Ridiculous, really. Let them talk.

At one point, while we were all sketching away in silence, Miss Wilkes said to no one in particular, "I really must see about getting Gregory back to model for us. He's such a wonderful model, and it's been such a long time since he sat for us."

"Oh, yes, do," said Maurice, "he's my favourite."

There was an interminable silence during which I could virtually feel the physical weight of their anticipation, but I said nothing and the intensity waned. The conversation moved elsewhere. It always strikes me as odd the way they all chatter quite openly in front of the model, as if he or she were not really there. It must be the way the aristocracy behave in front of servants, acting as if they are deaf or aren't really human. I barely say a word when I'm drawing there—the complete opposite of when I am drawing Gore alone, when I can't keep quiet.

So I decided on the way home never to go there again. It will be awkward; my absence will undoubtedly be commented upon, and I shall no doubt bump into one or more of them in the street on occasion. Barnes is like a medieval village sometimes. But I don't need them. Shan't miss them. It'll give me more time to work on my paintings at home. I never produce anything very interesting at the group; it was always more of a social thing, strangely enough. Now the social element has gone to the dogs, there hardly seems any point in pursuing it.

I always reassured myself that at least I acquired wisdom as my youthful ignorance was replaced by knowledge and experience. Now, however, having met a man half my age who has truly lived life to the full, I feel like a child again.

His appearance belies his knowledge—for there is a knowledge there, after all, which I have come to discover.

Much more there than meets the eye. He isn't as dim as he first appeared, just inarticulate, incapable of expressing the complexity of what he feels. How do I know? The rapidity with which his moods change, and the colour of his eyes with them; the world-weariness worn like a garment that ill fits the statuesque demeanour. His intelligence is of a different order—an intelligence of the body, if you will. An intelligence that shines unselfconsciously, wordlessly, and which would evaporate should he ever try to articulate it with anything *other* than his body. It is a logic of the blood-beat, a meaning held within the contours of his skin, coded within its tones and lines.

His face expresses such a joyful innocence when it breaks into a smile. His eyes sparkle with mischief, though not of a specifically sexual nature. His face and neck always discolour to a light shade of red when he is naked, making him look slightly embarrassed, even though his body language suggests the opposite. When he gets excited—which he does often when he talks—his hands move with wild abandon and his voice oscillates madly as he stumbles to find the right word. There is something extremely innocent about him that I wouldn't immediately associate with a whore, though what that says about my prejudices I daren't begin to imagine. He is like a beautiful child, and he makes me feel so jaded by comparison, so cynical and tired. His joy serves to remind me of my solitude, my self-enforced speechlessness—my monastic vow of silence that I took in my sleep one night, unaware of how much I'd miss engaging with the world. Until Gore's arrival into my narrow world, I had grown accustomed to expressing no further sounds than "good morning" or "good afternoon" to neighbours and shopkeepers, and the weekly banal small-talk of the drawing circle. And now this man has come into my life who seems to question all my beliefs, casting on them the light from his skin and bringing them under scrutiny—without even knowing he's doing it. I feel like a pupil with everything still to learn. Oh, I can hold my own, I'm well-read if not well-travelled, but everything I know seems anodyne in comparison to the side of life to which Gore has been exposed. His experiences are the stuff you never read about. He has a scar on his back, just underneath the right shoulder blade, from where he was stabbed in Johannesburg. He lost a toe from gangrene in a prison in Turkey after he was caught drug-smuggling. His body tells the story of his life. He seems to me the freest person I have ever met. How like a prison my little house seems once he has gone and I am left to rattle in it alone. How dull the light seems in his absence, how dim the rooms.

1998

I moved out of Edward's place after a few weeks and into a squat
near King's Cross. Edward and I crowbarred our way into it one
night and I found myself a home. It wasn't bad: it was adequately
decorated and had running water and electricity. Once we were
in, Edward nipped out to a friend of his who lived in the same
block, to invite him back for a smoke. This man, emaciated and
intense, was a poet named Dominic who dressed like a tramp and
told us stories about the history of the area. Queen Boadicea was
said to have fallen there, in the Battlebridge Basin, and the area,
he told us, was bisected by ley lines. The huge skeletal cylinders
of the black metal gasworks nearby, whose monolithic outlines
filled the sky, were listed buildings. Vast iron lungs, imperceptibly
moving up and down, up and down. The place was an ancient
site of spiritual energy, he told us, a historic gateway to the past,
a vital source of regeneration for the entire city. Periodically,
Edward would croon the word "fabulous" as he passed Dominic
the joint. In his soft, serious voice Dominic told us he was working on a long poem about the place and its history, and asked if

we would like to hear some of it. Edward nodded enthusiastically, and Dominic began reciting, his eyes fixed straight ahead as if he were reading from idiot boards. The only line I recall is, "He was mad by every measure of a standard man." Dominic told us that the earth, being older than us, holds us. He said that, however much we may feel that we have banished nature to the outskirts of the city, it inhabits the very buildings we construct to protect ourselves from it. There is nothing but nature. Culture is nature, he said. We are a recent natural phenomenon, and we may well prove to be transient. He said the next natural phenomenon will be the post-human, whatever form that takes. But the land, he said, is eternal. It moulds us in ways we couldn't begin to imagine. It makes maps of us, not the other way around. It traces patterns on our skin and takes its co-ordinates from our desires. We think, he said, that we locate the land, but the land, in truth, locates us.

Dominic worked for the housing co-operative that rented out the flats where I lived, and he managed to wangle it so that I could pay rent on my place and stay there indefinitely, which was perfect. Now that I had my own place, the career that had begun on that golf course with the Count could resume. I placed an ad in the free gay press, and pretty soon my phone was ringing. The first client was a rather timid old man, who spoke very softly and was rigid with nerves. I ushered him into my bedroom, which was at the front of the flat. Outside there was a narrow balcony upon which pigeons nested, and which I shared with the neighbouring flat. I'd yet to meet the neighbours. Before I'd had time to ask the man whether he wanted a drink first, the doorbell rang. He looked at me, terrified. I ignored it, but it rang again and again, persistently, until I had no choice but to answer the front door. Outside in the hallway stood two firemen and a young man who introduced himself as my neighbour. He explained that he'd locked himself out of his flat and needed access to the balcony in order to break into his flat. The three of them marched through the door and into my bedroom, where the old man was by now virtually palpitating with fright. They opened the sash window, clambered through and disappeared, the young man going last and thanking me for my help, casting a puzzled glance at the old man sitting fidgeting on my bed before disappearing through the window. I stood there flooded with relief at the timing. Ten minutes later and it would have been a different story. The man asked, "Does that happen often?" and I said, "No, it's the first time." Then he said, "Get it out, then, so I can suck on it."

Before long I was also posing naked for photographs and performing in pornographic films. These were the tools with which I slaughtered everything I had been. I removed myself—am still removing myself, even now. I became a whore in order, not to find myself, but to lose myself in the dense forest of that name. Words, by naming, claim a sovereignty not rightly theirs. In doing so, they mask a geography of possibilities. My first solo video was for a middle-aged man in Cambridge who worked as a tennis correspondent for one of the broadsheets. He picked me up at the train station and drove me back to his house. Over a cup of coffee, he began showing me photographs of other models, clothed and unclothed, solo and in pairs or groups, and giving me their names, asking me which ones I fancied doing a film with. Suddenly there was the sound of people coming in the front door, and the guy quickly scooped up the fan of photographs he had been showing me and hissed, "*My parents!*" He pushed the photos underneath the sofa before doing the same with the thick wad of photo wallets that lay beside me, telling me in quick whispers that I would have to pretend I'd come to discuss tennis, a subject about which I know absolutely nothing. His aged parents and an equally elderly aunt then shuffled their way into the room and he introduced me. The three of them settled down into the floral three-piece suite and the man offered tea, and then disappeared into the kitchen, leaving me alone with them.

"Which court do you use?" asked his mother, making small talk.

"Do you know Willesden Green?" I replied, to which she shook her head. "I use a court in Willesden Green."

They came around another time when I was just starting a duo, and at the sound of the key in the door, to which the middle-aged man had made himself particularly attuned, the boy and I were hurried into an office at the back of the house while he went off to entertain the parents. By the time he returned we had already fucked twice.

It was for him also that I had done my very first duo, and when he'd introduced me to my co-star, a six-foot-four, dark-haired, hairy-chested, chisel-jawed man, I was straining at the leash. The video guy, John, left us alone while he went off to fetch his camera, and this beautiful, sexy man leant across and whispered in my ear, "You can do anything you like but don't touch my hair." I found out later that he had had a hair transplant and was some kind of walking advert for the procedure.

After every shoot I did for him, John would cook us lunch and he, my co-star, and I would watch his recording of our performance as we ate from trays on our laps.

I did several films for a man in Hove, whose bed was encased in black leather sheets, and who always wore the tightest stone-washed jeans imaginable, and liked to go through a ritual of washing our genitals after we had cum for his camera. He would disappear to the bathroom to fetch a warm wet flannel with which to wipe us down.

Having sex in front of a camera was a curious process of self-objectification, whereby I would distance myself completely while remaining utterly within the present tense of what I was doing, within the moment of pleasure. I was in that state of being where only sex matters. I never doubted that I was in complete control, that I was doing what I wanted to be doing. It was falling in love with you that made me start questioning my life, made me stop wanting that way of life. Maybe love is always an aberration from what we take to be our normality. I can imagine you saying something like that.

In those days, all that mattered was fun. I didn't want to feel anything but constant stimulation, extreme pleasure. Dancing and fucking, that was all I lived for. The next drink, the next fuck, the next drug, the next client, the next party. London meant having everything. I wanted sex all the time, and found that it was possible to live this way. An entire network of men appeared, only too willing to thrust money into my hands for the pleasure of seeing or touching or tasting my flesh. To say that my vanity responded does not do justice to the vigour with which I pursued this line of work. I was doing two or three videos a week as well as servicing my clients, and because the life modelling didn't pay as well I eventually did less of that, preferring the more lucrative porn work. Slick with baby oil, I would slide from one encounter to another. I hid myself beneath that glistening skin, beneath that hunger for pleasure. Unknown desires were unearthed within me. I explored them and explained myself to myself through the coded messages that came from touching other men's bodies. Nothing about my life seemed real to me, and that was just how I liked it, just how I wanted it. On top of that, I was going out every night and having recreational sex once or twice a day, often with more than one person at a time. It never occurred to me that I might live life any other way. My body moved to an insistent blood-beat that never seemed to rest except perhaps for those brief catches at pleasure when I realized that nothing was easier than to live like this. My pleasure lay in getting what I wanted even though I wasn't sure why I wanted it. Sex became so habitual that I ceased getting much pleasure out of it, though I continued to act as if I did, and continued to pursue it constantly. Everywhere—parks, toilets, even the tube or the street—men are picking each other up, following each other home, undressing each other, and wordlessly exchanging pleasure. It thrilled me to be part of that unspoken, unseen network of activity.

There is something about that life that sours so easily after a while, and yet it remained impossible to leave. One party blurs into another, one encounter morphs into the next; you wonder what you are doing, but never enough to wonder why you aren't doing something else. When do you officially become a whore: when you first take money for sex, or when you first realize you've lost count of the men you've had sex with?

Something disconnects.

I'm not saying it wasn't a good life; I'm not saying I didn't have fun. What I'm saying is that I was in for a shock. I thought that pleasure would always manage to steer me clear of pain, not knowing then that the two walk together like mute Siamese twins, never talking to one another, though never able to separate, often thinking the same things, and always, always, inhabiting the same space. I tried to make sure pleasure was always one step ahead of pain. For a while at least, I suppose I succeeded.

One night, in a club in Leicester Square, I was approached by a paunchy middle-aged American sporting a moustache, Hawaiian shirt, baggy Bermuda shorts, and a baseball cap. It was toward the end of the night and somehow I had lost the people I'd arrived with, and he began chatting to me. I was speeding off my dial. He invited me to a party being held by a well-known male strip troupe that was appearing in town at the time. He mentioned a few celebrities who would also be there. He explained that he had been sent to find some boys, that it was only five minutes away. I'd already had sex in the toilets with a Brazilian, but I was still horny and it sounded like fun so we left the club and walked around to his car. I stopped, suddenly sober.

"I thought you said it was only five minutes away."

"In the car. Five minutes in the car."

I got in the passenger seat and we drove off. He asked what music I wanted on, and I said that if it was only a five-minute drive I didn't care. I began to feel uncertain. Some instinct was telling me to be wary. He put the radio on. Then he began telling me stories about the strippers, how they started by doing circle jerks at college. At one point he touched the top of my leg, to indicate how high-cut the strippers' shorts were. Eventually he pulled into a large block of flats on Kensington Gore and drove into an underground car park through a remote-controlled door that slid shut behind us. Inside the car park, he stopped the car and asked me to get out and open the gate that closed off his individual parking space. I did so. My unease had increased, and I found myself imagining what gruesome fate might await me in that flat. Scenarios of slaughter filled my thoughts, with parts of me ending up in skips, in the river, scattered across the city. Once he had driven into his parking space I pushed the gate closed and ran to the door. Instinct made me run. Set into the larger garage door through which we had just driven was a smaller door. As I approached it, I wondered what I would do if it was locked, but it opened and I ran out into the night.

Anxious that he might come after me, I ducked into Hyde Park. Within ten minutes I was picked up by a biker in full leathers, and we rode back to his place in Wimbledon on the back of his Yamaha, me breathing in the smell of leather inside the helmet, holding onto him. Back at his, he hooded me in a studded leather mask and handcuffed me to the bed while he fucked me, spitting at me all the time, trying to aim it at the eyeholes and unzipped mouth. You find danger if you need it. After I had cum, he uncuffed me and asked me to choke him as tightly as I could. "*Tighter*," he hissed as I increased the pressure, his fist pumping furiously at his cock, his face getting redder and redder. I watched him lying there panting afterward, my white handprints vivid against his crimson neck, a huge smile on his face, and thought about the fragility of this life.

I have no idea what time it is now. The whole prison is shrouded in silence, apart from the occasional scream or eruption of rage, and the steady snorts from Tony below me. How I envy him his lack of consciousness right now. Sleep is a country that has just cancelled my visa. All I have to my name are these useless memories. Because of them I am here now. They form a path that leads both backward and forward. That's the strange thing about prison: there doesn't ever seem much point in looking forward, not even to the day you get out. It seems like a liberation to which you can no longer lay any claim. And the present is so unbearable that the only safe place to look is behind you, both literally and metaphorically. But my memories give me nothing resembling safety. I feel a rush of vertigo every time I think of you.

1894

They held us in remand for a whole fuckin' week, the miserable bastards. You ever been in the clink? It's no party, especially if you're young and pretty, surrounded by men who've not seen a woman in years. None of them would touch Taylor, but they were all over me and other boys. Ironic, when you think about it, that we were up to the kind of stuff in there that had got us locked up in the first place. But we weren't getting paid.

None of us was charged with anything though, thank God. Taylor thinks they just wanted to scare us—scare him—and they did for a while. I've never seen him look so fuckin' terrified. Yet the first thing he did on our release was set off to find new lodgings. And guess where we live now. Only right in the dirty fuckin' heart of Westminster, no less. Little College Street. Slap bang behind the Houses of Parliament, right under their fuckin' noses. I can't believe the front of that man. But it makes absolute sense. Now we've got all the trade we need right on our doorstep, and they don't have far to travel for a little relief from the tedium of running this country.

So we're all here now apart from Walter, who had it bad in the slam, pretty thing. Me and the others didn't mind the attention, but poor Walt kept refusing, so he'd get duffed up as well as fucked. I put up no resistance, being the shameless whore that I am. But when we got out Walter didn't want to risk getting thrown in the clink again and so he's gone back to Manchester, though he'll be worse off there, I don't doubt.

We may even see him again, soon as boredom sets in. And so with sadness we said goodbye, though he said he'd come visit us whenever he was in need of a good time and I for one hope he does.

So we're back in the game and this new place is even swankier, though a bit smaller, and we still have to share a bed—though now at least, with Walter gone, it's two in each.

The night we moved here, Oscar came to investigate the new premises. Said he wanted to make sure we had the right wallpaper, though I think he missed us. He's become a regular at the house since that first night at Kettner's. The next week a repeat performance and the next week and the next, a regular little earner it's turned out to be, entertaining this Mr Oscar Wilde. At the start I was no fonder of him than any of the others, though he's more amusing than the other swells, who're always so bloody serious and humourless. To begin with he was just another fool easily parted from his ackers, but he has grown on me, I have to admit, though it took a while, and it took till we were alone, but then I realized that without an audience, once he stops posing and trying to impress, to make people laugh, then he ain't half bad. But the first time, when it was just me and him, at first I was dreading it because he's not much to look at, let's face it, and anyway, all he usually does is watch us perform, so I thought I was in for a dull old time, but I was wrong. He has this way about him that brings out a good feeling, not like some of them who, after kissing them it leaves you feeling dirty and full of regret, and you kind of feel unwell. With him it wasn't like that. It might sound peculiar but he treated me like I was a girl, sitting me on his knee and wooing me and the like. At first it was funny and I was laughing, but then it became nice and it was a good feeling, the way he petted me and worked at getting me feeling special and all ready to be touched. It sounds queer saying it like that, but that's how it was, how it is with him.

I didn't catch on at first just how famous he is, but I soon clocked on that he's known all over London. He's been to America and France and Italy and Greece, and everybloodywhere. Places I've never heard of and have no clue where they are.

We aren't alone often because that poncy little prick Bosie's nearly always with him, but luckily they're always falling out, and when they do he comes here to see me alone and then he's like a different person. Bigger, warmer, kinder. He's a way about him, gentle, I'd say, if that didn't sound so soft, but he is a *gentleman,* whereas *Lord* fuckin' Alfred treats me like shit on his shoe.

Either way, though, I get paid, so what's the bleedin' difference—rough or gentle, *they* call the tune, though it's always him that pays, always. I've never see the lord dip into his dusty upper-class pocket and I doubt I ever will.

Bosie likes nothing better than to spit in my face and bark obscenities as he spends, while Mr Wilde—or Oscar as he's requested I call him—will stroke my hair and call me his boy as he comes between my thighs, for he doesn't like to fuck, he likes to slide his prick between my spittle-slicked and hairless haunches. As he does it, he describes the curve of my roseleaf lips or the beaten gold of my hair, the blossoming bud of my cheeks—things like that. And to tell the truth such tenderness always makes me feel more unsettled than the lord's barked curses, but they also make me feel warm and strange.

Last night Oscar took me to an orgy held in the grand house of a Member of Parliament, a Tory. We had to travel somewhere way out west, way beyond anywhere I'd ever been. I lost recognition of the city not long after we passed Marble Arch, and as we rode there in a carriage he held forth as usual and I sat there listening, not understanding a word of it, as usual.

"Like plants we strive toward the light," he began, and I settled back to enjoy listening. "If we don't understand something we say we are in the dark, or we ask for some light to be shed. Indeed, 'Let there be light,' was God's incantation for Life itself. The cold light of day as opposed to the dead of night, clarity versus obscurity, the purpose and virtue of the Enlightenment. The Light of Reason. Also, alas, its fatal flaw, for we are whole only when we take into account our shadow, for the shadow holds a knowledge all its own; the night contains another truth no less important for its occluded and tenebrous nature."

He lit an opium cigarette and filled the cab with the sickly-sweet smell. After taking several drags, he handed it to me and continued.

"Because the night makes us blind, we fear it, forgetting that the blind develop other senses, forgetting that in the night-time, during those brief sightless hours, we *feel* so much more. In the blackened, cabbalistic looking-glass of the night hours, our own faces appear. Incarcerated in the dark cell of night are the things we wish to hide, a wisdom the daylight hours refute or disavow. Light and dark, like good and evil, far from being opposites, turn out to be complements. And it is the task of the artist to enter the dank cave of the sunless hours and recount everything that he sees there."

He turned to me and stroked my cheek, offering the smallest of smiles as he plucked the cigarette from my lips. "Only in darkness can men truly be themselves, and therefore night is holier than day," he said. "As Michelangelo tells us, knowing only too well of what he speaks, I have no doubt."

Suddenly the carriage stopped, and he gave my balls a quick squeeze before the door was opened by the driver. I stepped down onto the gravel. The horses rubbed their noses together and shook their bells. Before us stood a large white stone house. Each of the eight windows facing us was shuttered like a closed eye. A wide gravel path led up to a large black front door, flanked by two white stone pillars. The house stood in its own grounds, the lawn around it populated with full green trees. There was the faintest trace of some strange music seeping through the still summer air, and my stomach danced to its rhythm. Me and Oscar walked to the front door. Oscar rang the bell, and I could feel the familiar hunger for pleasure stirring in my privates. A small window opened in the black wood, and a solitary eyeball surveyed us, blue as the moon. The hole blinked shut again and the door fell open, revealing a bearded man dressed as a shepherdess with a heavily painted face, who admitted us into a large entrance hall. Before us rose a wide staircase.

The bearded shepherdess told me I had to undress the minute

we were inside, which I did while Oscar remained clothed.

"Aren't you joining in?" I asked.

"No, Jack," he said, "I'm here purely for research purposes," and he wandered off, turning around to say, "Prepare to meet the Bacchae."

I had no idea what on earth he meant by that. I stood and watched him begin to climb the stairs until Bo Peep pushed me forward and pointed to a set of double doors to the left. I staggered forward as two naked young men with golden pricks strapped to them pulled the doors open and, as I stepped inside, I was for a moment if not dazzled at least bewildered. A thousand lamps of varied form filled the room with a strong yet hazy light. There were wax tapers glowing in massive candlesticks, and lamps covered with jewels hung from the ceilings, illuminating the scene below. Although the room was very large, the walls were all covered with dirty pictures, every imaginable mixing of bodies and species. The outskirts of the room were furnished with faded old couches, and men, young and old, and almost all naked, were lounging in twos and threes. I walked slowly around the room, taking it all in. I watched one young lad eat caviar from the puckered hole of another (at least I hoped it was caviar). Another man drank wine from a boy's backside as if he were a fountain. One man was popping grapes into his arsehole and shooting them into the gaping mouth of another. I saw a man spooning honey onto his erection and pushing the sticky member into the waiting mouth of another. In one corner a circle of men were frigging themselves and passing a golden goblet from one to the other, filling it with their relish. Once it was full, they passed the goblet again, only this time each man drank from it. I saw a man pull a string of pearls from his lover's fundament and then wrap them around the neck of his lover before placing his tongue where the pearls had been. One man was pushing a lit candle up another, who was positioned upside down on a divan, transformed into a human candlestick. The wax began to run down the sides of the candle-shaft and pour across the boy's flesh to solidify in thick white tears.

At the sight of all this action I need hardly say my own cock fairly crowed, and I leapt upon the nearest group to have some fun, knowing that, somewhere up there in the dark of the balcony that ran around the top of the room, Oscar was sitting watching. Somehow that seemed to add to my pleasure.

A band of musicians, naked but for turbans out of which sprang the blue and silver eyes of peacock feathers, played rhythmic and hypnotically strange music to which one young man danced, peeling veils from his body to reveal his cock standing to attention, strings of pearls coiled around his neck and looping underneath his bollocks. He thrust and moved his hips to the music. Smoke from opium pipes filled the air, and I sidled up to one man who was smoking and took a drag. I lay back and was immediately lost in a sea of bodies, all stroking and licking and nibbling me. Pleasure became the air I breathed and my flesh became a wave in which I bathed. I lay there as prick after prick erupted onto me and I drowned in that hot pleasure and my body shook.

As I lay there, spent, there was a sudden crash of cymbals and a floorshow began. The gold curtains against the far wall parted, and two men walked in carrying a third trussed like a sow, hanging upside down by his ankles and wrists from a pole yoked between the shoulders of the two carriers. All three men were naked, and the two carriers both had standing rods already. They stopped in the middle of the room, and the two carriers turned to face the third. Then they moved nearer to him till the cock of one could be pushed into his mouth and the cock of the other into his backside, as if he were being roasted on a spit. Then another man stood up from the crowd and pushed his cock into the boy's arse, also. I'd never before seen an arse accommodate two cocks. More naked men came from behind the curtain, each wearing a golden bull's head mask and each frigging himself furiously, hips moving to the music, which became more frantic as if in response to their movements. The crowd began cheering and clapping. A mouth on my cock stirred me from my reverie, and pretty soon the spectators had joined in with the spectacle.

In one corner, jets of water poured down from the open mouths of three cherubs, under which you could cleanse yourself, emerging refreshed and ready to start again. It was sunrise before we left, and I was well and truly spent, my head in the clouds and my body exhausted and exhilarated at one and the same time.

As I was dressing in the hallway, Oscar descended the staircase.

"Did you enjoy yourself, Jack?" he said with a smirk.

A grin split my face as I said I had, and I began recounting in my mind some of the joys of the evening.

"What about you?" I asked, as we climbed into the carriage. "Did you have a good time?"

"Oh, yes. I have enough material to keep me going for a long while. How's that adorable rump?" and he slid a hand under my nancy and gave it a squeeze. My arse was sore after being fucked every which way, though I mustered a brief smile for the old lech.

He looked out of the carriage window as we were rolling down Chelsea Embankment and said, "Ah this cold blue city, where danger is so near to pleasure." I looked out of the window too, at that teeming mysterious city bathed in the pink light of dawn, and gave a yawn, leaning into him and drifting into sleep.

1954

Before I married Joan, I went to see the family doctor, an elderly, no-nonsense man with a walrus moustache and matching eyebrows. I expressed my concern that I would not make a suitable husband, hinting at my lack of sexual interest in women and my desire for men. I had no word to express that desire, beyond derogatory and repellent terms I'd heard at work, words I could never in a million years apply to myself. Only last year a newspaper article referred to us as "these evil men." Back then, in the 1930s, it felt as if I was confessing to mass murder. I was racked with nerves as I stuttered my words, hardly able to speak, hoping above anything that he wouldn't mention it to my parents. He heard me out and then, after a pause, said, "Colin, such anxiety is understandable, all men go through it, but believe me, when it comes to it, John Thomas will be raring to go and nature's way will lead him to where he needs to be."

I asked whether there was a cure for men like me.

He said, "Marriage is the best cure. Once you've got a lovely wife providing all you need, you'll soon forget all this silliness.

You don't want to go meddling in all that, or you'll find yourself behind bars quicker than you can say 'Oscar Wilde.' Trust me."

But, of course, he was wrong.

It shocks me and thrills me to hear Gore's stories. I've always been too ashamed of my desires, too crushed by my onerous flesh. Always too terrified of losing control. What an idiot I've been. Here is this young man whose body is available to anyone with the cash to spend, or those he takes a shine to when he's up on Hampstead Heath, or in Russell Square, who is so devoid of shame without being what those who call themselves moral would call shameless, that one simply cannot see anything but limitless joy in what he does. He holds the key to pleasure, and lives, it seems to me, a long, long way from the shadows we expect to be cast by such sin.

His recklessness shocks and intrigues me, and fills me with envy too. He recounts these escapades of his with a childlike glee, seeming not to care that he's done something most people would consider not simply wrong but depraved, evil, immoral. He told me today about his adventures in a darkened toilet last night, and my face must have betrayed me because he said, "Oh, Colin, have I shocked you?" and laughed. And yet to see his body laid out before me, twisted and knotted into a conundrum of skin, one would almost think him a virgin, so pure, so unsoiled does he look. He is a paradox made flesh, a living question mark, a breath of fresh air compared to the death rattle I feel myself to be. He makes me wonder what I've done with my life. And he knows not at all that all these emotions, all these unanswerables, have arisen in me since we met, like an army of skeletons from scattered teeth.

Gore's curiosity is for pleasure and is pursued with a hunger so huge I cannot fathom it. Yet I cannot accuse him of anything other than following his desires—something, surely, for which I at least have to commend him, having never dared open myself up to the possibility of unadulterated pleasure. I've always been too much of a coward, held in check by my fear of blackmail or prosecution. And most of all by guilt—that most futile of emotions. The danger appears to mean nothing to him. If anything, it would seem to goad him on to greater recklessness. Yet such recklessness is as attractive as it is shocking.

Ironically (though, perhaps not), I have found myself thinking a lot about my death since I met Gore. I suppose it is because I have also been thinking more about my life, which his throws into a relief so stark it terrifies me. There is no such thing as security, I know that now. We think that there is, or that it is something we can construct: a safe life, a secure life. But that turns out to be no life at all. I feel as if I have lived in a state of catatonia all my life, an automaton. For I have lived without joy, terrified of feeling anything strange or unknown, battening down my emotions and my hunger and my curiosity like a door against a coming storm. This beautiful, inarticulate boy has shown me what it means to feel alive. And he doesn't have the first clue about this chaos I can feel dancing within me. Doesn't know that he is responsible for instigating this tempest in my soul.

Today I found myself pondering something that it surprises me I haven't contemplated already, for its inevitability strikes me as so patently obvious it seems foolish to deny it. It occurred to me upon reading the above that it would be so easy to unfurl a few bank notes and taste that flesh that lies before me each week like a meal of which I deprive myself, that flesh that glows and glistens and haunts my dreams. What, I ask myself, is to stop me becoming just another of Gore's customers or whatever he calls these men who buy him? He frequently gets erections in my presence and my palms sweat so much I can't hold the pencil, and my mouth runs dry. But it would be so easy to reach across and touch it, touch him. Perhaps too easy. Do I want to become just another old man whose hungry mouth repulses? Whose presence deadens? Whose adoration means nothing unless represented by money? That fate is one I dare not risk.

The problem, of course, is that in my own stupid and pompous way I've convinced myself that we are friends, and I fear that sex, even as the most straightforward financial transaction, would scupper that. He talks to me so openly, and seems to like my company. I am flattered, I admit. I get the impression that very few people he meets ever pay much attention to what Gore has between his ears, so busy are they contemplating what he has between his legs. He's not the brightest button in the tin, I'll admit, but he likes to talk. The three hours we work together go so quickly. He shames me into admitting there's a world out there of which I know very little. Perhaps I should just offer him the money, and do exactly what I want to do, if I am honest with myself. I'm a bigger fool than I imagine if I think he might do it out of love or friendship. Perhaps to be paid is exactly what he is angling for. It would certainly pay better than simply modelling for me. What's to stop me?

Recently, I have been putting aside my drawings more and more and sidling up to him when we take a break. It's become quite natural to hold him as we talk, hold that warm naked flesh in my arms, against my chest, and though I fear he may detect the violence of my heartbeat, or the hardness in my crotch, I do not move away. I know it makes him uncomfortable, but his discomfort pleases me, makes me want to do it more.

Today, though, he began crying all of a sudden, as I held him. I didn't know what to do, he was sobbing like a baby. Eventually he calmed down enough to explain that today is the twentieth anniversary of his brother's death. He said that he'd been trying not to think about it all day. It seems the brother died in an accident when they were small children and Gore blames himself somehow. I reassured him that it wasn't his fault. I suggested we call it a day and go for a walk down by the river, and I stood up and left him to get dressed in private, which seems so silly in retrospect.

It was a beautiful day, and as we walked, Gore told me about his brother, recounting pranks they had played and adventures they had shared. They were so close in age as to be practically twins. I'd never thought to ask about siblings, perhaps because I lack any, but it seems he is from a large family. Ten on the last count, though he hasn't seen his family in thirteen years, and has never mentioned them before.

A little routine has developed during his visits. After a couple of hours' drawing, he dresses, and we go down to the kitchen. I start to prepare some food for us to share, while he uncorks a bottle of wine and pours out two glasses. We talk some more, and he tells me about his sex life once the wine has loosened his tongue, and I laugh to mask my jealousy. I laugh. But I don't know if I am jealous or envious. Do I want him, or the experiences he recounts with such attention to detail that I am aroused by them? I don't know.

The Greeks placed greater value on the emotion of love than on the object. If one felt love, that was enough, and there was never any question of whether the object of one's love deserved such adoration. The emotion justified the object, not *vice versa*. The beloved was good because he was loved, not loved because he was good. Nowadays, when the notion of love has become so desecrated, and the chances of its existence made almost impossible as a consequence, one must love only the good. To love the bad is considered a pathology. To love the bad is to reveal one's sickness, one's own badness, and that revelation is tantamount to the peal of a leper's bell.

I am unclean. I love this vulgar, inarticulate male, with his coarse tongue and his wolfish grin. I love his crude and immediate attitude to life, his lack of respect for authority, his cynical negativity toward everything, coupled with a limitless curiosity and hunger for joy. I love the rugged contempt in which he holds me and those like me, coupled with a reverence characteristic of his class. A mocking reverence, a loosely veiled contempt. As if I represent a world for which he feels nothing but a mixture of pity and anger.

I showed him some of my drawings today, and he was so genuinely enthusiastic about them that I signed one and gave it to him. He was so appreciative that it was touching, the way he read what I had written at the bottom of the sketch, some words about how inspirational he has been. He stood there staring at the drawing like a child on Christmas morning.

I lie awake at night, feeling his absence as if he were a lover I have woken up to find gone. I imagine him returning from the bathroom and crawling back in beside me, caressing me for warmth, moaning with sleepy contentedness. It is strange, because I have always loved to sleep alone. Even during my years with Joan, we slept in separate beds, apart from on our honeymoon, when we found ourselves rolling to opposite sides of the bed every night to place as great a distance as possible between our bodies. But now all I feel is lonely. I lie on my back in this bed and imagine it is a coffin.

1998

Being in prison has hardened me, it's true. I realize now how much I needed it, because I thought I had it, but I didn't, I didn't know a thing about survival. I do now. You'll no doubt want to know all about how I survived in here, what I've done to survive in a place like this. All I can say is, I did. I have.

I never wanted to need anyone, nor for anyone to need me. I thought it was best to travel light, never get too close. The lifestyle I chose for myself kept boredom at bay, but more importantly it kept intimacy at bay too. Everyone I knew was busy avoiding it: Edward with his twin beds, Lilli with her violent mood swings. Whoring diminished the chances of intimacy. I didn't consider the sex I was having to be in any way intimate, and that was the way I liked it. I never had relationships, very rarely going past a one-night stand—certainly no more than twice. I had more intimacy with some of my regular clients, though it was a sham, for I told them nothing true about my life if I could help it, and yet I might end up knowing virtually everything about them. One of my earliest clients, soon after moving to London, was a black choreographer who asked in a plaintive voice as we began having sex, "Can I be your friend?" Inwardly, I recoiled in horror from his naked desperation, while outwardly I said, "Sure." He paid me with a cheque that bounced and, remembering where he had told me he was rehearsing, I went around there and demanded cash. He was genuinely shocked to see me and gave me the money straight away. I never saw him again, and I always insisted on payment in cash from then on.

London made me, but it made me invisibly, like a roll of film that once developed reveals nothing more than an identical series of blanked or blurred over-exposures. I try to think back to when I first arrived, and I find myself holding onto pictures with my own face cut out, a resistance of memory that just leaves me guessing. My body feels as grubby as the notes for which it was exchanged, my heart as shopworn.

The hotels exist—I can take you there—where I stripped and revealed nothing real about myself, where I pressed my body into servicing a fraudulent intimacy that depleted my resources for real love. The affluent houses, the council flats, the restaurants and cinemas and parks, all can be found in any *A–Z*, if you care to look; but what went on there, and who I was, have been lost forever. The deaf man in jam-jar glasses whose hearing-aid screamed all through the comical sex we performed, who got me to piss on him in his muck-ringed bath, before fucking him with a dildo as he screamed, "Oh, you bastard, oh, you bastard," with each thrust. The Hungarian hunchback who still lived with his mother at the age of fifty, and who fellated me so inexpertly I had to smack his head and snarl, "Watch the teeth!" The film distributor whose flat in Surrey Quays, all cream shag pile and mirrored wardrobe doors, was the place in which I experienced my first kiss with a client, an act which haunted my dreams for weeks afterward, bringing with it each time the acrid stench of his aftershave and the blunt stab of his rigid little tongue. Or the old hippie in Kensal Rise, who would be blindfolded in a chair when I arrived, door on the latch, and who would lick my boots till he came and then smoke a joint with me afterward. A man in Cricklewood wanted nothing more than to sit in a wornout old armchair in his garage masturbating through his trousers while I punched him repeatedly in the stomach as he yelled, "Harder!"

Like the bandages on the Invisible Man, I remove these stories to reveal nothing but a shocking absence. *My* absence. My words unravel and expose beneath their covering anonymous air, through which you can pass your hand. I am not here. These words can only explain how I disappeared completely, how I moved through this city like a ghost.

It is right that a man who turned away from his family should end up with no family. My mother's death remains too abstract, and my own present too painful, for me to grieve. Although I'm sure I will. I know now that grief cannot be avoided. Not even by the most selfish.

I can see the sky getting lighter through the window. Inexorably.

1894

Today I helped Oscar write one of his smutty books. He told me it's a game he plays with some friends. He explained that they take it in turns to write a chapter and pass it on. Today he wrote his contribution with the script spread out across my bare arse. He read the filthy passages out to me as soon as he had written them and reached his hand around to see what reaction it had on me. If my rod wasn't stiff, he crossed out what he'd written and started again. When I complimented him on a particular passage, I'm not ashamed to say that he claimed my own sweet arse had been his inspiration.

I told him today as he lay with his head on my bare buttocks that I try and remember the funny things he says so I can use them for my own, but that I always forget them. He kissed my rump and said, "Jack, my dear boy, a sense of humour cannot be coutured; it has to be cultured, like a pearl." And with that he buried his face between my cheeks as if he were diving for pearls, and we were off for a second coming.

He also likes to pen short lewd plays for me and the other boys to act out before a small select audience of his friends. They're always hilariously debauched versions of classic plays whose titles he reworks. *'Tis a Pity He's Not a Whore* and *He Stoops To Be Conquered.* Last time we performed one in French called *Nostalgie de la boue.* There weren't many words in it, thankfully. I played the part of a bored and decadent aristocrat who seeks adventure with some stable boys. I asked him in bed afterward what the title meant and he said, "It means 'a longing for filth,' Jackie. Isn't that the very essence of life?"

I love these performances. Oscar always insists on the authenticity of our costumes and dresses us up early in the afternoon in order to spend a couple of hours getting a photographer friend of his to take our likeness. He gave me one of himself yesterday. He wrote on it, "*To Jack, my favourite writing desk, O.W.*"

This afternoon, after he'd dropped the manuscript off at a bookshop in the Strand, he whisked me off in a hansom to a travelling circus in Smithfield.

"I've something to show you which might amuse you as it amused me, or disturb you forever and haunt your dreams. We shall see."

I wasn't sure I liked the sound of that, but as always my curiosity got the better of me.

"What is it, Oscar?" I asked, "Where are we going?"

But he wouldn't tell me. "Patience, pretty one, patience," was all he would say.

During the entire journey he refused to tell me anything of where we were going, and when I saw that it was a circus I was ecstatic. I had always wanted to go to the circus but could never afford it—had only snatched brief glimpses by sneaking in, before being caught and hurled out. But then to my disappointment he marched me past the entrance to the big top and led me behind the giant circus tent to where there were stalls in rows selling all manner of things, gingerbreads and whelks. The air stank of straw and dung mixed with fish and tobacco, of sweat and burnt potatoes, and this mix of scents carried upon its back a cacophony of sounds. Mountebanks stood sentry outside each small tent shouting for attention, their voices cutting across each other in a storm of exaggerated claims, like gamblers raising their bets ever higher, shouting things like, "From darkest Africa," "Ferocious as a tigress and captured in the forests of India," "You will not believe your eyes, ladies and gentlemen: from our very own London town a specimen the likes of which...," and so on. Gaudy placards displayed portraits of the tents' inhabitants. Human freaks. There was the bearded lady, the human skeleton, Siamese twins, pinheads and dog-faced boys, dwarves and tattooed ladies. I'd heard of such things, but had never been to one. I had seen the drawings of the Elephant Man in the news-sheets but had imagined the pictures a fraud.

A hurdy-gurdy played somewhere, sinister in its cheerless monotony. Boys and girls laughed and screamed, women and men cried and swore, bells were rung, and applause from the Big Top cut through the sounds surrounding us. One by one, Oscar led me in and out of the tents, and as I observed the freaks he observed me, amused by my awe and horror. I saw a woman with three legs, the third growing atop her right thigh, hanging there smaller, thinner, useless. I saw a boy with thick, coarse fur covering his entire face, a woman with a black curly beard down to her waist, another with every inch of her flesh coloured with flowers and dragons and scrolls and mythical creatures, a beautiful mermaid curving down her back.

"Is a mermaid a woman with a fish's tail or a fish with a woman's torso?" Oscar quizzed me, and I couldn't for the life of me come up with an answer.

I saw a hermaphrodite, half-man, half-woman, its breasts and penis on display.

"Tell me, Jack, what is the opposite sex for a hermaphrodite?" Oscar teased.

I saw two little girls, Sadie and Maisie, whose shaven skulls tapered to a point, accentuated by a tiny sprig of hair tied in a ribbon. I saw a fully grown man no taller than a child, his voice a squeak, and a girl whose skin was spotted like a leopard and who snarled and scratched the earth in her pen like a wild thing. I saw a boy with big pink lobster claws where his hands should be, scissoring them open and closed, open and closed, his face a mask of boredom. There was a human giant who towered above us, making even Oscar look small in comparison.

"Do you think he's all in proportion?" I said.

Then Oscar said, tipping me a wink, "I wonder how much it would cost to find out." He offered the giant ten shillings, and without wasting any time he had whipped out the biggest I ever saw. He said that for an extra five shillings we could hold it, so Oscar paid up and we took the heft of it in our hands. It started to grow, but we heard some other people entering the tent and the giant had to put it away and we left.

In the next tent we saw a hunchback, almost folded double, buckling under the weight of his burden. Oscar told me that the French consider hunchbacks to be angels whose wings have yet to hatch and they touch the hump for good luck. I placed my hand on it, expecting soft, feathery turnings beneath, but nothing stirred. Next were two boys joined at the hip, their torsos springing from the same waist, sharing everything from the navel down, though their upper halves branched off to form two separate individuals. I wondered what it's like to live like that, to feel so divided within one body. As we left Oscar turned to me and said, "You know, Jack, there are those who would have the likes of you and me exhibited in such a show as that—those for whom our love is a monstrous thing, a grotesquery to be mocked and spat at and rejected from the human world. Such people are the enemy; they believe only in what can be seen with the naked eye, never thinking for themselves nor imagining anything other than what they can see and comprehend. They have the imagination of cattle. Never forget, you are a freak in this world the minute you think for yourself, the moment you act on desires not deemed worthy of this shoddy herd. Take pride in that."

I looked at him, not really grasping what he was saying, hearing only the words "our love," though trying hard to look as if I understood. "And never forget that the role of the freak is to sustain the illusion that such a thing as normality even exists in this world. Yet we know better, don't we, my friend? We know that the role of the paradox, be it one of flesh or word, is to reveal the anomalies that parade as truth, to declare the freaks as the true rulers of the earth."

And then, hailing a cab, he said, "I hope you enjoyed our little excursion. Now I, for one, am ravenous. Let's eat, then fuck." He never fucked, he didn't like to fuck, though he loves to use the word, he says, because it tastes so good in the mouth.

As we rode back to Taylor's place he carried on talking. I was amazed at first that he bothers to talk in such a way in front of me, for he must have known I was incapable of understanding the most of it, but I think he uses me to rehearse, like an actor, for the evening to come, when he dines with and entertains important people. In front of me he's just trying out his speeches, trying out his words, but I don't mind; in fact it's like watching someone perform on a stage, truth be told.

"There is a way of living that's completely outside the law; there's a world in which you can do whatever you want, a world of no laws but those of the body, no government but that provided by your appetites. You can be free, free to pursue any desire, acquire any knowledge. It's the most terrifying place to live. It's dangerously beautiful, this way of life, dangerous the way only beauty can be, that is, blindly refusing to see the full extent of the danger."

This is the kind of thing he comes out with all the time, and it's both fascinating and irritating in equal parts.

The thing is, I've never met anyone before who I wanted to *be*. I've met people who made me laugh, people who impressed me, but the majority I try my hardest to be unlike.

I reckon most for fools or hypocrites, just like Taylor said I would, but never before have I looked at another's life and thought, that's exactly what I'd like to be. Would like to be but know I never could be.

When it's just the two of us, on those occasions when Lord Muck isn't around, Oscar seems so much happier, and I am too. It feels different somehow, less sordid, less like a financial transaction. And though part of me likes the adoration, still, when I'm alone I find myself vowing never to let him make me feel that way again, cursing myself for my sentimental weakness.

1954

I was carted off to boarding school at such a preposterously young age that I cannot now recall anything about my life before that, try as I might. Fleeting scenes of ambrosia, paradise lost, Eden before the fall, that kind of thing. An innocent brightness before the descent of darkness, like a last glimpse of sun from the edge of a cloud as it sinks out of sight. Boarding school is not a place for children. Indeed, one is actively discouraged from being a child the minute one arrives. One must replace joy with discipline, freedom with submission, and curiosity with a deadened obedience to umpteen rules and regulations, facts and figures. It is a painful process, growing up by force, becoming an adult at the age of six, becoming a "little man," as they called us. How we became little men, though, was through a brutalisation of the highest order. If you weren't willing or able to beat others into submission, you were beaten into submission yourself. I was weak by nature and physically small for my age and so it was my lot to suffer during my time there, caught as I was between the barbarity of the staff and the decadence of the older boys. I think now that I and the other weak boys were punished for not conforming, or for not being able to conform. I never breathed a word of it to my parents and, of course, my experience of boarding school made me long to conform even more, rather than the reverse. I used to pray every night for God to kill me, or save me. When he did neither, I became an atheist. Since that time I've never once doubted the non-existence of God.

The sexual indignities I had to endure at the hands of the older boys were made even more unbearable by the fact that, for the most part, I took a shameful delight in them. I even looked forward to some of the encounters, had crushes on some of those older boys, though none ever showed me a scrap of affection.

The only thing about becoming an adult that I rushed toward with open arms was that I would no longer suffer the brutality of school and could blot the experience from my memory, along with my desires. Life seemed so much easier for adults. In many ways, I was much more capable of conforming to the accepted behaviour of middle-class adults, though I say that with absolutely no feeling of pride whatsoever. I've always been too frightened to do anything else. My timidity shames me all the more since I met Gore.

Sis ut videris was our school motto. "Be as you seem." No pretence, no airs, no affectations. We would become good, solid, bourgeois men, reliable, capable, honest, and true. Masculine. Transparent. *Be as you seem.* Ah, but we seemed, and still do, so much less than we really are or might be. Right down to marrying Joan, I did exactly as expected. I moved placidly within the narrow parameters set down during my childhood. I never once questioned whether anything lay beyond, never dared articulate my own desires or ambitions. My only outlet from this prison has been art, though until recently I was never anything other than an observer. Once I'd left art school, outside of work I never picked up a pencil, let alone a brush. Although I still visited galleries voraciously, I no longer thought to sketch those paintings that moved me the way I had when I was young, let alone attempt to create my own. I had locked away my joy in creating art when I began working. And yet now I cannot stop, producing countless sketches, good sketches, and finding myself itching to work in oils. For the first time in I don't know how long—perhaps ever—I feel exhilarated.

This morning I finally began to prepare for a large oil painting of Gore. I haven't worked in oils for years, not since my art school days. The smell of the paints took me back instantly to a time when I was still able to dream of my life as an artist. Over the last few weeks, I've been working on preliminary sketches. A year ago I would never have believed that I would ever paint again.

I stretched the canvas myself, relying only on memory, and am quite proud of the results. After over thirty years I could still remember each stage of the process. When I touched the coarse fabric, the past contracted into an instant and I was full of youth and optimism and I felt a pang of pity for that young man I was and wished that I could speak to him now and tell him to follow his dream. In this life, dreams are all we have to remind us of who we really are or should be. How different my life would have been if I'd been strong enough to defy everyone in the pursuit of freedom. How difficult life is without the freedom to discover who you are meant to be. I refuse to believe I was meant to be so unhappy. Making that canvas this morning felt like an act of rebellion and, in choosing to portray a beautiful man in my painting, I feel another sense of vertigo. Freedom is always vertiginous, just like desire.

When you work as a designer you spend all your time pleasing others, those clients upon whose patronage you rely. It is, I suppose, a form of prostitution. You work hard at keeping them happy, doing what they want, at the expense of your own creativity. There is little scope for making *yourself* happy. Your happiness defers to that of another. The artist is as far away from this position as possible: the artist spends all his time and energy making himself happy. I please myself now. There is no one to tell me what to do, and that is quite frightening. Freedom is always frightening; that's why most people choose not to be free. I wouldn't say I'm any exception, but with these new paintings I'm planning, I feel as if I have no choice. I either paint what I see, the way I see it, or I don't bother.

I've been thinking a lot about freedom since reading yesterday the outcome of the Montagu case. He has been given twelve months, whilst Wildeblood and Pitt-Rivers each received eighteen. Harsh sentences, I thought, though I've read of other men recently who have been handed seven years' imprisonment for such activities. I worry about Gore. It's a miracle he hasn't been caught. Judging from the papers, the police must be everywhere. I wish there were some way to change the way the world sees us.

1998

For almost the next ten years, this was my life, this pursuit of pleasure and avoidance of pain. The names changed, but the patterns remained the same. Lilli ended up in a mental hospital for a while before eventually moving back home to Newcastle to live with her mother. One night Edward and I had arranged to go round to her place after a club, only to find her drug-fucked and lost, staggering around with bare feet, and leaving bloody footprints everywhere from treading on broken glass in the kitchen. She wasn't even aware of the pain. I went to visit her in hospital only once, and she was unrecognizable. Devoid of make-up, devoid of life, pale as ash, and silent, so silent, where once laughter and joy had reigned. She looked like a little girl, as fragile as a child, skinless and lost. When I said hello and asked how she was, she said nothing. I put the flowers and magazines I'd brought on the bed, but she didn't look at them. She was elsewhere. Somewhere unreachable, somewhere off the map. Somewhere lost to any language. I watched her vacant face flicker with confusion, and I thought of all the times we had danced together across this city's skyline, striding with the purpose of gods; of all the nights lost to that wild intense joy we found and threw about us like robbers laughing in a snow of banknotes. I wanted to cry. I wanted to hold her and tell her it would all be all right. Instead I sat in that silence, installed myself into its comfort, and simply held her hand as she stared into space, enraptured by something she no longer wished, or was able, to share.

That was the last time I ever saw her. A week later she moved back home.

Not long after, Edward got a real job, working for an art gallery in the West End, and started partying with another, richer crowd. I hardly ever saw him, just the odd postcard from some far-flung place. I hung out with other whores who would come and go, staying around just long enough to earn the money to take them elsewhere. But I had no real friends. I'm sure the only people that have missed me while I've been inside are my clients.

Do you miss me? I wonder.

I'd grown up feeling invisible, making myself invisible by every means possible. I had wanted to remove myself, to become some-one else. Sex became a way of avoiding a great many things. I didn't recognize myself. I didn't want to recognize myself. I wore it like a badge, or a medal, this desire. I heightened it, and cheap-ened it, and worked it like a slave. I wore men's names like scalps around an Indian's waist. There was no victory because there was no challenge. It was my path of least resistance. I thought I wanted half the things I have forgotten even doing. Even the brutal sex I've experienced in here has been a welcome form of attention. I can pretend I am wanted. I can imagine that it's me they want and not some quick relief. Perhaps that's what I've always done, imagining a particularity in another's desire for me when in truth anyone would have sufficed. Perhaps that's what I did with you. To accept that would be the hardest lesson, but perhaps that is exactly what I am supposed to learn from all this.

The day before we met, I saw a regular client, an Irishman, the owner of a record shop outside Dublin. Once a month he travelled over to buy stock, and usually gave me a call. He was younger than the majority of the men who hired me, not bad-looking. One of the few I enjoyed. For that reason, it was much harder to differentiate between work and pleasure. It was with mixed feelings that I went to visit him at his hotel in Piccadilly. The previous time I'd seen him, he'd suggested flying me over to Dublin for a weekend, paying not only for the flight but my time. Although I'd agreed, I'd known that I would probably have gone even if he weren't paying, and that made me uncomfortable. I'd never considered that I might be lonely. Not that anything emotional was involved, at least not on my part. That never happened. But I knew that my curiosity alone would take me. Sometimes, my curiosity knows no bounds.

We went to his hotel. I knew it well. In the same hotel I would often meet another client, an older man, a married Scottish businessman who once showed me a snapshot from his wallet of the wife and kids, just after peeling off the rectal examination gloves he had worn while his fingers worked the lubricated edges of my arsehole. A polite man, who always began the session taking Polaroids of my arse before asking, "May I insert a finger?" his voice tentative and uncertain. The Irish record shop owner had no such kink, it was straight down to fucking, first me him, then him me. I wondered where my life was going, not knowing that, a week later, an answer would present itself in the shape of you.

(But what kind of answer was that?)

The first time we met was by daylight, though it always feels like night when I think of you. It was a freakishly sunny day in late January when you appeared. 1996. I had been doing videos on a regular basis over the past couple of years for a man in Clapham named Harry. Harry wanted me to "recruit some new models," as he called it. So he placed an ad in the gay press, using my phone number as the contact. My job was to screen out the uglies, to pan for gold. You came to me that way, my love, a glint in the silt. I'd get them to strip off and pose for a Polaroid. Of course, I had sex with most of the guys who came over. I'd say something like, "How would you feel about posing with a hard-on?" And that was that.

I opened the door to let you in, and you were every bit as sexy as you had sounded on the phone. Tall and dark. Tight white T-shirt and turned-up Levis, black leather jacket. I couldn't wait to see you naked. And when you took off your jacket I knew then, I think, that this was dangerous. Nice arms. Nice tattoos. I itched to taste your sweat. Such a pull, such a wrench, such a light-headed, dry-mouthed need to touch another. I thought that that had died in me, that thrill, that excitement. I made us some coffee and talked about the modelling. You were new to the game, but showed no nerves when it came to shedding your clothes so I could take the obligatory snapshot for Harry. You were more beautiful unclothed than I'd imagined.

After I had taken the picture, you sat down, still naked, on the floor by the window, where your clothes lay in a pile, and rummaged in your jacket for a cigarette, and said, after lighting it and exhaling the first lungful, "So, how did you get into this game?"

I was enjoying the excuse to look at you that talking allowed. You asked if I had any pictures from the porn modelling I had done, and when I said yes, you asked to see them. I went and fetched them from the bedroom, these pictures I had never shown anyone before. We'd been talking for about half an hour before you commented on how strange it felt, this situation of you being naked with me fully clothed.

"I'll take mine off too, if it'll even things out," I offered.

"I don't know about evening things out, but I'd sure like that."

I shed my clothes, and you asked if I had any grass. I sat there naked at the kitchen table, rolling a joint. When I looked up, you were smiling at me, a smile so bright it was as if you'd eaten stars.

"What?" I questioned, suddenly paranoid.

"Nothing," you replied, and I mirrored your smile.

I thought I knew all there was to know about sex, but I'd never experienced before that dissolving of skin till nothing exists but a network of sensations that glow and sparkle, turning you inside out and back again, somersaulting rapids of touch and taste that you never want to end. Never knew this blending of selves, this fading into you. This cannibal, animal hunger and joy.

By the time you left, a couple of hours later, something had happened that had never happened before. I'd found myself thinking, I'd really like to see this man again. But before I'd had time to ask for a phone number, you had said goodbye, kissed me, and gone, off into the drab evening, which began working its insipid way through the windows. You'd been in the flat for hours. We'd chatted before, during, and after sex, and it had all actually made sense, and been funny, and felt good. I didn't want you to leave. And this was unheard of in my experience. With you it felt like meeting an old friend, someone I hadn't seen for years. Someone I was so glad to see because not only do we share a perfect familiarity already, but we have so much to tell each other, we could spend a lifetime recounting all those things we've done since we last met. And still it wouldn't be enough time. With you, my spirit danced. A face and a body I could never tire of looking at, and a soul it seemed I could never tire of exploring. We laughed like children and tore the world apart. Because of you, I am beautiful. Because of you, my body is a possibility. My body is a gift. My flesh reconstituted in your hands, your mouth.

After your departure, my phone rang and I was called out to a regular client in Earl's Court, a man who liked to be scrubbed all over his body with wire wool. I quickly dressed and left.

1894

I feel unsettled after spending this last weekend with Oscar. He invited me to Paris and arranged it with Taylor for me to go. I've never before left London, let alone the country, and it was the most bizarre experience of my life so far. Away from London, and in the thick of such a strange tongue, my life became more and more peculiar, took on more and more bizarre patterns. What a world I've been born into. To think that there are places and people and languages beyond anything I could ever imagine. It makes you want to make the most of what you have.

He took care of me in a way no one ever has before. I'd been so used to looking after myself that I was a bit suspicious at first, wondering why would anyone bother being nice to the likes of me, even if he is infatuated with that petalled jewel I sit on, that smells, he tells me, like no other? He claims to be able to tell a boy's age simply by the scent of his arse, and said he would be able to tell my arse apart from any other simply by the smell alone. "It emits a unique perfume, dear boy. If you could bottle it you'd have wealth and love beyond imagination," he told me.

In Paris he was everything to me—lover, companion, guide, even my voice. I'd have starved if I'd been on my own. Instead I was treated to the most incredible delights. I couldn't wait to get back and tell the other boys I'd eaten snails, though the thought disgusted me at first, and I didn't want to touch them till Oscar scooped one up and popped it in my mouth. It tasted like butter.

As soon as we arrived, he took me to have my hair done. It was the first time I'd ever been in a hairdresser's. Taylor normally cuts it with blunt scissors as we take it in turns sitting on a stool outside in the street, our locks blowing away in the breeze. But in Paris Oscar left me there to be pampered and preened while he went off to meet some fellow about one of his plays. In the afternoon, after the haircut, I entertained myself exploring that strange city. I wandered down by the river to watch the boats go by. I like to do that in London when I can. Then I found myself in some gardens where, between the orange trees, young men loitered suggestively. They say it takes one to know one, and I knew one when I saw it. My own kind. Their availability was written all over their faces, and I was instantly alert to their desire. It wasn't not having a word of the lingo that stopped me having some fun, none of them said much to one another anyhow, but I was having enough fun just taking in the show, watching the chorus line of older gentlemen billing and cooing around the young bits of rough, who played the part of the leading ladies. I amused myself watching their courtship rituals and their pairings, and I was surprised how similar it was to London, a universal language of lust written on the body and spoken by the eyes and fingers. I whiled away a pleasurable couple of hours trying to predict who would swallow whom.

On the Saturday evening we went to a show. We didn't see a play 'cos I wouldn't understand a bleedin' word—instead we went to Pigalle and the kind of show that delighted Oscar because it was bawdy and lively. A line of girls dancing to frantic music, lifting their skirts and kicking their legs high over their heads, showing the frills that frothed beneath, and just for a cheeky moment you could see that they wore no knickers. They were coarse and loud, them girls, their faces painted in heavy bright colours. Between shows they cavorted with the gents in the audience. Many of them sat on laps in various states of disarray; some fucked or sucked, curling up the banknotes afterward and sliding them inside the garters they all wore. I sat there watching, drinking one absinthe after another, and when I turned to Oscar he was watching me, not the goings on around us. He smiled and said that for him the greatest pleasure of all is witnessing the joyful corruption of another.

Late at night in bed, he whispered strange words to me in French. I asked him what he was saying and he told me. "You are a treasure." It made me sad, though, the way he said it. For too brief a time London and Bosie seemed a million miles away, but I knew it must end. On the boat back to England I was quiet. I could feel tears swimming in my eyes, and though I tried hard not to let it show, I'm pretty sure he saw. When Southampton came into view he sighed and said under his breath, "Ah, this septic isle." When I got back to Taylor's, I looked the word up in the dictionary he give me, and had to agree with him. And as I lie here in bed with Johnnycakes snoring beside me, I find myself thinking about last night, with Oscar sleeping at my side, and I wish he was here with me now.

I just got back from seeing Oscar and am so full of rage I could kill a man with my bare hands. That's the only way to describe how I feel. I swear I could tear the world apart and still not be calm.

For the last few months, as the old year turned to the new, he's taken me places and spent time with me and made me feel special in a way no one ever did before, actually listening to me when I spoke and even asking me my thoughts and opinions, flattering me, making me feel things for him. l thought I meant something, and I know this sounds stupid coming from a whore, but it's the truth. I wish it wasn't, but it is. I don't know whether I would call it love because I'm certain I don't know what that word means, but something happened to me inside and a storm of emotions has awoken in me like never before, like a flock of roosting birds shaken from a tree. I know he also sees the other boys here, but I flattered myself that they meant nothing to him compared to me. And now he's told me he can't see me any more. I feel such pain and panic that the only word that comes to mind is rage.

Tonight, he took me to Kettner's and I found myself remembering how ridiculous he appeared to me on that first time I'd met him, and it seemed like old news from another country. It was just me and him this time, though a friend who introduced himself as Robbie joined us for coffee and his intrusion started the anger I now feel.

Throughout the meal Oscar had been quiet and tense and I knew that all was not well, though we don't ever really talk of such things. His personal life is a mystery to me. I knew that if Bosie wasn't there it meant things weren't good between them, though for my part I was glad of it for I prefer it that way. Most times, even in the little bastard's absence, he is still in good spirits, but tonight he was somewhere else entirely, not with me at all. His laughter had no life to it and, as a result, neither did mine. He seemed to light up when Robbie imposed on us, which was probably planned and not the coincidence they both pretended it to be.

We were at a table in a private room upstairs. Oscar had just been to see his clairvoyant, an old bird called Madame Cybele. I could see he was agitated, and after a few glasses of champagne he told me what the tarot cards had revealed. Smoking one cigarette after another, he told me the stupid old sow's predictions.

"It couldn't have been worse," he said, "it really couldn't. I had the Page of Wands reversed, indicating the presence of a young man who will be my downfall, a youth who perpetrates scandal, a superficial creature with no thought for others. Who else could it be but dear Bosie? I had the Nine of Swords, which signifies miscarriages of fortune and unbearable mental torment. Card after card, all signifying separation and loss. And then, curse my luck, I dealt Death, *La Mort*, the grim reaper, which in itself doesn't necessarily bode ill, but then I dealt the Tower reversed—which can only mean one thing. I'm in for a fall. The Tower reversed, my dear boy, spells prison."

I tried my best to comfort him, saying it's all a load of old hokum, but he insisted that the cards were never wrong. He was seriously scared, and I'd never thought he could feel fear. He always seemed so fearless.

"Every prediction that woman has ever made has come true so far," he said, "and tonight not one card spoke well of the future. I am doomed. Next came the Five of Swords, signifying loss, affliction, defeat. Then I turned over the Fool reversed, the end of a journey, suffering by reckless action. I was petrified by this point, positively drenched in perspiration, and did not want to pick another card. My hand trembled as it hovered above the stack, and when I plucked one and turned it over I cried out and my heart sank, for it was the Wheel of Fortune reversed: ill-fortune, failure, another portent for the end of a cycle. My life is over, Jack. I sat there trembling with fear as she spoke in grave tones, thinking, Will there be no end to this nightmare? Have I angered the gods so profoundly that now I must pay with my life? Am I to be punished for the life I have led? I am not a bad man, am I, Jack?"

I assured him he was not. I said that he was never anything but kind and generous to me. But he was stricken with inconsolable grief and would not be cheered even when I made jokes and acted like a wizened and toothless old fortune-teller, fashioning a headscarf from my napkin. Never have I seen him so crushed.

"Separation and loss," he kept saying, and stared down at the table as if he could see still the cards laid out before him spelling out his fate.

Then he started on and on about that fucking Bosie and his maniac father. Said something about them both being the death of him, and his tirade lasted until the food arrived. It seems that the father's accused him of corrupting his son, and he is going to have to defend his honour and take the old bastard to court. He kept on calling him a damned interfering ignorant fool.

"Oh, the rules of love," he sighed. "It takes us a lifetime to learn them, and when we do we find we no longer wish to play the game. A revolting paradox, to be sure. How lucky you and I are not to be cursed with loving each other, Jack," he said. "How easy life would be if one could live without love—how easy and how dull."

I don't know why, it was probably the champagne, but I found myself blurting out that I was scared and, to be honest, I didn't even know I was until I said it, and then I felt really scared—the words seemed to bring about the emotion they named.

He said, "To admit that one is scared is the beginning of bravery."

He asked what I had to be scared of, saying that the young have nothing to fear because the world is on their side, time is on their side, and no one can tell them what to do because to be young is always to be right.

"Never ruin yourself with love, Jack, for you are a fountain of youth, and love would only age you as it has aged me."

Then he told me the thing that turned my sadness into rage.

"I won't be seeing you for a while," he said. "All this nonsense has started to interfere and it is best for now if I am not seen cavorting around London with dangerous, beautiful creatures like you." And then, after a pause, he added, "Enjoyable as that might be," and gave me a weak smile.

I don't know why this should make me feel so angry. Maybe it was that I wanted him to defy the world and not want us to part, or maybe it was the conversation with Taylor earlier today when he told me not to see so much of Oscar.

"You know, Jack," Taylor had said after breakfast, "Mr Wilde is a fickle man. You might think that you're special, but you're not. You mean no more to him than any of the other boys he rents. You're a whore—a very good whore, mind, but don't lose sight of that. Don't go getting all sentimental on me, now." I didn't know what he meant at the time, and I said it was up to Oscar how much we saw of each other. Taylor arched his eyebrows and said, "Oscar, is it? Don't be a stupid tart, Jack. You've no idea how much danger you're in. Just keep away from him for a while."

It all seemed suddenly to make sense as I sat there hours later staring across the table at Oscar, and it all seemed to indicate a plan to keep us apart. But I can't for the life of me understand why, and that makes me want to rave and scream and smash things in a way I've never felt before.

Then comes the time for me to leave. No hansom to the Savoy tonight, no frolic in the sheets. He explained he couldn't risk being seen with me, so I left on my own feeling so torn up inside.

And that was when I had another surprise, one more thing to feed the furnace of my rage. Oscar and Robbie stayed behind. I couldn't say for sure what made me wait across the street. I think, stupidly, that I wanted one more look at him, which sounds pathetic, I know, but that was why I didn't return home straight away, but hid in a shadowy doorway opposite Kettner's. And I'm damned glad I did, for not more than five minutes later a cab pulls up, and out of it steps Sidney, dressed up to the nines. My jaw fell as I watched him swan straight into Kettner's. The cab didn't pull away, though, and before all this had sunk in, I clocked the three of them emerge, laughing, and watched them climb into the cab, and watched it pull away, and then my fury was complete.

1954

I was working on some preliminary sketches of Gore this afternoon, selecting which of these sinewy charcoal outlines would
translate best to oil on canvas, when I was assaulted by a memory
I haven't recalled for a long time. It seems like a lifetime ago, a different person altogether. I was thirty-nine years old, and Joan and
I had been married for about eight years. It was early 1939, and
I'd just started working for an advertising company near Charing
Cross. It was my first managerial post, and I was doing remarkably well. We had our art supplies, pens and inks and so forth,
supplied by a company based in Long Acre, around the corner
from our offices. This meant they could deliver at a moment's
notice, which was very handy. One of the delivery boys, Billy, was
a handsome youth in his early twenties, and I took a shine to his
rugged and uncultured appeal. He must have been about six feet,
four inches tall, with broad shoulders and dark hair, and the most
dazzling black eyes. Many a time I had a vision of him in my head
as I masturbated.

One evening, working overtime, I needed some supplies, and

so I telephoned to order what I required. They were just about to close, but promised to deliver within the half-hour. Billy arrived with the order. I was in the office alone. It was February, I think, definitely the winter months, the sun long since set, the office shrouded in shadows, and I thanked him for staying late, gave him a tip as usual. He said, "You look like you could do with a drink, my friend." I agreed, but said I needed to finish this job by the morning. He held up the money I had just given him and offered to buy me a drink. I declined, stressing the urgency of the job. He smiled and held my gaze, and I faltered, flustered. "One drink won't do any harm," he goaded.

I sat in the pub, waiting for him to return from the bar, wondering what on earth I was doing, cursing myself for my lack of resolve but excited to be in his company, thrilled he wanted mine. If I didn't deliver this job the next morning, I was in danger of losing one of my top clients, and here I was drinking with some bit of rough, and loving every minute of it. The risk made me feel alive in a way I'd never felt before.

When he returned with the drinks—a gin and tonic for me, a pint of bitter for him—we made some small talk about the business. He told a funny story about the warehouse boys. Then he turned to me and said, "There's one or two of them lads'd do anything for a bit of extra cash. Anything." The mood of the conversation changed with that statement. I tried not to look as flustered as I felt. Was he soliciting? And if so, what about me had given the game away? I modelled myself on all the other men I met. I dressed soberly, perhaps too soberly. I policed every gesture, every intonation. I never lisped or acted effeminately, never went to queer pubs, nor had any queer friends. I was impeccably ordinary, even dull, priding myself on my mediocrity.

He continued, leaning forward conspiratorially. "A couple of 'em reckons to know gentlemen who pay a fair price if a lad is willing." His eyes held mine. "What do you say to that, Mr Read?"

"Each to his own," I replied, averting my gaze.

He changed his tack. "I could tell straight away the first time I saw you."

"Tell what?" I stuttered.

"What you like."

I stood up to go. He grabbed my wrist and pulled me back into my seat.

"What do you want?" I whispered. "Money?" Suddenly angry at having been coaxed into this situation, I growled at him, "I will not be intimidated like this."

He laughed at that. "You wanna know what I want?" he asked, leaning back in his chair, rubbing a hand on his belly, a lascivious grin on his face. "I wanna fuck you."

I could hardly believe my ears, but his words hung between the two of us in that smoky pub like a cloud of gun smoke rising from an emptied barrel. I didn't know what to do. Was it a trap? If I admitted that I wanted him too, would I be lost, imprisoned, shamed by all society—or would I find the love I could not even dare to admit I craved?

My initial response was to laugh at the absurdity of the situation. Then, without responding to what he'd just said, I stood up and told him I had to return to work. I was terrified. This was wrong. All wrong. He asked if he could walk back with me. Of course I agreed. Some terrible, overwhelming desire made me agree. When we got to the front door of the office, he asked if he could come upstairs. He came back up to the office, and before I had even switched on a light he had grabbed me and was kissing me. He tasted of cigarettes and beer. He told me to leave the light off. The street-lamps cast a dim light by which we made our way over to my office. Once there, he removed my glasses and my jacket and kissed me again.

I was disoriented with desire. I became someone else entirely, someone who could touch another man's body, respond to another man's body, unreservedly, and without shame. But that feeling didn't last long. The minute the act was over, I found myself overcome with remorse and was incapable of looking him in the eye. I could barely bring myself to speak to him, this being with whom I had just seconds earlier known such intimacy. The joy his body had given me evaporated into a shame in which I sweated and steamed. We dressed wordlessly, and I let him out, feeling almost physically sick with disgust at myself. He went to kiss me, but I backed off callously. I knew that I wanted to, but knew equally well that I could never allow myself even to register that wish. I knew I must kill it, as I had killed all the other wishes I had ever had. My parents had trained me well. I went back to my drawing board and finished my work.

I never spoke to Billy again, and began sending one of the office juniors around to collect our supplies rather than have them delivered. On the rare occasions when this was not possible, I would get someone else to take the delivery, and would make myself busy if it was Billy. I wanted to avoid him at all costs, though at the same time I longed to see him. I was a coward, and that cowardice shames me now. I think eventually he must have left, because someone new started to appear before long. Then, of course, the war began, and I've no idea what happened to him, whether he survived or not.

Despite my closeness to Joan, this was one episode I kept to myself. Emotions were not a topic of conversation for Joan and me. I wonder whether I should tell Gore about Billy, about my one attempt at taking a risk, my one grab at pleasure.

When Gore arrived, I didn't feel like drawing straight away so I suggested we take a trip to Kew Gardens. I'd mentioned it last week and he'd remarked that he'd never been. The weather was glorious so I took along my box Brownie and snapped some pictures of him amongst the flowers as we walked and talked. He wanted one of us together and asked a passing stranger, a middle-aged man, to take it. Boldly, Gore placed his arm across my shoulder and, whilst it thrilled me to feel it there, I felt self-conscious in front of this stranger, scared that my joy, my love, would show too clearly on my face. I dread seeing the developed photograph, though Gore insists he wants a copy.

I mentioned I'd started preparing to do some oil paintings, and he got very excited at the idea. I said I wanted to do a triptych of him, though of course he had no idea what one is. I explained, telling him about the symbolic and spiritual significance of the number three: the Father, the Son, and the Holy Ghost, for example, or the three kingdoms of matter; animal, mineral, vegetable. He seemed genuinely intrigued and interested. I said I'd show him when the three canvases were finished.

When we got back and started drawing, Gore dropped off to sleep as I sketched. His breathing changed, becoming shallower—and I stopped sketching and watched him sleeping, wondering what he was dreaming about and thinking about whether any of my dreams could ever have come true, if maybe I'd believed in them a bit more, been a little braver. It is wonderful to be able to witness someone you love sleeping, naked, before you. It's a joyous sight. As quietly as I could, I collected the camera from downstairs and sneaked a photograph of him.

1998

I didn't see you again for about a month after that first encounter. Harry, the man in Clapham for whom I had already done several videos and photo shoots over the years, booked me to do a group video, something I always enjoyed doing. I was horny and anxious for days leading up to it, wondering if you would be there, though I tried my best not to raise my hopes.

Harry led me into the lounge, where several boys were sitting around smoking and drinking, all naked. I was introduced to the other three boys in the room. I felt a jolt of disappointment that you weren't there and decided I didn't fancy any of the others much. In the centre of the room, on a white sheepskin rug, there was a smoked-glass-topped table, upon which stood a large brass ashtray and a marble cigarette holder. Along one wall, there was a unit holding an expensive hi-fi and several reproductions of Greco-Roman busts and bronzes of naked young men, individually lit from above. Harry began pouring me a drink. In one corner of the room, a large cheese plant stood in a copper pot. A labyrinthine hallway, its walls mirrored, led to the bedroom, which also contained one wall of mirrors. Classical music was always playing and this was also piped into the bedroom. Harry always had plenty of cigarettes and alcohol. Once I'd stripped off and plonked myself down he handed me a large whisky and I helped myself to one of the cigarettes from the ornate silver box on the glass coffee table.

He asked me some inane questions about my life, to which I responded with the minimum of detail and truth. While this was going on, the other three continued a conversation they'd evidently been having prior to my arrival. They were discussing a book one of them had read, some New Age nonsense. Harry refuted every single "argument" the boys had been making in a loud and pompous, though highly logical, manner. Before he'd retired, he'd been a physicist. Did you ever notice the way he slapped his lips together—only he doesn't actually have any lips, just these hard edges to his mouth which, when he smacks them together, make a noise like a pop or a click? He disagreed with nearly everything the three boys said. The boys argued back. He interrupted by standing up excitedly and clapping his hands together, turning to me, and saying, "David, follow me." I put my drink down and followed him out of the room. He led me to the bedroom, where on the bed lay a naked man, spread-eagled on his back, his hands and feet bound to the bedposts, his eyes hidden beneath a black leather blindfold. It was you. Even with the blindfold on, I could see it was you.

"Suck him off," Harry said, fiddling with the video camera.

In the mirrored wall, I watched myself crawl onto the bed and take your already hard dick in my mouth, recognizing its taste and shape. I could see Harry behind me, switching on a spotlight that flashed back from the mirrored wall in front of me, blinding me momentarily. I closed my eyes and continued sucking. You started to groan.

"Okay, that's enough," Harry barked, and I reluctantly stopped. I looked at your face—what I could see of it beneath the blindfold. Your strong nose. Your Cupid's bow mouth. A rosebud pushed from between your lips and burst into vibrant colour. I imagined that you were falling in love with me, and pretended I could hear you gasp my name. I wanted to take the blindfold off. I wanted to see your eyes.

I wanted you to see me. I suddenly wished we were alone.

"Send Darren in," Harry said officiously.

I returned to the living room and told Darren to go to the bedroom. I lit a cigarette and refilled my glass, my erection wilting. The other boys had clearly been getting down to something while I'd been out of the room, as all three of them now had hard-ons. When Darren had gone, the other two asked me what went on in the bedroom. I told them. They started to kiss, and I walked over and joined in, thinking to myself, at least they're not still discussing that stupid book.

One of the boys rummaged in his jacket and pulled a joint from one of the pockets. After a couple of drags he passed it around. The two boys kissed and played with each other while I stood there smoking. I crushed the finished joint into the ashtray and half-heartedly joined in.

Shortly, we were all called into the bedroom, and I was glad that I wouldn't have to wait while they all went in one by one until I could see you again.

When we got to the bedroom, the blindfold was off. Our eyes

met and smiled. That same look of brand-new recognition. The same face, the same response.

Harry said, "Jake, this is David." We shook hands, and I was struck by the absurdity of the situation around the same time that you were. Our grins were equally broad.

Afterward, you and I shared a cab with one of the other boys, and you got out first. I wanted to ask for your number, but not in front of him. I felt a sudden irrational hatred for this boy. I didn't say a word to him during the rest of the journey, other than, "See you," when he climbed out. I stayed on to Soho, seeking something other than rest. It's not difficult to find in this city. Not if you are restless enough.

The day after, I rang Harry to get your phone number, and when he started asking questions I wished I'd been bold enough to ask you myself the previous evening. I felt vulnerable, as if Harry knew how much I wanted the number, and I was annoyed that I had to rely on him to get it. He mentioned getting the two of us to do a video together, and I said that I'd like that and hung up. I rolled a joint and wondered how long I could reasonably leave it before ringing you. As I sat there, playing with the piece of paper bearing your number, I started to imagine you in my life, dreaming of the two of us beginning a career together, only doing films with each other, only doing escort work as a duo. I had turned into something I was not. It wasn't long then before I realized that I didn't want you to touch anyone else, and that this meant I was possessive, even though I remain unsure exactly what that means. Jealousy is not good in this game. Of course, it happens. I've seen rent boys tear each other's hair out over a man, thinking to myself, why bother? Sometimes it feels as if I have spent my entire life thinking, why bother?

Even though we had barely spent more than a few hours together in total, I had mapped out an entire life together, with the colours and trajectory of a rainbow. The greatest thing about being a prostitute was the freedom. I couldn't imagine having to explain myself to anyone. Perhaps your being a whore too made me think it would somehow be easier, I don't know. I can't really remember how I justified calling you. But I remember that the second I decided to dial your number my telephone rang and I was required elsewhere. A distraction. Calling you would have to wait.

I arrived back at the flat around midnight, and as I approached the entrance to my block I heard a car horn beep behind me and saw the momentary flash of headlights. I turned around, and there you were, in a red Porsche, beaming your biggest smile. I walked over to the car, and you wound the window down.

"Hey there, handsome."

"Hi."

"I've just watched a girl and her client fucking over there by your bins," you said, laughing. "It was hot."

"That goes on all the time," I said.

"How you doin'?"

"Fine," I replied. "You?"

"Yeah, great." You banged the steering wheel. "Listen, I've got this beauty for the night—gotta deliver it in the morning. Fancy a spin?"

I walked around to the passenger door and, as I did so, you reached across and opened it. I climbed in. You leant over and kissed me. As we left my road behind us you said, "Open your mouth," and popped in a tab of acid. I immediately thought of Spike and our acid-fuelled joy-rides to the moor a hundred years ago. I was already stoned and relaxed back into the smell of the leather and the thrill of being with you, embracing like a lover the night to come.

"I thought we'd go up to Highgate Cemetery," you said. "Ever been?"

"Not at night," I said.

"You're in for a treat," you said, grinning to yourself, your hand squeezing my knee on its way to the gearstick. Hole's *Live Through This* was playing.

The cemetery was locked, of course, but after parking the car by the main gates and waiting for a clear road, you hoisted yourself up the wall and I followed. We dropped down into the shadows. The moonlight painted each leaf fluorescent till the trees glowed enough to light our way, and you led me through the labyrinth of trees and headstones to a sunken circular arena of private mausoleums. Graves yawned. The darkness was thick with the sounds of the night: with owls and silence, the occasional fox crying like some abandoned baby. You pulled me to you, drawing my face close to yours till our mouths met in a kiss that made lights appear in my head. It was a cold night, but when your hands reached under my clothes to touch the small of my back, they were warm and massive, and I responded by holding your head in my hands and eating your kisses as a starving man might wolf down his first food for weeks. And the sky was made of amethyst, and all the stars were just like little fish. Not feeling the cold, we unfastened our trousers and pushed them to our ankles, grabbing and tasting each other's flesh. This cannibalism made time itself more edible a concept. Nipple, belly, cock, scrotum, armpit, arsehole. I wanted to eat you as badly as you wanted to eat me. Waves broke against me in sudden splashes. Sea-spray flecked my hair. Salt stung my skin. Your warm hands passed over me and your mouth tasted good. Your hair smelt atomic. A bright forest of tall white candles grew up around us, lighting up the sky. *Go on, take everything, take everything, I want you to.* When you pulled away, silver webs appeared between us, which dissolved almost as soon as they were spun. It was suddenly as bright as day and a shoal of stars swam off into this vast sea of light, leaving trails of bubbles that rose and burst. My hands passed right through you. We walked through each other's bodies like walking through corridors, opening doors that led to other corridors and other doors. Your moans transformed into a flotilla of butterflies, and as they flew away they spelled out the word "danger" with their dark bodies. I am here without knowing how. Suddenly, terrifyingly present. Here, now, lost and hot, my heart in my head, and my cock warm and wet in your mouth. I held your head in my hands, your black curls thick between my fingers, and as I slid down your throat toward my orgasm, I remembered who I was, who you were, and I didn't know whether to feel safety or fear.

In bed, afterward, we stayed up until sunrise, describing to each other the visions we could see.

1895

Odd the way some people froth with anger at the sight of a man in a woman's clothes, as if some law of nature were being trespassed or the end of the world were on its fuckin' way. I've never understood it myself, but then Taylor often swans about the house in a dress, and I've even worn a frock myself. To a drag ball. You can't get in without one. The first time was strange, I'll admit, but it was great fun. The costumes turn us into something more extreme—I hardly feel myself at all. To begin with it felt like sin, and I was embarrassed and awkward, not sure how to act, trying to be myself, but just feeling stupid. After a few drinks and a bit of hashish, this other character takes over, some fishwife or harlot. The drag creates a whole new state of being within me. With a bit of slap and a skirt, we all unleash a slattern.

We all have women's names at these parties. Mine's Penny Dreadful. The lengths that some people go to, making themselves elaborate gowns like Marie Antoinette or Anne of Cleves. We always look like a gaggle of scullery maids by comparison, decked in Taylor's ratty cast-offs.

Last night, Taylor got wed at a drag ball to a handsome young fellow called Eddie. We call him Steady because he is one of the most unstable people you could ever wish to meet. He flies into a rage without any reason. I saw him bark at a total stranger in Oxford Street once, just because he thought the man had looked at him funny. His temper is worse than Pa's. I've seen him threaten Taylor with a knife many times, and he's always getting into fights, turning up with black eyes and a split lip. But Taylor's in love, so they got married. Any excuse for a party.

Taylor was dressed in white and Steady wore a suit. He's a good-looking chap, it has to be said. Burly and hairy, with dark eyes and thick eyebrows, and hung like a shire horse. He needs no excuse to whip it out and show it off, and I guess if I had that between my legs, I'd do the same. It's just a shame he has the personality of a mad dog.

I was maid of honour.

Oscar wasn't there. He's still keeping out of our way owing to all the trouble with Bosie's father, but he sent Taylor a huge bouquet and a bottle of champagne. Frederika Faithless, as Taylor called himself, played the part of the blushing bride perfectly, tossing her bouquet of paper flowers at the excited bridesmaids. I tried my best to grab it, but Lottie caught it and was giddy from the event all evening. Silly cow. Anyone would think she was the one getting hitched. One of the regulars who's a real priest came dressed in his robes and did the ceremony before we showered the happy couple in a snow of torn paper pieces as they retired to one of the bedrooms upstairs. The wedding took place in a huge house in Victoria owned by one of Taylor's better-class acquaintances, a duke known to us as the Duchess. Last night she was dressed like Queen Vic. "Don't you fucking bleed on my clean sheets!" she screamed as Steady and Taylor made their way upstairs, standing with her hands on her hips at the foot of the stairs.

"Don't worry, dear," said the bearded man dressed as a shepherdess who had welcomed Oscar and me at the orgy that night, adjusting the bow under his chin. "She cracked her pot when Queen Vic was still sucking the milk out of a wet nurse's tittie."

"Well, I wouldn't put it past the godless whore to grow another plug just to spite me," the Duchess snapped back before floating off across the room with her fan fluttering in front of her face.

George, a fat jolly blacksmith dressed like a scrubber, with thick black hair bursting from his bodice, bashed out filthy songs on the piano and we sang along. One or two of the guests who work on the stage put on a show and they were very good. The songs were all as crude as hell and they told dirty stories in between that had us falling over with laughing. We all drank and danced and flirted. Those queens are always viciously funny when they're kanurd. At one point Nell Gwynn, with breasts made of two huge oranges, ran to the foot of the stairs and yelled up to the newly-weds, "Is it in yet?"

By the end of the party, most of the queens had either passed out from too much booze and opium or retired to a bedroom with one of the boys. Johnnycakes came up to me and pointed to a bulge at the front of his dress, saying with a smirk, "Do you want to help me get rid of this?" I certainly did. He led me to the kitchen, where we pulled off our frocks, naked as nature beneath, and set to covering each other in sweet sauces and creams from the pantry till we were sticky from head to toe, then like cubs we licked each other clean all over. By the time we'd finished we both shone from the spittle, grinning at each other like idiots. I know Taylor robs us blind, but it isn't a bad life sometimes. I even forgot my rage over Sidney for a brief moment.

Johnnycakes asked me if I'd ever go through with a wedding, and I thought to myself that if Oscar asked me, I'd marry him, but I said, "Nah, that stuff is just for the queens." We never considered ourselves to be queens, always pretended to be interested in girls, though I'd never been anywhere near one. Johnnycakes taught me to read men. He liked sleep and tobacco, and as he sat there on that kitchen floor with the sun coming up through the window behind him, I watched him roll a cigarette between yellow finger and thumb and wondered whether I'd ever know him or ever hear his life story. He never said much about himself, and none of us, not even Taylor, really knew anything about him. He'd been a merchant seaman and had jumped ship at Portsmouth and made his way to London, that was all he'd say. But once in a while he'd come out with these tiny fragments that spoke of a life beyond anything I could begin to imagine. "Know your men," is something he always said. "Know your men." And as he lit the cigarette and took the first pull, sitting there looking so handsome, he said, in that silky rich American drawl of his, "Sometimes the most important thing is that you don't betray yourself."

I wasn't sure if this related to anything else we'd said to one another, but it clearly made sense to him and he assumed it would make sense to me on its own without further explanation. He leant back contemplating his own wisdom, judging by the look on his face, and I said nothing. I just reached across and plucked the cigarette from his rosy fat lips and brought it to my own, repeating his words to myself in my head, trying to make something of them. But then Taylor appeared in the doorway, dressed in his regular clothes, and said, "Come on, you two reprobates, get yer kecks on, we're goin' 'ome."

We'd only just fallen into our beds when a fuckin' gang of crushers stormed into the house and nibbed us all again. Sidney was still in full drag from the party, which caused a certain amount of confusion, I can tell you. They threw him in with the tarts at first till he lifted his skirts and flashed an officer his privates, and I wished they'd left him in there for I don't want to clap eyes on him ever again. Since that night outside Kettner's I've tried my best to avoid him. Not easy when we live together.

At first we all just thought it was a regular raid, like before. Occupational hazard. We were in the clink for hours before anyone even mentioned Oscar's name. I was still filled with rage and confusion over last week's betrayal when I heard it, and I flushed scarlet like a bride. What did he have to do with it? As far as I knew, he was prosecuting Bosie's father, so what did it have to do with us? In time, piece by precious piece, the story came to us through some elaborate chain of hurried Chinese whispers from cell to cell.

It seems someone talked, some she-whore narked at the marked decline in her trade (same old story: arse preferred to cunt), and it turned her bitter. With her mouth puckered to the shape of a sour grape she spat out Taylor's address like a pip, and lo and behold, the bluebottles descend and cart us off like stray dogs. When I'd pieced it all together I vomited, much to everyone else's annoyance—as if it didn't stink enough in here already. I couldn't believe it was all out in the open, what we did for a living. How long before my mother knows? What will she think of me?

Just then a bobby came and dragged me off and I was taken to a room where a senior bobby and a man in a black suit were seated and a grizzle-chopped old man in tweed was pacing furiously, his face red and his manic eyes bulging, his head surrounded by a thick cloud of smoke from the pipe he was angrily sucking. So this is the old man, Bosie's father, the mad marquess.

I was pushed into a chair, and the old man turned to me and screwed up his red-veined nose like he was suffering the presence of a bad odour.

"Master Rose," said the man in the black suit, "you are in very grave trouble, and depending on how well you co-operate you will either get yourself out of trouble or sink yourself further in it. The outcome entirely depends on you."

I hadn't the first idea what he was talking about so I said nothing.

The old aristocrat was pacing back and forth by the window gnashing his teeth and chewing his pipe.

"Are you acquainted with Mr Oscar Wilde?" the bluebottle asked.

I said I was.

"Were you aware he's a bugger?" snarled the marquess, pushing his fat red angry face down into mine and wrapping my head in a cloud of smoke as the words sprayed like spittle from his mouth. He was terrifying. Reminded me of Steady in one of his moods.

"This gentleman is the Marquess of Queensberry," the man in the black suit said, "and I am his lawyer, Edward Carson. Mr

Wilde is prosecuting my client for libel and, unhappily, stands a good chance of success. We, however, believe that the claim Lord Queensberry has made about Mr Wilde can be substantiated and we are seeking witnesses to give evidence. Do you understand what that means?"

I nodded.

"Good," he said. "Now tell us, what is the nature of your acquaintance with Mr Wilde?"

I wasn't sure what to say at this point, but before I could say anything the red-faced aristocrat screamed at me, "Has he sodded you, lad? Has he put it in your arse?"

"No, sir, he hasn't," I said, for that was the truth.

Carson then said, "Master Rose, you are in terrible trouble and stand to be convicted for practising an illicit profession. We know all about what goes on in Mr Taylor's lodgings. There's no use denying anything. The point is that you can get out of that trouble if you help us. Wilde is going down, there is no question of that. The question is, who does he take with him? Now, you can give evidence and be granted immunity—that means you can walk away a free man—or you can refuse to co-operate, in which case you will go to prison. Have I made myself clear?"

"Yes, sir."

So I told all. I didn't need to think about it. My anger was still intense and I wanted to hurt him; I wanted him to suffer the way I was suffering. Yes, I told them, I had met him often, yes, he had given me gifts and money and yes, he touched me in an indecent manner, but no, I insisted, he never sodded me. Although plenty of others have, I added. I spared no details other than the details of my own suffering since seeing him walk out of that restaurant with Sidney last Wednesday night.

They lapped it up, and Queensberry, who paced around the room barking and muttering to himself as I spoke, slapped guineas down on the table in front of me till I was performing like a seal hungry for another fish, erasing from my memory the time I spent with Oscar, the things he showed me, the things he taught me. What took me months to learn took an hour to forget. I cannot deny it, though it shames me to say it. But I was angry at Oscar for not loving me and for loving instead that arrogant, self-centred, thoughtless little turd that had sprung from the loins of this insane chimpanzee chattering fish-eyed before me. I was angry at Taylor for interfering, and I was angry at Sidney for taking my place in Oscar's shallow affections, but most of all I was angry at myself for ever getting involved in this stupid game in the first place.

Maybe, I thought to myself as I walked away with a thick column of gold coins like a stiff yard in my trouser pocket, maybe this is my way out, my way to a better life, a way to forget all about it. Forget about him. What do I care about the consequences of giving Queen's evidence against an old queen? Particularly an old queen so rich, so famous, so important that he is above anything, certainly above the law. So, like the whore I am, I thought only of the money as the grizzled old Queensberry held out that fat fist of push so close I swear I could smell it.

I knew I couldn't very well go back to Taylor's, but nor did I feel I could return home, as I had no notion of how much news had reached my ma. For all I know she could have completely disowned me by now. So I hung around outside Bow Street Police Station until I saw Sidney come out. He was the last person I wanted to see, but all the same he might have news of what was going on, news of Taylor and the others, so I jumped down off the wall I'd been sitting on and called his name. He was happy to see me or at least acted that way, and I didn't tell him I'd seen him with Oscar that night, so as far as he's concerned everything between us is fine, I imagine. Don't suppose he has a clue about my feelings for Oscar. He told me that they'd forced him to give a statement and I didn't feel so bad about my own loose tongue, but then he told me that Taylor had refused to give evidence, even for immunity, and so had been arrested and would be put in the dock with Oscar. He'd heard no word of Charlie or Johnnycakes.

"What are you going to do now?" Sidney asked, and I said I didn't know. I felt bad about being angry with him; after all, it isn't his fault, he was just doing his job. So when he suggested that we walk together back to the house and decide what to do, I agreed. I hadn't the courage to ask him if he too had been given a pile of ackers in case he hadn't. I walked all the way with my hands in my pockets so the coins wouldn't make a sound.

The lock on the door was busted, of course, and the house was empty. Ghostly quiet. We hadn't been given any food at all in the clink and were starving. But neither of us knows how to cook, so we had some stale bread washed down with the dregs from a bottle of red wine we found in the pantry. It was strange being in the house without the others. It seemed so empty and joyless, and there was nothing we could do about the broken door so we were fearful, too, of strangers coming in while we slept. We decided to go to bed, and I jammed a chair under the door handle once we were in our room. We climbed into bed together and held each other and when he asked if everything would be all right I said it would, though I wasn't at all sure. At one point he started to get fruity, his hands wandering to my privates, but I was not in the mood at all, and took pleasure in rejecting him.

In the night we were woken by banging on the door and jumped out of our skins with fright. We lay there clinging together in the dark thinking it must be a ghost or a murderer or the devil himself come to claim us for the flames of hell. But it were only Charlie and Johnnycakes wanting to bed down. I got up and let them in and all four of us climbed into the one bed. Johnnycakes had some baccy so we rolled cigarettes and started exchanging stories of our day. No one had seen Taylor. Johnnycakes told us he's going back to America on the first passage he can get. So the family has broken up. Mother is locked up and the children have to fend for themselves in the wilderness. And as I lay there trying to sleep after we'd nished the chat, I couldn't help thinking it was all my fault.

This morning we woke to a beautiful spring day. April 3rd, 1895. It's two weeks since we've seen Taylor and bade farewell to Johnnycakes. He may well be in America by now and it's sad to think we'll probably never see him again. He did ask if I wanted to go with him, and I must admit I was sorely tempted, though to be honest I can't imagine living anywhere but here, even now, with all this fuss going on. And I need to see Oscar again, need to know the outcome. I don't know why but I do.

We've fixed the front door, and have taken to begging and nicking food when we can. Neither Charlie nor Sidney have mentioned receiving money, so I've kept my mouth shut about mine. They must've made as much as I did, surely. But it's been too long now for any one of us to come out with the truth. We'd rather keep up this pretence at poverty. Charlie has taken to picking pockets, which is something he says he grew up doing.

After a breakfast of piss-weak porridge, we made our way to the Old Bailey, Charlie purloining a few wallets and watches along the way. At one point Sidney ran off and came back with three shiny red apples, and I felt guilty accepting one when he held it out. But I was that hungry I wolfed it down, pips and all.

I'd never been in the Old Bailey before, and as you can imagine anything to do with the law leaves a bad taste in my mouth. It's a fuckin' vast place. As we entered, Charlie cracked a joke about the importance of being early and Sidney laughed. Some crusher led us into a small room where we were told we'd be spending the day. We're not allowed into the courtroom. Fuck. Two crushers stood guard at the door and there was just one small bench for us to sit on, but we were given all the cigarettes we wanted and of course we stuffed our pockets and smoked ourselves stupid. Sidney and Charlie joked and laughed the whole time, of course, and I longed for them to shut up. I smiled half-heartedly at their lame jokes, but all I could think about was what was going on in the courtroom. I couldn't wait to get out and find out. It was worse than being in prison.

Outside, we ran into Taylor's mate George, who'd been to loads of our drag parties. We hardly recognized him out of his frock. He'd sat through the whole day, and he told us about it over an ale. He said that in the morning it'd been quite jovial, with Oscar in good spirits, but that in the afternoon Queensberry's defence, Carson, went in for the kill, and after grilling Oscar over his books he started naming some boys Wilde'd befriended and given gifts to, including myself. He said that Oscar's face had run deathly white. "I fear the worst for him, the poor bugger. He'll go down for this, I'm certain. I'm leaving for France tomorrow. Wish me luck, boys." And with a solemn goodbye he stood up and walked out. The ground beneath my feet disappeared.

"What d'ya make of that?" asked Sidney, and as Charlie started saying he thought Wilde was done for, I felt the bile rise and I had to dash to the shitter.

When I came out I couldn't see Charlie and Sidney anywhere, so I walked home, feeling terrified and confused and dreading the next day in court.

How I curse that he taught me to read. For I do think that ignorance is bliss. This morning, in the papers, I was able to read the details of his arrest. Last night at some posh hotel in Knightsbridge, it was. It seems that Oscar withdrew his case yesterday and soon after a warrant was issued for his arrest. He'll stand trial for "gross indecency."

I'd only wanted to punish him and had thought that once he lost his case against Queensberry then that would be the end of that. Never imagined it would lead to this. I read that he was being held at Bow Street, so I told the boys I had some errands to run and I made my way there. We've been locked up in that room in the Old Bailey during the trial, so the boys wanted nothing more than to stay at home and sleep.

When I arrived at Bow Street, there was a mob gathered, shouting obscene names. I've never seen such a foulmouthed and frightening gaggle. I thought at one point they were going to storm the place. They were fearsome and I felt ashamed to be near them, to be amongst them, so I turned to leave and ran right into Bosie and he started hissing that I was a vile Judas scum of the earth, that I didn't deserve to lick the dirt off Oscar's shoes. Then he begged me not to give evidence, and I said I was only telling the truth and he said, "No, what you are doing, *Jack*, is killing him." Then he turned and disappeared inside the police station.

On the way home, I took a detour into St James's Park. It was as busy as ever, running alive with guards and trade. I needed to distract myself from the ghosts of Taylor and Oscar and the way they were darkening my mood. I got into a chat with a burly young butcher and before long we were frigging each other in the bushes, trousers pushed down around our ankles. He delivered the primest beef, it has to be said, and I walked back feeling a little better in mood, though the ghosts still hovered and would not go. Perhaps they never will.

1954

I spent last night in a police cell.

Gore had taken me to my first queer pub, the Lord Barrymore, near Regent's Park. I've walked past it on several occasions, never imagining for a minute what it was, and not being a pub person I'd never had cause to go in. But last night we went for a drink there.

A few weeks ago, Gore was astonished to hear that I'd never been inside a queer pub. He refused even to believe me to begin with. Once I convinced him that it was true, he insisted the situation be rectified. I agreed to go to one with him. A few weeks went by and nothing more was said about it. But yesterday, I brought the subject up and asked whether he was free that evening. He said yes, so after our meal we got a cab into town.

I felt a great deal of trepidation during the cab ride, and despite all the wine we'd drunk with our meal I was incredibly nervous as we entered. There was a lot of rococo carved glass over and behind the counter and a number of mahogany chairs with red leather upholstery. A fog of cigarette smoke blurred the air. Apparently it had only gone queer in the last few months; before that it was an ordinary public house. Gore informed me that once a place has become established as a queer pub, the police start raiding it on a regular basis so that the clientele have to move on to another pub.

There were about thirty people there when we arrived. All of them turned to look at us when we walked in. As we made our way to the bar I noticed Gore nod acquaintance to a few men and I wondered if any of them were his punters, but dismissed the thought. There were two or three young soldiers by the dartboard, and a clutch of young men standing by the fire who seemed to be wearing make-up, the paint illuminated by the firelight. The rest were an unremarkable and fairly typical crowd of men. I overheard bits of conversations as I followed Gore. Dog-ends, my mother used to call them.

"She said, 'Well, don't ask me, dear, I've only got two inches of vagina left'…"

"So, by the time I finally got to Kathmandu …"

"If I catch you strolling and caterwauling I'll beat the milk out of your breasts, so I will."

"Smell her!"

Gore ordered the drinks and I gave him the money to pay for them. As he took it, I noticed those around us watching the transaction, and knew how it must seem to them. A feeling of both pride and shame washed through me.

If only.

It was easy enough finding a seat, and Gore said it was because most people preferred to stand so they could observe everything, or rather everyone, in the room. There didn't seem much to observe to me. Just a regular public house, except perhaps for the occasional shriek of hysterical laughter and the absence of women. I said as much to Gore when he returned with the drinks, and he explained that glances were being constantly exchanged and rendezvous being arranged without a word being spoken— an invisible web being spun around us of covert eye movements and facial gestures you'd be hard-pushed to notice. The soldiers, apparently, are well known for letting you fellate them in the gents', if you slip them a couple of quid.

Gore told me that the regulars call the landlord Mother. And in these places most of the punters are regulars. He explained that all eyes had been on us because they had never seen me before. I said I found the attention rather strange. He laughed, and I wasn't sure if he was laughing at me.

At that point, a grey-haired old man in an extremely tight burgundy velvet jacket and blue cravat, who had been staring and blinking at Gore ever since we'd sat down, came up to the table and grabbed Gore's hand. In the fruitiest voice, he said, "*Young man,* when *you* have a few spare hours and *I* have a few spare pounds of plaster of Paris, you *must* let me make a cast of your hands. They're divine."

"Away with you, Jack!" Gore laughed, pulling his hand free.

"I'm serious, Gregory, I intend to immortalise them in bronze." A lascivious grin spread across his face. "And your cock too, if you'd let me." He gave Gore a nudge.

"Behave," Gore said, "there'll be none of that talk in front of my friend here. He's an artist. A real artist." Gore nodded in my direction.

Jack held out a limp hand for me to shake. "Jack Rose."

"Colin Read. Pleased to meet you." I shook his hand.

"I knew an artist once," he said.

"Sure you did, Jack, sure you did," Gore teased, looking at me. "Didn't you meet Mr Oscar Wilde himself, now?"

"No word of a lie," he said, dropping the genteel accent and trowelling on the Cockney. "I was a beautiful boy, not ashamed to say it, a shiny ripe apple in this veritable Eden, and Mr Wilde liked beautiful boys, as did all the swells that came my way. But we had something special, Mr Wilde and I. Treated me like gold, he did. Here, take a vada at this," he said, plunging his hand into his inside jacket pocket and plucking out a tatty sepia photograph. He handed it over and said, "Just you read what's written on the back of that, Mr Read, go on, read it. Aloud, if you don't mind."

I read. "'To Jack, my favourite writing desk, O.W.'"

I said I was impressed, that I had enjoyed many of Wilde's writings.

"I had a silver cigarette case, too, what he gave me. But the filth took that." He helped himself to a sip from my drink. "It's a crime what this country did to that man, a crime!" he hissed.

Then without further encouragement he launched into a monologue. "When they locked 'im up, London sank to its knees, five years before the century did, tatty and knackered, as grey as Victoria's hair. The inns were empty, the drag balls wiped off the face of the city like a tart's panstick. Most of the well-to-do queens had sodded off abroad, the ones who stayed too scared to play out their lust. The party was over. I fucked off up to Manchester, but I had such a miserable time I came back after a year. You ever been? Don't bother. I missed London. But the

London I missed was no more."

He paused for dramatic effect.

"But then," he said, moving closer, "ever so gradually, legions of Oscars started to spring up like flowers all over London, on every street corner in town from the Dilly to Oxford Street. So many Oscars. Vivid and proud." His hands started to dance, stressing certain words with an invisible stitch of the smoky air. "More timid than he had been, mind you, but taking their cue nevertheless from his former glory, before Lily Law kicked the living daylights out of him. And the resilience of this desire fascinated me. I heard the song of its voice and joined in the chorus. They were back: the taverns, and the drag parties, and the swells. You could suddenly make out a sparkle of gold feathers beneath the ash-grey pelt of London town."

He paused, lost in some long-forgotten memory, a beatific smile lighting his wrinkled, powdered face.

"D'y'know, it was as if he had to die so as to be reincarnated not just as a person, but as a whole new century. That's how big he was."

Then he turned to Gore and said, "Can this old ponce ponce a Vogue off you, duckie?" And while Gore was fishing in his jacket pocket Jack lifted Gore's glass and took a swig.

As Gore handed Jack a cigarette, there was a sudden burst of noise and half a dozen policemen crashed through the doors. Everybody froze. Absolute silence. My heart was racing. Jack just rolled his eyes as if to say, *here we go again*, and tilted forward to light his cigarette in the flame that Gore offered.

"Goodnight, sweet ladies," Jack hissed before slinking off to the back of the room, gliding like a phantom.

"Good evening, gents," said one of the policemen.

"How can we help you, officer?" asked the landlord.

"We're here to seek your co-operation."

"Oh, yes?"

"If you'd all be so kind as to supply us with your names and addresses, then we'll be on our way."

"Why?"

"Just procedure, sir."

"But you've got them already. You were in here last week. There's nobody here tonight who wasn't here then. No one." I looked at the floor.

"It won't take a minute, sir."

Our table was nearest to the door and a policeman sat down in the seat Jack had vacated. I looked at Gore; he looked calm as anything.

"Evenin', ladies," he said with an imbecilic grin. Neither of us spoke. "If I could have your name, please, sir."

"Gregory Moretti."

"And where do you live, Mr Moretti?"

"With him," he said, pointing at me. I couldn't believe my ears. I was confused as to why Gore would say that. But I didn't have much time to reflect on it, for the policeman turned immediately to me.

"Does he live with you, sir?"

"Yes," I blurted out.

"You don't sound so sure, sir."

"Yes, he does, he lives with me."

"And what is your relationship with this young man, sir, if I may ask?"

I was momentarily flummoxed, and by the time I came out with "friend," Gregory had already said "son" the smallest fraction of a second faster.

The policeman closed his notepad, put away his pencil, stood up and asked us to accompany him to the station. I felt so humiliated I could hardly stand.

"Leave 'em alone, they've done no harm. Only having a bleedin' drink. It's not a crime," yelled the landlord.

"Stay out of this, Mother."

"Mr Wilson to you."

They took us away in a Black Maria, and I felt as if I were being driven to my execution. Gore suddenly seemed like a complete stranger about whose life I knew absolutely nothing. To compound my humiliation, there were two men with us in the back of the van dressed in women's clothes, their faces covered in make-up. One of them explained that they'd just been arrested for soliciting in the park. They introduced themselves as Lady Godiva and Gilda Lily. Gilda did all the talking, explaining that Lady Godiva was still upset that the police had accosted her in the middle of a particularly enjoyable encounter, servicing a serviceman in possession of what Gilda termed "the biggest cazzo in Christendom." He leant across and said quietly, "She takes her work too seriously, if you ask me." He put a hand on my knee and said, "There are two things I can't stand: size queens and small cocks."

I looked at Lady Godiva. He looked at me and smiled weakly, exposing teeth so bucked I couldn't imagine anyone wanting to be fellated by him. My grandmother would have described them by saying he could eat an apple through a letterbox.

Gore and I exchanged not one word during the entire journey. The sounds of the traffic as we travelled through the city filled me with sadness. At the station we were separated immediately and taken into different rooms. I don't think I have ever been quite so petrified in my entire life. A police officer took down my details and then put me in a cell with Gilda and Lady Godiva, who still hadn't said a word. I was in there for what seemed hours. I wondered if they would interview me first and then Gore, or Gore first and then me, or both simultaneously, but concluded it didn't really matter. Our stories would not match. I wasn't about to start fabricating a life in which he was my son. Besides, what if he had decided to pretend he had simply used the wrong word accidentally in the pub and had meant to say friend? What if he was about to tell the truth? And what was the truth? Could I say he was a friend; could I lie and say he lived with me?

My mind was spinning with so many thoughts, and all the while Gilda was beside me recounting stories about the cock size of various members of parliament. "They don't call them members for nothing, love, believe you me!" he roared.

And still the only torture was his absence.

I wondered what Gore was doing, why he hadn't been put in with us.

Finally, I was taken to an interview room, where I maintained that his current address was with me.

"Why did he say he was your son, do you think?" The policeman arched an eyebrow.

"I imagine he used the wrong word accidentally. He is multi-lingual and is prone to mistakes on occasion."

"That's what he said."

I relaxed a little.

"You know that the Lord Barrymore is frequented by homosexuals, do you, Mr Read?"

I said I did.

"And do you frequent the Lord Barrymore, Mr Read?"

I said that it was my first time there.

"It always is, sir, it always is." He grinned and I was as tense as ever.

Then he pushed a sheet of text toward me and said, "If you could just read through and sign this statement for me, Miss—sorry, *Mister* Read." I read through it, considered pointing out the numerous errors in spelling, punctuation, and grammar, but thought better of it. I signed it and pushed it back toward him and he declared me a free man.

"And Gregory?"

"He's waiting outside for you." And he gave me that knowing grin again, and I thought to myself, *You don't know anything, you filthy Yahoo.* That was what my father used to say under his breath whenever anyone tried to talk to him whom he didn't like, which was almost everybody. I remember as a child thinking it a terrible name to call anyone. But, by Christ, that ape before me was a filthy Yahoo if ever I saw one. Where do they find them?

I found Gore skulking around outside, kicking the curb like a naughty bored child.

"Come on," I said, "let's get home." We took a black cab home in silence, and I found myself thinking about Frank Symonds sitting in all those cabs with all those boys years ago, and wondering what he might have talked to them about, or whether they too sat in a silence as deadly as this, like two creatures who had yet to develop a means to communicate. My mind was racing with words, but none of them seemed the right thing to say. Not in front of a cabbie. As soon as we were in the house I asked Gore why he hadn't simply given his own address and he said he didn't have one. He told me he had run away from his place in Islington without paying his rent and is sleeping in parks or with friends. I told him that I was sorry about his situation, and would help as much as I could, but that there was absolutely no way he could stay here.

He laughed.

"Gore, this is no joking matter."

I knew that, compared to the scrapes he'd regularly found himself in and the dangerous situations he'd placed himself in, a London bobby was child's play, but I still felt sick from the whole experience. I tried to keep a stern face, but he carried on laughing and eventually I found myself succumbing to a smile and then I myself began to laugh. In some curious way I felt the experience had brought us closer, though God alone knows how or why. I was very cross with him, and he knew it, I could tell. I can't help feeling a little unsettled by the whole affair. Especially the police having my details. I imagine that they have a huge ledger in which they record the details of every homosexual they've ever unearthed, and I keep picturing the policeman who interviewed me scratching my name in it and blotting it dry with a grin of triumph. I thought of Montagu, Wildeblood, and Pitt-Rivers in their cells. There but for the grace of God go I, I thought, even though I'm an atheist.

We were both in need of some sleep, so Gore took the couch and I took to my bed. Although I left my door open, he didn't take the hint. Just as well, for we were woken in the early morning by an almighty banging on the front door.

1998

After the cemetery, nothing. You left in the morning without offering any hope that we might meet again. There followed what seemed like weeks of deserted time, stretched out between the last sight of you and the next sight of you, dune upon dune of pointless space, waiting to be crawled across in the vain hope that your face might rise like an oasis as I scaled the summit. I busied myself, though nothing could bring me joy.

I cannot recall now how long until the next encounter—perhaps no more than a week. You pulled up outside on a motorbike, making enough noise to raise the dead. It was late at night. I was stoned and bored, waiting for the phone to ring, for the distraction of a client. I leant out of the window to see you looking up at me, visor up, holding out a spare helmet. I grabbed a jacket and ran down the three flights of stairs so fast I felt dizzy and breathless by the time I reached you. There are no words for what followed. I don't know if you felt anything like what I felt that night, with my arms around your waist, my hands nestled in your denimed crotch, my legs sealed against yours, the heat between us bonding our surfaces like adhesive, like two pieces of a whole being mended. The aroma of your leather jacket. The click of our helmets like a clumsy attempt at a kiss. The night air tearing through us as we sped across the flyover and out of the city, leaving the earth behind us as we traced a flight path beyond the speed of light, slowing down time till we could taste each nanosecond as it passed through our lips. When we stopped and climbed off and removed our helmets, somewhere west of the city, I felt such a spin of adrenaline that, when you grabbed my face and kissed the mouth off me, I lost myself in that dissolving of reality that makes you believe that life after all might be worth something, if only it could last. We made love on Barnes Common and smoked a joint, talking about things I can no longer recall, things that made sense of the madness of our lives, if only temporarily. Things that pulled me further in.

"So I guess we're fuck buddies, now, huh?" you said with that ironic tone of yours that I only now realize contained a distance I myself was trying to bridge. At the time I thought you craved a cleaving of the gap between us as much as I did.

"I never had a fuck buddy before," I said, mirroring your tone, ever reluctant to let the real emotion show lest it not be reciprocated. "What are the rules?"

"There are no rules," you said. "Rules are for people who have no imagination, who fear freedom." I remained silent. "You and me, we're free as birds."

"Free to do what?" I asked.

"Whatever you want."

On the way back, more than once I was assailed by a strong urge to loosen my grip on you and let the wind rip me from the bike and send me out into space, to a place from which I could never return. Somehow I knew that, whatever it was that existed between us, it could not be preserved, or could only be preserved if we were to collide with a tree or a truck and be crushed into an instant that could keep this love locked up tight forever, never to go stale. I wanted to be a child again, standing on a railway track, waiting for the impact of the train. You dropped me off outside my flat and roared off into the night.

We met again the next night. It was raining lightly. I walked past Price Check, crossed the road, past the Scala, toward the Bell, the place where it all began. I passed a man and a woman standing in front of a shop window, a huge reflective surface, in the crude glare of the streetlights. The drizzle shone like glass on the young man's bare, hairless torso. She turned his gaze toward his image. His blue jeans were unbuttoned, the root of his cock visible in the gap. "Look at you," she said. "Just look at you. You're fuckin' beautiful." And he looked at himself. And smiled. A stupid, drunken, narcissistic smile.

I walked into the bar. Already stoned. Looked around but you weren't there. I thought of the first time I walked in here, over nine years ago. Friendless and ignorant and nervous as hell. I thought of Edward, whom I hadn't seen for years, other than the occasional fleeting chat in a club, or at a party; of Lilli, who'd burned too bright to last. I thought about my family, whom I hadn't seen for nearly a decade. All the people from my life crowded around me, repeating like a mantra the one word: conform. Over and over, conform, conform, *conform*. I ordered a drink from a barman who wore the face of a man I had sex with a decade ago. The whole place was packed with everyone

I'd ever fucked, all the inhabitants of my memory, repeating that word: *conform*. It curled up within the shell of my ear and slid to the pit of my heart. Shame and excitement, fear and desire, all staked their claim there. When it gets to the point when there is no memory, that's where memory begins.

As I was daydreaming all of this, you arrived, to hand me a torch with which to banish these demons. Never thought this was possible, this tug-tug-tugging of the heart. A face I didn't want to take my eyes from. That face can never, will never leave me. A face to light up my own. My piece of treasure. A nail to pierce the hands and feet. *Always be with me*, I thought to myself. Always be with me and always look this glad to see me.

I felt scared for the first time in years. I tasted danger when I looked at your face. I smelt the unknown. I wonder now how much of it showed. Wonder when it got too hot, when you felt the intensity become unbearable for the first time. When did it all become too much and you decide to chicken out? I certainly imagined at the time that I always kept it well hidden, how good it was to see you. Thought I was playing it cool—at least to begin with. I was used, of course, to performing in the opposite manner, feigning a pleasure I didn't feel. Perhaps we always give the game away, despite ourselves, to spite ourselves. You bought a drink and sat down next to me, kissing me on the lips. You had just done a client and were glowing with after-sex. I wanted you. Still want you. Will always want you, perhaps. I felt a stab of jealousy. The air I breathed got thinner. It was a feeling that remained for the longest time indescribable. I dismissed it.

"How was your day?" you asked, and I told you, though I cannot recall what I said. Very little of that time remains with me that didn't contain you. My life had long ceased to be memorable. I would never have admitted it at the time, but I was bored. My days had become an utterly pointless quest for cash and cock. The brief thrill of the cruise. Even sex rarely moved me any more, unless it involved you. The anticipation was more enjoyable than the actual thing. How many times during that period did I conjure your face to make myself cum?

After a couple of pints, we returned to my flat, and I lit a candle before climbing into the bed beside you. Several minutes into the sex, the room became suddenly illuminated with a dancing orange light—the candle had set fire to some newspapers in my room. You leapt up and used your T-shirt to beat out the flames, rendering it scorched and unwearable. You managed to stop the fire, but the wall was black and the room full of acrid smoke. I opened the window, coughing.

We pulled on our pants and left the flat, going upstairs onto the roof to get some fresh air. The familiar smog of London greeted us affectionately. Some of the residents from the other flats had planted little container gardens up there, but no one in our section had bothered. Ours was the slum end. There was one pot that served as the last resting place for a dried-up stump of a plant. There was a red British Rail bench. On one side of us the lights from the trains were moving in and out of King's Cross station; on the other, the staccato architecture of St Pancras was silhouetted against a burgundy sky. I tried not to imagine what might have happened if we hadn't spotted the fire in time. I didn't want to think about that. I wanted to return to the moment, so I started to kiss you. We fucked standing up, both facing out onto the open city, your cock connecting us, our bodies welded with sweat, alone, together, facing what lay before us, like the figure-head of a ship about to sink.

There have been many times over the past eighteen months when I've lain here, thinking of the enormity of the city outside, of the expanse of life taking place in all those buildings scattered across the city, and of my tiny life here, in this cell. I have thought a lot about the outside, what it means to live outside. Outside the law, for example. Outside respectable society. About how difficult it can be to live there. I like these dark, vast hours, when most people are sleeping. During these hours, I feel I can breathe and think more freely, till my breath and my thoughts expand to fill the empty space left vacant by the sleepers. I've always loved the night; my blood responds to its call. As a teenager, I would slink out of the house as my parents and my brother slept and I would walk the empty streets feeling free and invisible. The occasional car would pass as I made my way to the railway embankment near our house. At night, the place was dense with silence. I might see a family of foxes emerge, watch the tiny cubs scrap and tumble in the starlight. And I would feel more alive than I ever did when the sun shone.

It seems so unfair that we can only have one life. So much remains uncharted. So we look for ways to erase reality to make it more manageable, to avoid the madness that comes with con-fronting raw multiplicity. But those familiar paths of fake reality hold their own harsh realities. I was forever in clap clinics, forever on antibiotics, forever warding off the bite of the comedown with the taste of something else, forever running from the black cloud of psychosis that I had seen descend on others. Forever losing myself. The life I thought I wanted had become as monotonous as that from which I thought I had escaped. Is that why I lost myself in you?

The next night we met in the West End. Meal at Pollo's, drinks at the Edge, a cab back to your flat in Limehouse, during which you pointed out your favourite buildings or recounted stories about the history of the area. I think if I had to pick the first moment when I expressed to myself how much I had fallen in love, it would be then, when you talked excitedly about what you knew.

Your flat was enormous, with a balcony overlooking the river. I remember wondering to myself what you must think of my poky, untidy flat. The bathroom was painted black, with hundreds of silver stars covering the walls and ceiling. You showed me a table you made while studying furniture design when you were younger, a huge, kidney-shaped hunk of wood, and some strange but fascinating vases you had made recently. Your accent betrayed the fact that you grew up partly in America when you said *vayse* instead of *varze*.

I said that I thought they were beautiful, though I wasn't really sure I meant it.

"Would you like one?"

I didn't say anything.

"Here, have one, I want you to have one," and you held out a green vase. "Matches your eyes," you said with a smile. Why do I feel so unlike myself when I am near you?

Pointing to a small mirror on the table, upon which lay two fat lines of cocaine, you said, "Help yourself," and I did. You came over and made short shrift of the other line, before dabbing your finger in the remaining dust and rubbing it against my gums, then kissing me. You lay back on the sofa and whispered, "Come here," pulling me to you. I lay on top of you and we kissed for a long time, grinding our erections together through our jeans. You slid your right hand inside the back of my jeans. You said, "Let's sit on the balcony—it's beautiful out there at this time of night."

So we stood up and you walked over to the open-plan kitchen and grabbed a bottle of red wine from the rack, scooping up two inverted wine glasses from the draining board. I remember wondering who else had been around here drinking wine with you, and how recently. You nodded down at the table as you passed it, saying, "Grab that box," and continued on toward the glass doors leading outside. I picked it up and followed you out onto the balcony. The sky was a dark, dark blue. Starless and moonless. Across the water, a galaxy of orange-lit windows, blinking lights, strings of street lamps and the brazen beams of cars. This city is constructed of points of light, like a madrigal.

You opened the box and removed Rizlas and a pebble of hash. There are lots of ways to roll a joint. In my life, I have probably witnessed them all. But no one has ever rolled a joint the way you did. It was an art to rival origami, the way you ripped and licked your way through six small Rizlas. You handed it to me, and I set a flame to its magnificence.

You stood up quickly and said, "Let's have some music. What do you fancy?"

"You," I said, feeling like a prick immediately the word was out.

"Got any Radiohead?" I asked, to cover the word that hung there in the silence between us.

You disappeared indoors, returning as the first notes of *The*

Bends crashed in. I handed you the joint. You were carrying a CD case, and I watched as you carefully cracked open the two parts of clear plastic to expose the hollow of its spine. There, like vertebrae, lay a row of white pills.

"I posted them over last time I was in L.A. You get the best ecstasy there." You necked one and held another out for me to take. I closed my mouth around your fingertip and swallowed the pill. Across the river, two spotlights appeared in the black sky, their beams cutting across the darkness, and dancing, now close, now far apart, their diagonals dissecting my vision. The music intensified the sight.

Everything started to fragment.

You told me it was your mother's flat. She's English, your dead father Venezuelan. You didn't have a flat in London. "I don't like to feel tied down to one city," you said, mysteriously. You told me that your mother, a professor of art history, was away, lecturing in the States. You told me that your younger brother died of AIDS four years earlier, just months after your father died of a heart attack. You recounted these details without any visible or audible emotion. I have no Great Tragedy to recount in return, only the uneventful blandness of my childhood. The fact that I haven't seen my family in ten years doesn't strike me as a Great Tragedy. I told you one or two stories about myself. You told me about the three months you spend each year in Venezuela, staying in your dead grandmother's house, taking the purest cocaine and sleeping your way through the local boys. You told me about hanging out at a bus depot there, where they have showers for the drivers to freshen up before going home after a shift, recounting how you befriended the son of the depot manager, and how one day when the manager was absent and the son was in charge, you talked him into locking the door while the two of you and a few of the drivers stripped off and had sex in the showers. I wondered whether to believe a word of it, and concluded that it didn't really matter.

"It's like Joe Orton said," you smirked, "you'll only regret not having fun with your genitals."

You promised to take me to Venezuela. I'd heard that one before. I looked at the sky. I could hear and smell the pelt of the Thames passing by us not too far below, like a beast pacing the forest floor.

"You know, you're not at all like the other British men I've met."

"Really? In what way?" I asked.

You laughed. "Well, the way you have sex, for a start. You really go for it. I like that."

"Is that unusual?" I asked, wondering what kind of person wouldn't really go for it with you.

"You're very passionate. I like that. I don't find that very often in Brits." Although what you said made me feel good, I didn't know what to say in response, so for something to do I lit a cigarette. Just at that moment you held out the joint and I swapped it for the cigarette.

"Shouldn't I have said that?" you asked, a slight note of worry in your voice.

"No, it's cool."

"You're a rare breed." You reached for the ornate wooden box. "You have the most amazing aura." From the green packet, you plucked out six skins in quick succession.

"Sorry?" I immediately remembered the night at Harry's and that dreadful New Age book those boys were discussing. Had you been involved in their conversation before spread-eagling on the bed? Had you begun it? Read it? *Believed* it?

"Your aura. It's the most amazing colour. I've never seen another like it."

You started to lick a Rizla's edge and begin to construct that strange configuration of papers.

"And what colour is it?" (*What colour is it?*)

In the distance, the Thames was striped in gold like a tiger. A black and gold tiger.

"It's kinda orange. Like a flame. Really hot," you said, with a grin on your face fresh enough to eat.

I could hear the river tiger breathing in low slow rasps. I didn't know what to say so I didn't say anything.

"David isn't my real name," I said, after a long silence, apropos of nothing and sounding far more mysterious than I had intended. Just at that moment, you shouted, "*Oh, shit!*" and drowned out my statement. I looked at you.

"I just dropped the dope, man."

"You didn't!"

"I did. It fell right down between the fuckin' boards!"

We both looked down at the balcony floor. It was constructed of widely spaced wooden beams between which the resin had just dropped, down onto the beach below. The tide was out, luckily, the Thames revealing its bed, like a whore disrobing. A carpet of shingle stretched out beneath us, millions of dark brown lumps of rock worn smooth by the river's suck. Each and every one of them looked just like a lump of hash.

I said, "Whoops."

"Whoops?" you yelled. "No, 'whoops' is for when you've accidentally electrocuted your grandmother. 'Whoops' is for when you realize you've just outed your boyfriend to his parents, or when you catch your foreskin in your zipper. The only possible response to this situation is…" And you emitted a bloodcurdling scream that had us in fits of giggles, which you cut short by saying, "It's not funny, man, that was a big fuckin' lump."

"Oh, well." I took a sip of red wine in commiseration. I was already rolling from the E.

From the living room drifted the sound of Thom Yorke tearing his heart out.

"I'm gonna fuckin' find it!" you said, standing up and disappearing inside.

"Okay," I said, joining in the lunacy and following. We went down a flight of stairs into the bedroom, a large room with two massive vertical wooden beams. You disappeared into a cupboard and reappeared with a rope, which you tied around one of the beams as if you were Errol Flynn, testing your handiwork before trailing the rope toward the open window. I watched you thread it through and down to the beach below. "A flashlight," you said, running past me and out of the room.

You returned holding out a bunch of five white candles like a ghost's hand. "Couldn't find a flashlight. Here." You handed me one.

You went first, disappearing through the window, and I heard the wet crunch of you landing on shingle. I followed, smelling the damp brine, crystalline in the warm air. Clumps of green mush and debris were scattered about—tin cans, plastic bottles, crisp packets, a bicycle wheel—looking strangely beautiful in the faint candlelight. On our hands and knees, faces pressed close to the circle of orange light as it made its way across that impossibly homogenous landscape, we began our search for the lump of hash. There was no sound except the rustle of the tiger's fur.

It was hard not to laugh, so we did. The tiger laughed too. Quietly.

A long and profound silence descended, until…

"This is like looking for a needle in a fuckin' hay—" I said, the sentence broken off by the absolute beauty of the brown nugget I had just panned. "I've fuckin' *found* it!" I yelled, holding it up inside the candle's halo, feeling it give as I squeezed it gently, gently squeezed it. Yes. I tested it on my teeth like a jeweller. Yes. You ran over and kissed me, leaving diamonds in my mouth. Mmm. We rooted the candles amongst the stones and you began to skin up our prize, saying, "What did I say? You're fuckin' amazing." The river purred at our feet.

I looked at you and heard an echo: *you're fuckin' amazing*. And the river purred at our feet.

1895

Before the start of this second trial, we were told that we'd have to give evidence, me and Charlie and Sidney. I was up first, and I was practically shitting myself with fear. My heart was banging so much that for the longest time I thought they must all be able to hear it, all those people with their beady eyes on me, and my legs wouldn't keep still. It unnerved me, knowing his eyes were on me, and it made me think of that time at the orgy when the opposite was true, when I rejoiced in his gaze. But how different his thoughts would be now, I thought. How much he must hate the sight of me now.

I couldn't even once bring myself to look over at him.

It was painful to have to repeat in public the things I'd said in his presence. It made me feel sick, truth be told. But it'd all gone too far and I could never now admit to the truth anyway, so I stood there and told that courtroom all about my times with him at Kettner's and the Savoy and the Café Royal. That shocked them more, I think, than when I mentioned the orgy and the sex games—the fact that scum like me'd been to such grand places. As if that were the greater crime.

Each word I spoke was offered like a mouthful of vomit and received like a priceless jewel.

The questions were easy enough, but it shocked me to the quick when they produced the silver cigarette case he had given me with an engraved inscription. I felt my face redden as it was passed amongst the jury, for it became in my eyes a symbol for what I'd done to him. It seemed that with the appearance of that gift everyone in that room knew exactly how I felt about him and why I was betraying him this way, as if my heart were transparent and revealed itself to contain nothing but a handful of silver.

After me, Sidney took the stand. And what a sly bastard he's turned out to be. He denied absolutely that anything untoward had ever occurred between him and Oscar. I couldn't believe it. The prosecution was furious. You could see it on his face—this was not supposed to happen. They had paid him to ensure he collaborated, but Sidney just sat there with a determined set to his mouth and said no, nothing happened, even when they spent the night together at the Albermarle Hotel. And I know for a fact that something went on, for wasn't I there as well?

"No impropriety has ever taken place between me and Mr Wilde," he said, "and Mr Wilde has never given me any money. I was always glad of Mr Wilde's friendship."

The lying cunt.

He claimed he'd been forced to give a statement but that his statement was a pack of lies. A tense, awkward silence settled on the court, then a hissing of whispers like a whole load of snakes had just slithered in, and he was asked to step down and I slipped out of the courtroom just in time to catch him and some well-dressed fellow shaking hands before Sidney walked away, out of the Old Bailey and I thought to myself, *Well, was it that easy?* Would it have been that easy to walk away from this whole fuckin' mess? Could I have done the same?

I don't know.

I walked home, buying a paper on the way. I lay on my bed reading it, thinking about Oscar. He told me once, "It is best to believe almost everything one writes and almost nothing one reads, because in order to believe something completely one must have lived it, and one does not live a book one has read, only a book one has written."

Another time he told me this story:

"There once lived a carpenter who had a piece of wood that he wanted to keep, for he valued it above all the other pieces of wood in his workshop. So he decided to build a box in which to keep this wood, for it was too precious to leave lying around. It might get chipped or dented, stained or dirty, so he looked around for a piece of wood with which to make a box fit for this precious block. It couldn't be a box made of any old wood. 'But all these pieces are not worthy of being made into a box in which to keep my precious block of wood!' he cried. 'They are all gnarled and ugly, worm-eaten and old.' So he decided to use the only wood worthy enough of the honour of housing his wooden jewel: the precious block itself. He sawed and planed, hammered and sanded until eventually the box was complete. It was a beautiful object, the grain perfect beneath the polished varnish. The carpenter was so proud of his handiwork that he couldn't refrain from planting a kiss on its shining surface, leaving an imprint of his lips upon its lid. Yet the box, he reflected with a stab of pain, must remain empty.

"And this is what we have done with our words," Oscar ended. "They are beautiful but hollow."

I shouldn't be thinking of these things, not now, not when he's stuck where he is. I've no right to feel sorry for myself.

1954

The banging was incessant. I looked at my watch. Six a.m. I dragged myself out of bed and pulled on my bathrobe and made my way downstairs. When I opened the front door, there were two policemen standing there. A furious sense of irritation arose and I was determined not to let them in, though at the same time I was terrified lest the neighbours spotted them. No doubt it was too late. I'm sure curtains were already twitching.

"Mr Read?" the uglier of the two enquired.

"Yes."

"We have a warrant to search these premises."

"What for?"

"I think you know the reason."

At that point Gore appeared in the hallway, bleary-eyed and dressed only in his underwear. My heart sank. The two policemen smirked.

"I suppose you'd better come in, then." I stepped aside to let them enter.

They were here for hours, going through everything. All my

letters and correspondence, of which there is very little. I do not possess an address book for I have no friends. I do not keep a diary for my life is without event—or at least it was until recently. They went through all my sketchbooks and drawings in the studio, seemingly fascinated by my artwork. All the while my mind was racing with fears that this was it, I was going to prison. I was practically holding out my hands for the cuffs to be slapped on me. I found myself thinking about my parents, particularly my mother. The newspapers would relish the fact that a former mayoress's son had been arrested for immoral practices. I could see the headlines. Not that I'd done anything. I wondered if drawing the male nude was enough to get me. Was art a crime?

I asked if I could telephone a lawyer.

"That won't be necessary, Mr Read." There was a note of disappointment in the policeman's voice.

"We'd suggest you take more care about the company you keep," the other one said—the first time he'd spoken. They looked at Gore. They told him he was to report to the police station as soon as he had an address. Then they were gone. I sank into a chair and buried my face in my hands. Gore came over and put a hand on my shoulder, but I shrugged him off. He walked away and I burst into tears. I felt violated, exposed, shamed, intimidated. Which is just what they wanted. I was shaking with fear. I don't know how long I sat there like that, but when I had regained myself I couldn't find Gore anywhere. I called his name and his voice came from the bathroom. He was reclining in the bath, nonchalant as anything. I realized at that moment how far apart we were, how different our personalities. This young man had had scrapes with the law his entire life; the previous few hours hadn't affected him at all. He'd been in prison before. It was all water off a duck's back to him. He smiled up at me, with that angelic face of his.

"Would you scrub my back?" he said.

After a breakfast I hardly touched (but which he wolfed down), we went looking for lodgings for him. I wanted him out of the house. It suddenly seemed too dangerous, too much for me to deal with, having him here. I braced myself to greet the outside world, and as we left the house my neighbour, Mrs Wardle, a nosy old widow with a creased face, appeared from nowhere, asking if everything was all right. Feigning concern, when what she wanted was gossip. I politely told her everything was fine. She was staring at Gore, taking him in, the quiff, the clothes, the incongruity of him and me. I ignored her and we walked on, leaving her there, gawping.

We found him digs in a house in Hammersmith. I paid the first month's rent and left him there. I needed to be alone. I boarded a bus to the West End, craving the anonymity of crowds.

I have no explanation for what I did next. Perhaps I needed further humiliation; perhaps I needed some reason to feel so shamed, needed to commit the crime for which I was being pursued. After a couple of hours aimlessly drifting through the busy streets I found myself near a toilet that Gore had told me about in the West End, where men meet for sex. I hadn't planned to go there, certainly hadn't the slightest flicker of desire within me, but even as my rational self screamed against such folly I found myself entering it. Nervous as hell, I slipped from the noisy bustle of Oxford Street into this silent cavern.

The place stank of stale urine, a fog of ammonia that stung

as I inhaled. The drip, drip, drip of the pipes was like a metronome keeping time to the rhythm of my desire. The place was empty, and as I approached the urinal I nearly turned around and walked out, and oh, how I wish I had.

What stopped me was the sound of another man entering, and I stood there and unzipped, though I had no desire to urinate. I looked around at the other man and our eyes met momentarily. He was young and good-looking. I looked away in panic. He entered a cubicle behind me, and I stood and waited to see what would happen next. I heard noises from within the cubicle, and turned my head, my heart pounding, though of course I could see nothing but a closed door, the engaged sign staring at me like an unblinking eye in a spyhole. There was a flush, and he re-emerged and walked over to the sink and began to wash his hands. Still, I stood there, by now paralysed by fear more than curiosity, my shrunken penis in my hand. Leave, I told myself, leave now. Danger had bristled the hairs on my neck. He walked toward me, I looked around to meet his gaze, and his face, grimacing, startled me. "Are you a pervert?" he demanded.

"Sorry?" I stuttered, near to fainting.

"Are you a fucking pervert? You've been standing there for ages. Were you trying to peep at me?"

"No, I'm just having a piss," I said, nonchalantly, trying to downplay the accent, trying to wrap my tongue around the vernacular so foreign to it, trying to mask my fear.

"You're a fucking pervert," he shouted, and I zipped myself up and stepped away from the urinal, trying to get past him, my head faint and my heart racing. He grabbed me and pushed me up against the wall. "I've had this problem in here before and

I'm sick of it. Fucking queers!"

"I'm not qu—" I protested, but his fist hammered into my stomach and lodged the final syllable there. I doubled up in pain and he walked away. I wanted to cry, but I heard someone else entering so I darted into a cubicle and locked the door. After several unbearable minutes, I flushed and left. I was halfway down Oxford Street, walking toward the Underground, when I realized he was following me. I didn't know what to do. I turned down back streets, trying to lose him, but he remained on my tail. I emerged into Carnaby Street.

"See this man here," he started shouting at passers-by, "see this man here, he was peeping at me in the toilet. He's a pervert."

My head dizzy, my body sweating, I took another turning, other turnings, not even seeing where I was going, just walking, rapidly, down side streets, fleeing him. I re-emerged onto Oxford Street in time to see two things simultaneously: a policeman, drawn by the commotion this youth was making, and a cab pulling up and two people disembarking. I scrambled in the back of the cab and slammed the door, telling the driver to move. My pursuer was left standing on the pavement, shouting, as the cab pulled away, and I collapsed into a fit of shame and self-hatred such as I had not known for years, cursing myself for my stupidity, feeling as if I didn't know myself at all any more.

Then I caught the cabbie's eye in the rear-view mirror, and he gave me a wink and chuckled to himself. I don't know which incident caused me more shame, the one in the toilet or the complicity he had offered.

"Next time, just give him some money—that usually shuts them up."

I muttered a perplexed, "Thank you," and closed my eyes, the terrible scene replaying in my head. I craved the sanctity of my own home, but dreaded going back there, for it offered no haven any longer.

I only now realized that today is my birthday.

1998

After that night at your place, losing and then finding the dope and having sex on the shingle, I didn't hear from you for over a week. I tried your mobile a couple of times, but you never answered it. After the second message, I hadn't the heart to leave another. I got on with my life, with this tension in my heart like a rock, this concentrated point of absence. Then I received a phone call from Harry. He wanted to make that video with you and me. That weekend. So we did it. Afterward, I'd assumed we'd go home together, but you said you had something to do and we parted after leaving Harry's place. Later that night, after a joint, I rang your mobile.

"It was really good to see you again," I said.

"Yeah, you too. So what you doin'?"

"Nothing. You?"

"Oh, I've got another job. Earl's Court. I'm on my way."

"Well, I won't keep you."

"Okay ... listen, let's get together again soon."

"That'd be good." (Too keen? Too non-committal?)

"Sure. I'll call. See ya, David."

"See you."

Another week without a word. I live a different life now, with you in it, even though you're not really in it. I roast on the coals, hating that your life is going on without me. I tell myself that it's wrong to feel this way, right to keep people at arm's length, as if they were a dangerous chemical. How can a whore fall in love with a whore?

Then, one Sunday afternoon, the sun shining, while I was walking home from Camden Town, a gleaming black BMW pulled up with you in it, smiling hello. You said you were driving out to Heathrow to deliver the car to someone. Asked if I fancied a ride. I climbed in. Once we reached the Hammersmith flyover you asked if I wanted to take the wheel, telling me what a great drive it was, but I said no. I just wanted to relax. I pushed one of the CDs I'd just bought into the player, and turned the music up loud so we didn't have to speak. There were so many things I wanted to say to you, but the music, for now, was enough, the lightness I felt as London peeled off behind us like a skin we were shedding. That was enough, for now.

Once the car had been dropped off, we took the tube back into the West End for a drink, then back to yours for a smoke and a fuck. (See how language reduces complexity?)

Two weeks' absence this time: a fold of time, a duration of pain, of which I have no memory now, no memory at all. Since I set eyes on you, I seem to have gone blind.

1895

We haven't seen Sidney since he turned his coat. Although I'm glad about it, and I couldn't care less what happens to him, I'd've liked to have talked to him about why he did what he did. It's just Charlie and me in the house now, and my first thought this morning on waking up next to Charlie was that I have to leave, I have to get out of this house. I can't live here any longer. But it was Charlie's turn in the dock, first thing, so we made our way over to the courtroom, mostly in silence, though we did both wonder aloud where Sidney might be.

Charlie's always loved to perform, and today in the dock he put on a great show. I'd never before heard the story of how he and Taylor met, and it distracted me from my own feelings of guilt to listen to him tell it. He said that Taylor came up to him and his brother at the bar of the St James and bought them a drink, saying something about the tarts round the Dilly, something about how ridiculous it was for sensible men to waste their money on painted trash like that, and then he tells them they could make money in a certain way easily enough if they cared to, the dirty old goat. I nearly laughed out loud picturing him being so bold, and I started to admire his courage. But then I looked at him standing there in the dock looking so old and beaten and with Oscar next to him looking ill and wretched, and it suddenly sank in that it was all over, the party was over, for the two who threw the best were as good as dead and buried, and my heart sank and struggled like something held underwater and fighting for its life.

Charlie pulled no punches. He told them everything and seemed to gloat over the details. I was surprised when he said Oscar sodded him because Oscar never did that to me, and as far as I know he didn't even like to do it. I felt a pang of jealousy considering whether Charlie was telling the truth or embellishing for the sake of it, for he is prone to that and would, I've no doubt, like nothing better than to say the word *sodomy* in a court of law. But maybe Oscar was sodding all and sundry but me. That never occurred to me before. Christ, my head is in pieces. And my fucking heart is on the floor. How could I ever go home again?

I walked as far as Whitechapel and found cheap lodgings in some filthy paddyken in Brick Lane, all sorts of wild thoughts flooding my head. This secret life I've been a part of is suddenly being talked about and written about. Regret, panic, and loneliness kept me awake for hours, listening to the noise of the city, the screams and shouts and commotion of a typical London night. Unable to sleep, I made my way to an alehouse in Aldgate and drank five beers as quickly as I could, listening in to everyone in there chattering about Oscar and reading out from the newspapers and talking about how sick and evil he is. Someone said he'd probably get the maximum sentence, and I suddenly felt wretched and had to leave, my head spinning from the beer and the thoughts assailing me. "That'll wipe the smile off his fat Irish face," someone said as I walked to the door, and everyone laughed and cheered.

I've never felt so alone in the world nor so fearful of the future. What will I do when my money runs out? How will I live, now that I've appeared in court for all the world to know my face and my deeds? And him—I can't get his big face from my thoughts. What have I done? This question echoes around my head like a bell. What have I done to him?

I can hear his voice in my head, saying, "Morality makes a prisoner of men, makes men cruel and vicious, for behind the pretence of morality lurks the bitter heart of a life blighted, and often as not the most moralistic are the most cruel, for their sense of loss makes them hack at you with bladed words until your own life is as limbless and immobile as theirs. If you can live without morality then you are truly free." Yet I've lived without morality, and I've never felt less free.

1954

There were no repercussions from the law, but things between Gore and me have changed. He still comes over, but something within me has begun to resent him. I still desire him, but I find I cannot bear the sight of him. I have hardened, and dread his arrival, when once I longed to see him. His cocky, jokey demeanour irritates me now. On more than one occasion recently I have come very close to slapping the money down and demanding his services, longing to treat him like the whore he is.

It all started going wrong when I discovered that I painted Gore better from memory than I did from real life. I was working on the triptych this morning, and I suddenly realized that the drawings I did of him in his absence were so much better than those I did when he was there in front of me. I have committed every line, every plane of that flesh to memory, so that, when it was spread before me, my eye got bored while my hand traced out its contours almost without looking at him. Worse than that, I found myself getting irritated by his presence because it was ruining my art; his real flesh got in the way of the iridescent memory that guided my brush. The more I thought about the irritation his presence was starting to cause, the more I tried to hide it, and the more I discovered that all I wanted to do was put aside my paper and explore that body with my tongue, trace its outlines not with charcoal or lead but with my mouth, my hands, my penis. There is nothing I can do with this desire. It rises up within me, clawing for supremacy, and I feel weaker and weaker with every passing day, less able to conquer it, and less willing. It needs some release, and that makes me fearful and brave in equal measure. I no longer know who I am. All I can think about is Gore's body and the process of replicating it on canvas.

1998

One night, after too much drink and too many drugs, I took
a cab over to the flat in Limehouse. Knowing nothing of what
I'm worth, I rang the bell. There was no response. I crossed the
road and sat in a darkened doorway. Two hours and countless
cigarettes later, a black cab pulled up and you clambered out
with another man, laughing. You unlocked the front door and
the two of you tumbled into the flat like acrobats, oblivious to
my presence, oblivious to my pain. I sat there, smoking, recalling
all the times you'd put two cigarettes in your mouth and lit them
both before passing one to me. And then, with no star to guide
me, I walked all the way back to King's Cross, telling myself that
what we call love is nothing but a misguided notion of salvation,
a rescue fantasy so wildly unreal that desertion, betrayal, and suffering are the only way out of the delusion. I resolved never to
see you again.

You had pegged me out in the sun like a hide to dry.

I looked for my self, but it was nowhere to be seen.

The next day—but why am I telling you this? what am I hoping to achieve?—the next day I visited you. You weren't dressed. It was about three p.m. You came to the door with your lower half wrapped in a duvet. It suddenly occurred to me that perhaps he was still here, the other man, and I panicked. You stepped back to let me in, pressing the duvet down to make room for me to pass. As I walked through, I felt like a condemned man who knows he must go to the scaffold and yet begins to tremble on seeing it.

You kissed me. Said it was good to see me. Offered me a cup of coffee. I accepted. You dropped the duvet and poured out two cups. You stood there naked. I sat down and you brought the coffee over. And it all seemed so normal, so domestic, I wanted to scream. I watched you. Watched your cock swing as you walked toward me, plagued by visions of you and him.

"Gorgeous day, huh?" You nodded toward the sunlit window.

"Yeah. What's left of it."

"Yeah. Pretty late night." A grin pushed onto your face.

"Fun?"

"No—I was stuck in hospital for hours. I was with a friend of mine who's epileptic and he had a fit and I had to take him to hospital. Didn't get in till early this morning."

"How is he?"

"He's fine now. Freaked me out though. Never seen him fit before."

So I'd become someone you lie to. Perhaps I had always been that. At least I knew where I stood, I told myself.

You came over to where I was sitting. You had a semi-erection. It was at eye level, and as you ran a hand through my hair you said, "Fuck, am I pleased to see you, man. I've been horny all morning." Knowing no shame, feeling no desire, I took you in my mouth. You tasted of someone else. You held my head in your hands, thrusting forward, saying, "It's all yours, man, it's all yours," but I knew that it wasn't all mine. It never was and never will be all mine. I was a fool for thinking that it could be. You'd never said those words to me before, and I wondered if you had said them to him last night or whether he'd said them to you. Where did you learn them? Why was I thinking like this?

Afterward, you rolled a joint and we lay there naked, smoking it. Even though I knew it was pointless, I asked you what I meant to you. I still had so much to learn. You passed me the joint and I sucked on it as if I might suck back the words.

"You're cool—you know I think you're cool. What we have is cool. What do you want me to say?"

"I don't know."

I told you about the previous night, and I felt unhinged, like a stalker, or as if I was confessing to a murder. I sensed immediately that it was the wrong thing to have said. Hadn't I learnt by now that the truth is always the wrong thing to say? I used to be so good at lying—when it didn't matter. You made an honest man of me.

You sat there burning the hairs on your legs with the tip of the joint as I spoke. When I'd finished, you looked up at me and said, "I'm a whore, David. You're a whore. It's in our nature. Do you want me to say I'm sorry? I'm sorry I lied to you? Yeah, I picked someone up, I fucked him. Big deal. That's what I do. I assume that's what you do. I'm not in the market for a relationship. I didn't think you were. We have fun, don't we? Isn't that enough?"

"I'm sorry. I have no right."

"Monogamy doesn't work. Love doesn't work, wouldn't work.

Not for us. I don't want a boyfriend."

"Fine."

You handed me the joint. Its taste offered comfort.

"It's like those tapes and CDs over there." You gestured to an untidy pile by the stereo. "One day, I know I need to sort them out, tidy them up, put them in the right cases, in some kind of order. But I keep putting it off."

I struggled to pick up the meaning of this analogy, though I nodded as if the greatest truth were being delivered.

"This isn't about me, you don't really know me. It's about you. Maybe you've been on the game too long."

I realized I hadn't spoken for a long time, and worried that you might think you were breaking my heart. You were breaking my heart. I smiled, though I wore it like a battle scar.

"You're gorgeous and sexy, and I love it when we fuck. You're a fantastic fuck." And with those words I was dismissed, I knew my place, and it was not there.

"Listen, I'm off to Amsterdam tomorrow, pick up some cars. Why don't you come? I need another driver. It'll be fun."

With those words you rescued me from the hell into which you had just cast me.

With these words the end began.

1895

It was an endless three weeks from the second trial, when the
jury couldn't reach a verdict, to this final one, and I've hardly
slept for fear of the nightmares that descend the minute I do, like
an incubus sitting on my chest and sucking my blood. Dreams
in which the hounds are after me, and as I run from them gold
coins are falling from my pockets and I want to stop and pick
them up, but I know that if I do the dogs will get me, and I'm
woken by the snap of their jaws, covered in sweat and shivering. I
keep recalling that fourth day of the second trial, when he started
on about the intellectual purity of the love between an older man
and a younger, jabbering on about Plato and Shakespeare. Many
of the crowd started applauding, but I knew for a fact that when
he placed his tongue on my prick he wasn't bloody well thinking
of Plato.

This afternoon, when the judge read out the verdict of guilty
and then the sentence, two years' hard labour, I thought I was
gonna start crying. I felt like I was falling. Once, when I was out
in the countryside with a client who liked to do it in the open

air, we got stuck in a narrow lane filled with horse-riders on a hunt, a sea of dogs yapping madly around us. It was terrifying. In that courtroom today, the air hung heavy like the stench of that hunt, the crowds baying for blood like those hounds. It wasn't meant to be that way at all, and I've been a bloody fuckin' fool to think it could have been otherwise. Blinded by my own rage. They wanted him, hounding their quarry to exhaustion.

I knew that for Oscar hard labour would be as good as the hangman's noose. Even Taylor, who got the same, would have a hard time of it. The crowd's glee made me want to throw up, though I heard some cry, "Shame." Their petty victory made me weep and my role in it made me want to die. I sat in the balcony of the courtroom and wished it was me going to gaol.

Charlie and me left the Old Bailey and the streets outside were full of people cheering like it was a bloomin' coronation or something. A gaggle of whores were singing and dancing, linking arms and hitching their skirts up from the mud as they jigged with glee. Those girls have been slagging us off for ages, complaining that their trade was sparse because we had pilfered their clients. I suppose there always has to be someone to pay the price. As we passed them I heard one of them yelling, "'E'll 'ave 'is 'air cut regular now!" Charlie, who was beside me, laughed at that.

I pushed past them and walked away from Charlie without a word, off toward my lodgings, taking shanks's pony, as Walter called it. I'm free to walk away, a free man. Although I never felt less free, truth be told.

With my shame dragging behind me like a ball and chain, I can walk away. But to where? I know I can't stay here, not now my name's been in the paper. I won't be able to get work anywhere, and I can't go back to whoring. And my thirty pieces of silver have nearly run out.

I sit here. It is midnight. The moon outside is half closed, like a sleepy eye. I stare at it, imagining his face, his big white moon-face. How large it seemed close up, filling my field of vision like a planet or a god. I picture how scared he looked when the verdict was read out this afternoon. He didn't look so grand and important then, as the Old Bailey erupted in cheers and applause. I thought I'd feel a sense of victory, I must admit, seeing him broken like that, but I feel nothing but a bottomless sorrow.

1954

Despite my awful experience in the toilet, and my resolution never to step inside such a place ever again, today I took a trip to a cottage in Catherine Street, famed for its gloryhole, I'm reliably informed by Gore. He told me that regulars call it Cathy's for short and arrange to meet one another there as if it were a gentleman's club, which I suppose in a way it is. It's just off Aldwych. I'd actually used it countless times when I worked near there, but never imagined anything like that went on there. I felt light-headed with nerves as I approached, anticipation and fear churning my stomach over. I almost didn't go in, so strong was the memory of my last attempt.

It was empty, apart from one stall that was occupied. I walked into the neighbouring stall and closed the door. I lowered the seat and sat down, my head floating somewhere too high above my body. I cast a glance at the wall. About one third of the way up there was a hole the diameter of a tea mug, tucked behind the roll of toilet paper hanging from a bit of wire, through which I could make out part of a hairy leg. My heart began to beat faster.

I leant forward, my gaze travelling up the leg, until, framed by the sweating rim of the hole, I viewed a hand clutching an erect penis, gently rubbing it up and down. My mouth ran dry. I sat upright, staring ahead at the back of the door, wondering what the protocol might be in such a situation. Before I had decided what to do next, the penis began emerging from the brickwork, like something growing from the wall. There, like a coat hook, protruding from the wall. Almost comical. Without a thought, I reached out and touched it, wrapped my cold hand around its warm solidity. It felt good. I could feel it swell and stiffen in my grasp. I lowered myself onto my knees and worshipped what I have so long believed I could live without: pleasure. I found pleasure, my pleasure, and it lifted my heart from the floor of that urine-stinking cubicle and sent it soaring past the clouds. There is no shame, not at first, because there is no identity. A mouth, a cock. Here, and now, those body parts connect in such a connectionless way that there can be but one response, that of the body itself, a body pleasuring another body, heeding its call. That is all, and that is glorious—until the guilt appears, the sense that pleasure should not be this easy that hit me as I rose and fastened my trousers, the taste of him still on my tongue. There is a price, and I don't know I've paid it until I slink out of there, checking the knees of my trousers beforehand for dust, and hail a cab to take me straight home. This time, I can't even meet the cabbie's gaze in the rear-view mirror as I give him my address.

But still, even through the shame breaks this insolent feeling of joy. I did it. Wait till I tell Gore.

Something unbelievable has happened. I sucked Gore's cock. Even to write those words excites me. We were working as usual. I was sketching away, and Gore was chatting about what he'd been up to in some cottage with a brickie, when I suddenly said, "I've been doing a bit of that myself, lately."

Gore looked over at me and laughed in disbelief. Emboldened, I confessed that I had been visiting Cathy's for the past couple of days, sometimes several times a day. It felt as if I was making it up, but I wasn't. It's the truth. Since that first time, I had found myself drawn back again and again, each visit making me hungrier than before.

"You must be getting pretty good at it," he said with a grin, and before I knew it I had answered back, equally bold, "I'll show you if you like." My heart was racing, but my desire now dictated. He looked as startled by my boldness as I felt.

"All right, then," he smirked.

I put down my drawing and by the time I had sidled over to him he was semi-hard, and I took off my glasses and took him in my mouth. It quivered and flexed. I had dreamed of this moment. I savoured the taste and the feel of it. I breathed in the dark smell of it. I pressed my forehead against his warm, smooth belly. He groaned and the sound was like a reward to me. I didn't remove my mouth until I had swallowed every drop.

"How was that?" I asked, wiping my mouth on the back of my right hand.

"Not bad at all," he said, wiping the tip of his cock with his finger and sucking on it.

I replaced my spectacles and sidled back and resumed my drawing and no more was said of it. After he had gone, I masturbated, recalling the taste and the shape of him, hardly able to believe what had occurred. Afterward, I panicked, wondering if

I would ever see him again. A stupid thought, and one that took two generous gin and tonics before its malignancy dissolved.

1998

A friend of yours ran a car hire company near Waterloo Station, buying cars in Holland occasionally and paying friends to fly over and drive them back, because they were cheaper to buy out there, you told me. So we flew over to Amsterdam, you and I. One bright April evening, 1996. (Did I really know you for so short a time? Why does time solidify so easily in the chambers of the heart, taking on the density of stone?) We took a train to Luton Airport, and within two hours we were in the city. You knew Amsterdam well, having lived there for a couple of years. You led me to the city's vivid night-time heart through arteries of sound and light; you found us a room above a bar, a tiny room with a tiny bed. A stained mattress and a pile of sheets folded upon it. We had to make our own bed. And lie in it.

We went out, smoked a few joints, had some food, cruised a few of the bars. At the Blue Boy there was an amateur strip competition and the prize was a bottle of champagne. You entered, and as you climbed up onto the tiny stage in the corner some tacky disco tune burst into life. I laughed and you started to move.

You were wearing, I remember, a tight black cap-sleeved T-shirt and faded jeans. And bit by bit you revealed your perfect body. The champagne was yours, and after downing it we went somewhere else and you bought a balloon filled with nitrous oxide from behind the bar, and we inhaled it, talking in squeaks and laughing, getting high. We scored some ecstasy. We played around in a few of the dark rooms. You dared me to take a turn in the sling that hung from four chains in the middle of the playroom. The room was full of men having sex, but no one as yet was in the sling. I rose to the challenge and climbed in, already naked. Slowly, men gathered around and watched you fuck me. One after another they pushed their cocks into my mouth, pinched on my nipples, caressed me. I was drowning in a sea of touch. You withdrew and someone else stepped up and pushed into me, then another, and another. Someone—you?—began working me with your fingers. The drugs made everything suddenly unreal. I submitted to the fiction of what was happening. Pain intensified and twisted itself into pleasure, turning back into pain and then exploding into fireworks of intensity that held me aloft in their momentary bursts. I felt myself turn into something animal as I moved beyond thought and into the white heat of pure sensation, my body saturating my capacity for reason, my groans feral and untamed. I floated on a cloud of steaming flesh, lost to everything but that moment of blissful and precarious existence, suspended on your forearm.

Eventually we went back to that tiny, tiny room with that tiny, tiny bed and fucked into another dimension.

Sometimes, when the body is taken, taken elsewhere, by someone else's body, sometimes it can create a sense of euphoria so strong that the mouth ceases to utter anything approaching sense. The words *I love you*, spoken at such a moment, can be fatal. Perhaps this is a law of physics, I don't know. All I know is that I said it, I moaned it, I rolled it around my mouth like candy-sugar and it tasted just as sweet. I gasped it, I whispered it, till tears stung my eyes, as your body pressed into mine with the force of a miracle. I actually felt I was being taken possession of, and I was happy to belong to you. I didn't stand a fucking chance.

I lay beside you for the very last time, deliberately staying awake so I could watch you sleep, watch that face without fear of being caught staring. It was serene. And so was I. I spooned up next to you and slept with your cock's warm fragility in my hand. I had a dream that I was in my bed back at home in King's Cross, asleep on my front. In the dream, I am woken by the sounds of someone breaking into the flat, and, though I am suddenly wide awake in the dream, I don't move. I can hear heavy footsteps stomping across the kitchen floor toward my bedroom door, which is directly behind me. The door handle turns and still I don't move. Somehow I know that I am about to die, and somehow I welcome it with a quiet and paralysing resignation.

The following morning, red-eyed and thin-skinned, we sat and had coffee before getting on the train to reach the town from where we were to pick up the cars. I can't even remember the town's name. The woman serving us had cropped red hair, thickly kohl-rimmed eyes, a face as cracked as arid earth, teeth like a horse. We were the only customers, and as she made our coffees, a cigarette hanging from the corner of her mouth, she said, "You don't mind this, do you?"—gesturing to the cigarette, from which hung a lobe of ash. Her voice was a deep unfiltered rasp. We shook our heads. "These Americans, they moan about the cigarettes. I say, why come to Amsterdam if you don't like the smoke?"

We laughed. Exchanged a glance.

"And these English girls, they speak like little girls, in squeaky baby voices." She squeaked away, her mouth turned down in mockery, her eyes turned up. The ash dropped, missing one of the coffee cups by the force of my will. She handed us the coffees and proceeded to entertain us with her impersonations of tourists of all nationalities, bemoaning the crowding of her home town. We were both glad of this distraction, I think.

"It's all the year round now. Used to be, there was the season, and then peace. But now, it never ends." She crushed her cigarette out in a large metal ashtray with a violence that matched her bitter mood. We agreed that London was the same. I saw a woman when I first arrived in London wearing a badge that said "I Am Not a Tourist." Cities change. They are malleable. That's why they are cities. The energy comes from the people, like oxygen travelling through blood.

She invited us to have a shot of some liqueur, some Dutch speciality. She poured out three measures of the thick liquid and we necked it. You rolled a joint and we left Lotte Lenya to her day.

We sat at a bus stop near the train station, smoking the joint, a cramped silence between us. I don't think either of us knew where to begin, or, even if we did, where it would take us. The sun was shining, and a hurdy-gurdy was playing and the trams slid past each other in graceful choreography. The canal rustled by at our feet. I looked at you and knew that there was no way I could repeat the words *I love you* without the security of last night's oblivion. But I wish now that I had. With what was about to happen, I wish I had, for there was, I now realize, nothing to lose.

We got off the train at some small, flat, regulated town, trees in straight lines along geometric streets free of litter. You had all the information, all the documentation. You'd done this trip before. I never asked who with. I just followed you as you strode into the car showroom, sat while you talked to someone, signed my name where you told me to, took the keys you held out to me, got in the car and started the engine. You got in the other car and drove off. I followed you. I've already told the police all of this. I have no more details than this. I'm sorry. I was stoned. I was in love. I don't remember much. I do remember that the only CD in my car was R.E.M.'s *Out of Time*. I listened to it over and over during that long drive, following your car as if I were playing a video game. *Trying to keep an eye on you*. Like a hurt, lost, and blind poor fool. We stopped by the side of the road a couple of times and smoked some more weed. What can I say? It was a smooth, enjoyable, uneventful drive. The motorway sped beneath us, all the way through Holland and France, like huge grey wings bearing us along. I nearly lost you once or twice, nearly killed myself overtaking a long vehicle in order to keep your tail lights in sight, trying to keep an eye on you. But by four o'clock, I think it was, we arrived at Calais. We drove onto the ferry. We ate a forgettable meal. I do remember how happy I was, how fucking happy I felt. Happy as a lunatic. I even entertained the thought that you might be falling in love with me.

At Dover, we drove off the ferry. We had been smoking since about eight that morning. It was now about eight o'clock at night.

The white cliffs looked like the surface of the moon, pocked with blue shadows. I think back to that moment, that moment at Dover when I last saw you, and I wish I could remember the last thing you said to me. It was probably something inane like, "See you back in London." Something like that. Something utterly forgettable. I know it can't have been anything worth remembering, otherwise I would have, but I wish I could remember nonetheless. I think I might find comfort in it, sucking on the words as a man dying of thirst might suck on a wet rag.

I've had time to think about it all. But there isn't enough time to make sense of any of it. There'll never be enough time to make sense of any of it. Did you know? Did you receive a call as we left Dover telling you the police were on to us? Did you drive off deliberately without warning me? Or did I simply lose you? Tiredness was beginning to set in at this stage. All I remember is losing sight of the taillights and putting my foot down to try and catch up with your car. Then suddenly there were police sirens behind me and flashing lights in the rear-view mirror, the car's interior lighting up as they caught up with me, the headlights in the mirror momentarily blinding me. Of course I pulled over—I had no idea the car was packed with the finest cannabis money can buy. I thought I'd get a caution or a speeding fine at the most. So what if I had lost you? I knew the way to London, knew where we were going. So I wound down the window. Did you drive off so that only I would get caught? Did you save your own skin? Did you care at all what happened to me? Have you ever thought about that night, about my fate since last you saw me? I'll never have answers, and I'm sick to death of the questions, but they can still keep me awake all night.

I guess the police could tell straight away that I was completely mashed. Eyes albino-pink like a lab rat. And the fact that I had so little information about anything relating to the trip must have added to their suspicion. Moreover, my nervousness at my own lack of information must have made it look like I was hiding something. I must have appeared guilty as sin. I retrace those few minutes before they opened the boot, and I find there the logic that makes it all fall into place. Why did I never mention you, never try and phone you to get you to explain? I still have no answers other than the ones that tear and destroy, and I cannot live with those. I got two years. I've had eighteen months to map out the geography that led me here. And still I wish someone would spell it out for me. Still I wish I knew I'd see your face again. Perhaps greater strength lies in the broken places. As I said, this is an old story. I'm not sure what it means, but it comes nonetheless, this stream of words. With its emergence begins the long journey of forgetting you.

1895

This evening I went for a walk around Piccadilly Circus and Soho for the last time. I've decided to leave London, and I wanted one more look at the old place. A thick smog had descended over the city like a shroud, a peculiar London smell of smoke and rain. The gas lamps hovered like jack-o'-lanterns. I made my way up Shaftesbury Avenue and into Wardour Street in the darkness of the badly lit thoroughfares. Several cafés flared with red gaslights, and as I passed them, I could feel the clouds of warm close air, reeking with tobacco and sour beer.

It was getting late and all the shops were shut except for the fish shops selling fried fish, mussels, and potatoes, throwing out a smell of dirt, grease, and hot oil, which mingled with the stench of the gutters and that of the cesspools in the middle of the streets. The mist was a fur that had grown on the still air like mould on bread, and I wore it like a coat, wrapped it around my shoulders as if I could take it with me anywhere. As I walked, I could barely see my hand in front of my face, but still they were out in force, all the painted, swishing boys peppering the fog with their jagged voices. I could hear them, even if I couldn't see them.

"Like a baby's arm it was, Doris, a baby's arm holding an apple!"

"Christ, it's colder than a witch's titty out here."

"Why not bugger off 'ome then, Mary?"

"She won't budge. It's the only time she has any luck, when they can't see her face!"

Orange cigarette ends glowed and danced, and I could hear horses' hooves nearby and stopped to avoid being run over. All of Soho was thronged with city life. I could hear drunken men rowing with their sluts and half-starved children singing obscene songs.

I made my way to one of my old haunts in Frith Street and was surprised to find it still open, so I stopped in for one for old times' sake. I must have known every bastard in there, but not one of them returned my nod, and when the bar tart wouldn't serve me I left in a temper, wanting desperately to punch someone. I'm glad I'm leaving tomorrow.

1954

I am losing him. I know it. I have lost him. I have precipitated that which I most feared. It's never enough, is it? You always have to grab for more, taking what isn't yours and in the process losing what is.

I wanted a kiss.

I wanted him to kiss me.

Bloody fool.

This was something we never did. After that first time, sucking him had become a regular occurrence. Gore would get an erection and I would put down my drawing and sidle over. But today when he got hard, I didn't stir. Didn't respond on cue. Instead, I carried on drawing, sketching his phallus as rapidly as I could. Neither of us said anything, until he asked, "Don't yer want to suck it, then?"

I paused, my mouth suddenly dry. Our eyes met.

"On one condition, Gore."

"What?" he said warily.

"That you let me kiss you."

He thought about it. If I had shocked him, he didn't show it. His face was expressionless. His eyes held mine and I saw that familiar contempt grow. "All right," he said.

I put down my drawing and shuffled over there as if I'd lost the use of my legs.

When I'd finished, with his sperm still fresh in my mouth, I raised my face to his and kissed him, pushing my tongue deep between his reluctant lips. And even though I could sense immediately that every cell in his body was recoiling in horror, I continued, exploring that sweet, sweet mouth. Perhaps I should have kissed him first, while he was still aroused, before his desire had been satiated. Perhaps then the added horror of tasting his own seed might not have contributed to that revulsion. Or perhaps I am repulsive, and would have provoked the same response even had I done so. That uncertainty is something I will have to live with, I suppose. But I know that I wanted to punish him for that repulsion, for not being able even to hide it. I wanted to make him suffer at our intimacy the way I suffered at its absence.

All his previous affection toward me scurried away, like a receding tide of bed lice when the sheet is pulled back. I knew straight away that things had changed. The air in the studio was not the same air. It stank of rejection, loneliness, and age. *My* rejection, *my* loneliness, *my* age. Foolish to think that the affection could ever have been equal or reciprocated. Foolish to think that I would be any different from any of the others. Except I wasn't even paying; I wasn't offering the one thing that would have made such an act bearable. Or not paying enough, at any rate. What I had done wasn't included in the one pound I paid him. I could tell instantly that some boundary had been transgressed, some invisible mark overstepped. I had done something unforgivable. I knew I'd probably never see him again.

He left, after some stilted, polite conversation over lunch. The usual spark was missing as we chatted, and we were barely able to meet each other's gaze. Once I'd shut the front door on him, I went upstairs and sat in the studio, in the spot where we had kissed, and I masturbated, my hurried drawing of his erect penis by my side. I didn't take my eyes off it. Even after reaching my climax, my gaze remained transfixed, and I didn't move my head until the tears became too unbearable.

With my head in my hands and my limp prick still hanging out, I sobbed the bitterness away to make more room for my grief.

It took me a few hours to decide to go around to see him. It took me another hour and two double gin and tonics before I rang and spoke to his landlady, a Scottish woman who told me Gore wasn't in. I drained my glass, grabbed my jacket and keys, and ran out of the door.

I took a cab to the Lord Barrymore. I was too drunk to be nervous, so I strolled in and ordered a drink. The landlord served me, and he remembered me from last time and asked how it had gone at the police station, or the "nick," as he called it. I said it was all fine in the end, and asked if he'd seen Gore tonight. He didn't know who I meant, and when I said it was the young man I'd been with last time he said, "Oh, you mean Gracie? She was in here earlier, but she's gone now. God knows where. She's a one." And he gave a dirty laugh. It seems he has female names for all the regulars. "She owe you money?"

I assured him he didn't.

"Makes a change."

Just then, I heard a voice behind me say, "Hello, duckie. Mr Read, isn't it?"

I turned to find the old man we'd met last time. I said, "Hello, Jack."

"Couldn't buy us a drink, could you, Mr Read? Only I'm nanti-handbag."

"Sorry?"

"Flat broke. I'll have a G and T, ta very much. A large one."

I got him the drink.

"You're a gent," he said with a grin, before taking a slurp. I wondered how I could extricate myself without sounding impolite. I didn't want to exchange small talk with him, I wanted to find Gore.

"Looking for Gregory?" he asked. I said I was. I'd got so used to calling him Gore that it was a shock to hear his real name.

Jack gestured for me to follow him and we sat at a table. "He's not here."

"I know."

"You're in love with him, aren't you?"

I was taken aback, but I stuttered, "Yes."

"Poor bastard."

"Sorry?"

He took another slurp of his drink. "Old men fall in love with whores all the time. You're not the first, an' you won't be the last."

"But this is different."

"That's what they all say."

"I'm not a client. I'm an artist. Gore models for me."

"Same difference, once love's made an appearance. But as they say, there's no fool like an old fool."

I didn't need to be lectured. I didn't want to hear what he had to say, however well-intentioned. I asked him if he knew where Gore was, and he said Gore had told him he was heading back home.

"But who knows?" he said. "The young are so capricious."

I left the pub and took a cab to King Street, just around the corner from Gore's road. It was a quiet street, narrow and tree-less. I scouted around for a public telephone and found one. I rang the house again and asked if Gore was at home. No, he wasn't back yet. I walked back to King Street and found a pub and fortified my nerve with another gin and tonic. Back at his house I hung around in the shadows on the opposite side of the street, feeling like an incompetent spy. Scared that I might be arrested, wondering what on earth I thought I was doing there, what on earth I thought I would do when I saw him.

It was a full moon, I remember. It crossed my mind that I'd gone insane, that the bone-white face studding the midnight-blue sky had hypnotized me and made me do this. That it was out of my hands now, my fate. This is how men lose their reason: for love, or desire. I'm not the first and I won't be the last. There was nothing I could do but embrace this insanity. I pictured myself in a straitjacket, explaining my actions in a babble that made no sense, my voice a series of yelps and stutters, my speech reduced to total gibberish. I pictured myself behind bars, catching flies and swallowing them whole. Amongst the staff I will be known as the Flycatcher.

At that moment Gore walked around the corner into the street-light. I sensed him more than saw him, like the immediate presence of danger. I walked out from the shadows and into the moon's blue, still not sure what on earth I intended to say. He froze momentarily then continued toward the house, toward me. He nodded in recognition and said calmly, "Wotcha?"

"Is there somewhere we can go?" I asked. "Somewhere we can talk?"

"Sure," he said nonchalantly, as if nothing were amiss in my being here, requesting this. As if it were a regular occurrence.

He turned around and walked back into King Street. I followed.

He took me back to the pub I'd just been in. I'd been hoping for somewhere quieter. It was about half past nine, and people were sufficiently inebriated for there to be a loud level of noise: arguments, laughter, singing, shouting, all as impenetrable as the smoke hanging in the air. We managed to find a seat, and I bought a round of drinks. I made mine a double, and ordered two, knocking one back before I left the bar to return to Gore. I had no idea what I was going to say to him. No plan of action. No strategy. I simply knew I couldn't just let him walk out of my life, though I think I must have also known that nothing was more likely to encourage him to leave than to do exactly what I was doing.

I returned with the drinks and sat down opposite him at a small round table.

"Cheers," he said, offering his pint glass for me to chink. Bonhomie.

I think I started to say something like, "About today—"only he had already begun with, "I can only have the one. I'm off tomorrow, early, so I can't stay long." My words were cut off brutally by the edge in his voice, and what I had been about to say now lay slain at my feet.

"Off where?" I stammered.

"Dublin."

He took a sip of his beer, wiping off the moustache of froth with the back of his hand before saying, "I've a cousin there, reckons he can get me a job. I've had enough of London. I've got itchy feet. It's the Romany blood in my veins, isn't it?"

"I believe Dublin to be a wonderful city." I hated myself even as the words were coming out.

"That it is." He nodded. "Although it's years since I've been."

"Might I write to you there?" Had I no shame?

"I can't remember the address right now. I'll write to you with it as soon as I can."

His eyes darted away from mine, breaking the promise even as it was being made. When did he decide this?

"You didn't mention anything today."

"I spoke to him on the telephone this morning. I was going to tell you this afternoon, only..." He broke off. Only what? What words would he have chosen to describe what had happened? What version of events had he fabricated into his truth? How did he see it, how did he see *me*?

"You don't need to go. Not on account of... me."

"I was thinking of moving on anyway. Been here too long. You know how it is."

No, I don't. I don't know how it is. This city is my home. I could never think of leaving it. I have hardly ever left it. And it has never left me. But I nodded, as if I understood perfectly his sudden desire to get away from me.

There was a long silence during which he sipped his beer and looked at the floor. I gulped my gin and tonic and looked at him.

Or rather through him. I said, "You were just going to disappear, weren't you? You weren't going to let me know."

"Of course I was."

"I don't believe you, Gore."

"I *was*."

"I don't expect you to love me or anything. But, we get on, don't we? It must mean something, what we have? Doesn't it? Our friendship, doesn't it mean—"

"Forget it. It's nothing to do with that." He drained his glass and slammed it down. "*Friendship*," he said, mockingly. He stood up, pulling his jacket closed. "I'm off."

I recalled Billy and how I'd banished him to the wasteland in a similar manner, cavalier, cruel, perhaps the only way such rejection can be executed—with honesty. Short, sharp, like an executioner's axe. I thought about all the drawings I had done of Gore, like tiny ghosts, waiting back at home to haunt me. I thought about living for the rest of my life without seeing him again. I thought of my future without him in it, and all light drained from my vision. My future shrank to the size and colour of a full stop.

I followed him out of the pub into the empty street. He turned around and told me to go home. I begged him to stop walking. He wouldn't.

I caught up with him, and he barked at me, "Fuck off! Leave me alone!"

He shrugged me away, and, a trifle unsteady, I think I grabbed for him. He must have pushed me for I suddenly lost my balance completely. A bank of pain hit my body.

I was on my hands and knees, howling after his retreating back, howling his name, lost to my grief. House lights were coming on, heads appearing from out of windows. I could hear someone screaming and wondered what they were screaming for. I then realized it was I who was screaming. Someone shouted for me to stop.

I stopped.

I managed to stand and looked in Gore's direction. He was nowhere to be seen. I was disoriented. I turned around and started walking, my vision colliding with itself. I didn't even think about hailing a cab. I just walked, head down, through the streets, across the bridge, making my way back to Barnes on unsteady feet. In the invisible city through which I walked that night, I don't recall seeing a single soul. The rest of the human race, the *living* world, had slid into another dimension. I moved as if through water. I cried, and the rain that started gently to fall as I walked felt like an amplification of my sorrow. I cried till I felt better for having shed my grief. The rain became heavier and heavier as I walked, and by the time I reached home it felt as if my tears had soaked me entirely and washed me clean, and I was strangely joyous. *Reborn*, if that doesn't sound ridiculous. Birth would be a moment of absolute panic if we but knew it consciously, our emergence into a world about which we know nothing, about which we have everything to learn. Thankfully, we have no consciousness of our lack of knowledge either. Along with everything else, that is something we must learn. Perhaps some of us never learn. But I felt something akin to that panic as I peeled off my sodden clothes, and it felt strangely good, because in that shivering moment of uncertainty lay the possibility of something else, some other life. I think I even laughed before collapsing onto my bed and passing out.

1998

I must have momentarily dozed off, sinking into a brief, but deep, sleep. And I dreamt of you, spinning like a distant star, with the night sky purpling behind you. We are on the roof, high above the city, and you are dancing like a dervish, foolish and fearless, teetering on the edge of a wall, above a drop that would kill were you to trip and fall. It's a summer's evening, which is strange because I never knew you in summer. The air is furred with heat, and music is throbbing its way across to us in steady waves from Bagley's Warehouse, where, half an hour earlier, you pushed me against the sweating wall of the toilet cubicle and kissed me, crushing your mouth onto mine as the first rush of cocaine took effect (the taste of it is still in my throat). Within seconds we were fucking, right there, soundless and intense, making of our bodies a new depth of feeling, our pleasure spilling out in tiny, almost inaudible grunts of whispered, sighed, and gasped delight. Quick, urgent, as if nothing else mattered. I suppose nothing else did.

We left the club and walked back to mine, arms across each other's shoulders, sweat cooling in the summer air. We stopped to give a prostitute a cigarette on the corner of my road. Then we climbed the stairs up to the roof, the city spread out before us in fluid constellations of light, like stars reflected in a river. The sky above us was dark and immense, St Pancras menacing behind us like some beast crouching in the shadows. You climbed up onto the flat roof of the stairwell, precariously close to the edge, and started to dance. I see stars around you and I fear for your life as you spin on the lip of the drop, but your eyes and your smile as they meet mine say it all.

Love isn't meant to stand still.

Skin has a memory all its own. Mnemonic flesh, store-room of all experience. Fingerprints stored, traces of lips indelible, epidermic recollections of the hands and lips and teeth that have marked it, surfacing to annihilate, barely visible, a palimpsest that will not, cannot forget, that cannot be erased, despite age and soap and usurpers, a Braille of recollections: the warm trickle of your piss still licking across a nipple, your spit still dampening my chin, your dried cum still cracking like plaster on my belly, pulling hairs exquisitely; your kisses still in my teeth; your tongue still feeding between my buttocks, crawling lower and lower. Your cock warm and heavy on my knee as you suck me. The hair on your belly crackling against my forehead as I suck you. The storm of you against my body, inside my body. Your hands in my hair. Your hot heat upon me. Because of you, my body is the site of miracles, and my skin remembers as fiercely as my heart tries to forget.

It's morning. I can hear the screws approaching, banging on the doors one by one to wake us up. The prison comes to life. Tony stirs in the bunk beneath me. I suppose some people would say this is the first day of the rest of my life, or something inane like that. Some people would talk about "closure" or some such bullshit. A "window of opportunity." Fuck that. I'm still in pain. I'm still angry. I still love you. Where's the closure in that? I am locked inside this pain. Is that closure? I am broken.

I think about Gregory, who is coming to meet me at eleven o'clock outside the prison gates, to drive me home—his home, not mine. I am homeless. I have lost everything. And we will drive back to Gregory's home, where, above the mantelpiece in the living room, hangs a drawing of him as a young man. A drawing by some artist he modelled for and befriended in the mid-'50s, who had some success late in life. "I've hung in the Tate," he told me the first time I was there, and he showed me a catalogue of some exhibition of this guy's work from the late '50s. Three paintings. A triptych. *London Triptych 1956. Oil on canvas. Each 950 x 735mm. Colin Read (1900–1975).* None of the images is recognisably a young Gregory; they're in all sorts of strange contortions and poses, the head tucked into the curlicues of his body. But he was clearly proud of them. I have since heard the story of that episode in his life, as I have heard, by now, most of his stories. He showed me a small, tatty black-and-white photograph of him as a young man, bequiffed and smiling, with his arm around an older man.

"That's Colin," he said.

"Were you and he lovers?" I asked.

He paused, before shaking his head and taking back the photo and placing it back on the mantelpiece, and I had the feeling the question had thrown him somewhere he didn't want to go.

The first time we met he explained the scenario he wanted

with me. I was to pose nude while he drew me, but at some point I was to get a hard-on. Then he was to suck me off. While he was sucking me, I sneaked a look at the picture he had been drawing of me, and was astonished to see a simple stick man, no better than a child's. Although I'm not exactly sure what else I was expecting.

I've grown very fond of Gregory. I don't know how it will work out, us living together, but I can imagine a worse situation, certainly. He hadn't been a client of mine for a while at the time I was sentenced, so I don't imagine he'll expect sex. Although if he were to, I know that's one way I can repay him. I've learnt that much. His kindness is more than I feel I deserve. Who knows what his motivations are?

Perhaps he's lonely. Perhaps he's fallen in love with me. I'm just grateful for somewhere to stay.

As I watch Tony get up and grunt his good morning while he pisses, I think about the holding cell beneath the Old Bailey, that tiny room in which I stood with seven others that morning before my trial. I had no idea what was in store for me. All I felt was that my immediate future had been stolen. It seems, now, like a lifetime ago, and I feel, strangely, as close to you as ever. Perhaps these words have done that—kept you close. Four of the seven men in there with me had come straight from prison, on remand. One of them had just been given fifteen years for armed robbery. He sat there, in the corner, sobbing. I read the graffiti on the walls. "If you get out of here take my advice be good." Afterward, we were led single-file outside to the sweatboxes, where each of us stood up in his own box, so small that I was in agony the entire journey to Wandsworth, shifting my weight from side to side, my chin nearly touching my chest.

I think about that first night in prison. In a room with three other men. I'd never in my life been so terrified. But once I started to talk to them I found that they were easy to get on with, not scary at all. I didn't tell anyone I was gay, but I guess I didn't have to. It didn't take long before I was being hit on, made to do things. You once told me that I looked as if I was always up for it. As a whore, that was an advantage; in here, I'm not so sure. Even if I'd been straight they would've come for me, I guess. I discovered pretty quickly what a high premium I had, and was adopted by a series of seriously dangerous men. None of whom I'll ever see again. I've done as much whoring in here as I did outside. In here it was all about survival. If I wasn't HIV-positive before, I undoubtedly am now. I'm so underweight right now that you'd hardly recognize me, but that might be the shit food. I can't wait for my first decent meal.

I think about you. Where you are now. Whether I'll see you again. What I'd say if I did. What lies before you is my past. This is for you, Jake, to make of what you will. There may be a logic to it yet, though I have failed so far to find it. And as I climb out of bed and begin to dress, anxious about the freedom that is soon to be mine, I remember the time I told you that you were amazing and you replied, "No, I'm not. I'm mean." Should I have taken that as a warning? Should I have stayed away?

Love isn't meant to stand still.

1895

Oscar always said he preferred women with a past and men with a future. From now on, I'm going to try to live without either. I'm on a train rattling its smoky way to Manchester. I don't know for sure why I chose that city, but it seemed as good a place as any to start a new life. Perhaps I'll bump into Walter there. All I know is I can't live in London any more.

This morning I went to see my ma and give her some money, and tell her I'm leaving. She said, "Are you in trouble, Jack?" It seems she hasn't heard a thing about the trials, thank God. I said I was just visiting a friend. Gave her and the little ones a hug and left.

But as London recedes behind me like a lover I'm leaving behind, I can't stop thinking about what the bleedin' hell I'm going to do when I get there. I don't know a bloody soul there except Walter, and have no fuckin' idea where to find him. I'll start at the Post Office, I suppose; surely they have need of 'gram boys in Manchester. And failing that there's always renting. There must still be men on this septic isle willing to press a shilling into a lad's hand for the pleasure of tasting his flesh. And as I settle back into my seat, feeling less anxious about what's in store for me, I call to mind a scene at Taylor's when I hardly knew Oscar at all.

We were all in the parlour, with its shadowed and dusty grandeur, its worn and torn flock wallpaper and its worm-eaten furniture, which creaked and groaned under Oscar's weight. Oscar always liked to sit with us, not like the other swells who would pick a boy before they'd finished their drink and often as not decline the drink altogether and simply go upstairs. Oscar would sit and talk for hours before choosing one or two of us to take upstairs. He seemed to enjoy chatting with us more than anything we ever did with our bodies, and he said he loved watching us. He said we were like panthers. Daft bleeder. Most of all, though, he loved to hear stories about what we got up to with the other clients, especially royalty and aristocracy, or anyone well-known. He loved hearing what they liked to do with us and as we got more and more smutty he would laugh even more and clap his hands with glee, like a child. As we joked and cursed he would laugh long and loud. Nothing was too vulgar for him. I remember him once saying to us, "My dear panthers, if only you were running this country, what a joyous place it would be. People would flock here from all over southern Europe to admire how we had managed by some Herculean effort to overcome the most adverse climate and produce a truly Latin temperament. If only we had a government of whores!"

"But we do," said Charlie. "Didn't you know, Mr Wilde, we *do* run this country."

"For sure," I added, "and isn't this the Houses of Parliament you're in right now?"

"It's a little-known fact that no law is passed in this land," continued Charlie, quite taken with the idea and running with it, "no department of state may function, no decision of national importance is ever made without our say-so. All the heads of state consult us; crowned princes defer to our greater wisdom; high court judges and law lords pick our brains on all important matters of state."

And then Walter chipped in with, "Taylor's not just *a* queen, sir, he's *the* Queen."

"Long live the Queen!" cheered Oscar, raising his cracked champagne flute, pinkie aloft, sweaty face split in a fat grin.

"I know no greater pleasure than being with those who are young, bright, happy, careless, and free," he had said in court. "I do not like the sensible and I do not like the old."

I look out of the window to watch dusk unfolding, trying not to think that he has a very different view right now.

1954

I spent the next few days in my bed with a fever, sinking and surfacing, vanishing down long shadowed corridors of nightmares,
corridors with walls that suddenly sprouted other doors, other
corridors, and the floor dropped beneath my feet, or lifted me
higher, or turned to liquid, or sand. I twisted inside sweat-stained
sheets in temperatures that burned into a chill, a chill that ate
at my bones and chewed through my nerves like wires, causing
fires to erupt in my head. I heard voices calling me, taunting me,
caressing me, chastising me. It felt, at times, as if someone had
sneaked in and stolen all of my bones and my flesh lay there like
a wet rag unable to move; at other times every bone in my body
ached as if it had been put back in the wrong place. My eyeballs
were pulled from their sockets and placed on the ceiling above
me so I could view the wild thrashing of my fevered body below.
For what seemed like an eternity I was gnawed by nausea, and
crawled from my bed only to vomit into the white porcelain of
the toilet bowl or empty my burning bowels. The rain had soaked
down to my bones and floored me.

By the third day I felt well enough to go downstairs and make myself a cup of tea.

By the fourth day I felt as I had never felt before in my life. A horizon of possibility beckoned to me and a new fever gripped me: a fever to paint. After a quick wash and a hearty breakfast, I went straight to the studio. I'd been putting it off, I must admit, too preoccupied, I suppose, with other things—too busy thinking about Gore. Love (if that's what it was) is a kind of sickness, clouding perception. I had become totally distracted.

But now, for the first time ever, I feel totally energized and focused to a point as hard and sharp as a cut diamond. I am filling the hollowness I feel with an enthusiasm quite unfamiliar to me. I know not at all where it might be leading me; I am simply placing one foot in front of the other, much like an infant beginning to walk, unsteady but resilient, half-blind but curious. Yesterday I felt like a man about to take an ice-cold plunge; today I feel that being in the water isn't as bad as I'd imagined. I still have all the chaos within, but now I have the time to sift through to its hidden riches without worrying whether I should. I don't know if love and creativity are compatible, nor whether this devastation is part of my fate. But I am strangely exhilarated by my grief. It's liberated me, allowed me to experience things in a way I haven't since I was a child. Everything seems peculiarly vivid, the daylight a sign—though as yet I don't know of what exactly. Through the fog of my headache, I recall last week's events, and already they seem a hundred years ago.

I am driven to give vent to those emotions in a way I never have been before. I feel such intensity I'm scared I might die of it, or I'm scared it might go, or I might not have it in me to express it adequately. My fear and my desire collide and I paint and paint hour after hour in a blur of rapid strokes as if my life depended upon it. Perhaps it does. I have these visions inside, visions of Gore's flesh, glowing like a monstrance, drawing me like a spell. I need to get them out. Perhaps then I will be at peace. These strange, dark, distorted canvases have become some kind of abstract autobiography. Heaven knows what they say about me, but at least they say something. That, at least, is enough.

Each brush stroke charges me, and I don't know if I am still inebriated with fever, but my blood sings to the paint, and the paint sings to my blood, and I have become the air that carries their voices back and forth. I cannot, must not stop now. Not for anything. Not with the fire in me now. I must paint, paint, paint.

Afterword: A Government of Whores

London Triptych started out as a short story entitled "Pornocracy" that I wrote for a competition. I had always been intrigued by the secret histories of male prostitution, and this first attempt gave me the character and voice of Jack Rose. History is all too often seen as something that only people who wield power experience or create; the powerless are seen to lead lives of no consequence. I wanted to see things from the other side: to give voice to the voiceless. I was interested in viewing the Wilde scandal from the perspective of one of the young boys involved, in imagining the lives of these bit-players, this shadowy cohort whose fleeting appearance in the history books fascinated me. Who were these "panthers" with which Wilde "feasted"?

This is the story that has the most historical grounding, in the form of Wilde's life and the detailed accounts of the trials. Alfred Taylor's boyhouse existed at the addresses used here, and much of his personal history is the same; he was convicted along with Wilde, receiving the same sentence. It was, however, also the most difficult to research in terms of the lives of male prostitutes. Their invisibility was the very thing that drew me to them. The transcripts of the Wilde trials were very useful, as was Kellow Chesney's marvellous *The Victorian Underground.* I also relied on the pornography of the time, such as *Teleny,* a book Wilde was supposed to have had a hand in writing. There is no specific historical counterpart to Jack; I took his name from Jack Saul, the narrator of one of the very few homosexual porn novels of the time, *Sins of the Cities of the Plain,* published in 1881. Wilde actually owned a copy of this book, according to Thomas Wright in *Oscar's Books: A Journey through the Library of Oscar Wilde.* So Jack Rose is a fiction; but I wanted him to do what he did out of jealousy: to kill the thing he loved, and perhaps be the inspiration for Wilde's famous refrain.

The short story didn't win the competition, but pretty soon I had embarked on a novel on the same theme. I was keen to explore further than Jack's story alone would allow. I needed other voices from other times, and formed the idea of three lives spaced roughly fifty years apart but overlapping chronologically. It made sense to counterpoint Jack's exploits with a different, more mature voice, so I developed Colin. I knew several older artists who had fascinating stories about gay London in the 1950s and their experiences were invaluable to me, in particular those of the artist George Cayford.

The early '50s saw a great witch-hunt of homosexuals by the British press and the police, which included the arrest of Sir John Gielgud and the imprisonment of the writer Rupert Croft-Cooke (whose 1955 account of his prison experience, *The Verdict of You All,* is a wonderful read), and peaked with the 1954 scandal involving Lord Montagu and Peter Wildeblood as recounted in the latter's book, *Against the Law*. Colin's world view is shaped by that climate of fear. I wanted him to feel imprisoned by society, but to find, ultimately, his own way out. I wanted him to find some kind of salvation, acceptance, and recognition. And I wanted art and love to be the source of those things. Novels from the time, such as Rodney Garland's *The Heart in Exile* and Michael Nelson's *A Room in Chelsea Square*, provided additional inspiration and atmosphere.

These two characters then suggested a third. The work felt incomplete. It called for a more contemporary voice to offset the other two: a modern-day Jack, the voice of a man whose sexual freedoms, whilst having their precedent and forerunner in Jack, were nevertheless the fruits of late-twentieth-century gay liberation. It needed a voice from a more contemporary London, my London. This allowed me to draw from my own experiences of the city, though David's story is by no means my own. I've never been interested in writing autobiography, though I'm aware that most writing is, in some indirect and alchemical sense, autobiographical. I agree with Jeanette Winterson that "there is no such thing as autobiography, there is only art and lies." I like to think I included a bit of both in *London Triptych*. James Joyce's claim that memory is an act of creation resonates with me. Wilde himself said, "Give a man a mask and he will tell you the truth." These are my guiding lights. I think we need to believe more in the powers of fiction, to trust that some kind of truth lies in imagined stories, to believe that—to paraphrase Jean Cocteau—a lie can tell the truth. The modern-day obsession with reality is doing us no good. Wilde, certainly, would have abhorred it. It leads us to believe that there *is* such a thing as reality and that language can represent it accurately. I'm more inclined to think that language makes realit*ies* (in the plural), for better or for worse. Surely this is what storytellers do, fabricate other universes, places governed by different laws.

I'm not a historian, and I didn't want to write history (though some history books, such as Matt Cook's *London and the Culture of Homosexuality, 1885–1914*, were invaluable). I wanted to use history to provide some kind of backdrop for the lives of these three men, and I wanted to use the city almost as a fourth character. As such, the city too needed to change. Jack's London is not Colin's, and David's London is different again. Not simply because our experiences of cities are mostly subjective, but because cities themselves are fluid, impermanent entities, grounded in a historical specificity that is in a permanent state of flux. For me, cities are also profoundly sexual, and that sexuality is caught up in the anonymity they provide. I think there is a great deal of knowledge in the sexual, and it was crucial that this most sidelined and contentious aspect of urban life be central to the stories I was weaving. For Jack the city provides a way of having sex with men without needing to integrate such behaviour into his overall sense of self—and of making a decent enough living at it, too. He is uncomplicatedly libidinal—though there is little about the libido that is truly uncomplicated. Jack represents, I hope, a way of connecting with the body that is freer than, say, Colin's: a form of sexual consciousness that is bold and blunt, not shackled by psychology, nor by religious or bourgeois morality, all of which he has mercifully escaped, though he ends up as their victim, nevertheless. I reintroduced him within Colin's narrative because

I was interested in imagining how he would change as he grew older.

By comparison, Colin represents all that is destructive about the morality surrounding homosexuality—a morality that exists not only in the shape of his parents (as superego), but also in the form of the police and doctors and other people in his social group. For him, the city is a place to scavenge for visual scraps to be soaked up and used to populate his masturbation fantasies. For him Gore represents the antithesis of what he has come to expect from life, a kind of sexual freedom unimaginable to him. Like Jack, Gore is a mirror in which we see our own desires. Through Gore, Colin discovers another London, one that unsettles him as much as it fascinates him.

For David, the city represents escape. Like many gay men of my generation who grew up in the provinces, London reeked of freedom and decadence, standing as a beacon toward which we all made our merry way, like children dancing in a line behind the Pied Piper. The appeal was primarily, for me at least, that of anonymity—not just in terms of the sex available, but in terms of confronting and constructing one's self. One could be anonymous in London—in any big city—in a way that is unthinkable in a small town; one could wipe the slate clean and start anew if one wanted to. David's journey, like the journey of the ego, is one of negotiating the physical world and assessing one's place within it. I wanted it to be clear that he has learnt something from that journey, even if he fails, as yet, to see exactly what that lesson might be.

Wilde's life and work became a governing principle as I worked on the novel. I incorporated and adapted events from his life into the narrative. For example, Wilde's mother died during his incarceration, so I killed off David's mother not long after he is imprisoned. All the words attributed to Wilde are mine, apart from one line. David's story uses the second person—is addressed to the boy who was his downfall—in order to evoke *De Profundis*, Wilde's prison letter to Lord Alfred Douglas. I like the way it appeals to a singular recipient, a single reader—though in this case one who will never lay eyes upon it. And, of course, just like *The Picture of Dorian Gray*, a painting is at the heart of the story: representation as the embodiment of erotic thought. One of the games I've enjoyed playing whilst writing the novel is to scatter echoes and nods throughout the three narratives. Nods not just to one another, but also to Wilde's life and work.

I tried to incorporate certain constants in the three narratives. As well as the city, there is the law. The police play a part in all three stories, as they have in the lives of many gay men. Love is another constant, as is sex. Indeed, the two are the most tightly bound themes of the book. Whilst I concur with Foucault that the truth is never to be found in sex, the truth of sex is one that is often overlooked in our panicky rush to categorise and moralise. I was attempting to write about gay sex in new ways, ways more in line with writers such as Georges Bataille or Kathy Acker, or Neil Bartlett and Samuel R. Delany, where sex can become an opportunity to explore subjectivity and sometimes language.

I wrote the three narratives as separate stories—even separate files—but I knew pretty much as I worked through them where the breaks would be. Each one was episodic. It was just easier to manage that way. But they each had an almost identical dramatic arc, so that when they were intertwined they would peak and fall at roughly the same time in the overall narrative curve of the novel. What came across on reading it through for the first time after I had plaited the three narratives together were the many other ways the three voices echoed one another. Jack's story ends with him travelling from London to Manchester, whilst David's begins with the reverse journey. Having Jack reappear in Colin's strand, and then Gore reappear in David's, was not something I had planned from the start. It came late, as did the title. But once I had decided on it I enjoyed working out how it would manifest, how these characters would be as older men. In setting up Jack and Gore's reappearances as old men, I wanted to open a space for also imagining David as an old man, as someone different again from the person we meet in the pages of his narrative. Our lives as gay men are not necessarily scripted to the level of straight people—we don't tend to have children (though this is changing), and we tend to organize our sexual and personal lives very differently—and one thing I was trying to do was to imagine the lives of older gay men in ways that enable us to write our own scripts.

For all three men, their experience of London is, essentially, one of liberation. I repeated some locations to give a sense of different memories, different events, occurring within or upon the same geographical site, such as Highgate Cemetery or Barnes Common. The three men's lives unfold in tandem, as if simultaneously, transcending concrete time. It is, in that sense, very much a triptych.

Acknowledgments

Special thanks to my family for their constant love and support. To all my gorgeous friends for their years of encouragement and humour, and for never doubting I'd get there in the end, especially: Michael Atavar, Darius Amini, John Lee Bird, Helen Boulter, Pippa Brooks, George Cayford, Matthew Fennemore, Johnny Golding, Lucien Gouiran, Sally Gross, Hally, Gerry Hislop, James Killough, Louise Lambe, Sadie Lee, Clayton Littlewood, David Male, Steve Muscroft, Joe Pop, Clive Reeve, Chris Rose, Matthew Stradling, Sue Smallwood, Roy Woolley. Many thanks to Jim MacSweeney and Uli Lenart at Gay's the Word bookshop. Extracts from *London Triptych* appeared in *Chroma Journal* and *Polari Journal* (*polarijournal.com*). Many thanks to Shaun Levin and Pema Baker, the respective editors of those two publications. Thanks to Jake Arnott and Neil Bartlett.

Endless gratitude to my literary agent, Adrian Weston; Candida Lacey, Vicky Blunden, and Corinne Pearlman at Myriad Editions. And to Linda McQueen for her amazing copy-editing skills.

About the author

Jonathan Kemp lives in London, UK, where he currently teaches creative writing and comparative literature at Birkbeck College. *London Triptych*, his first novel, was published in the UK in 2010 and won the Authors' Club Best First Novel Award. His second book, *Twentysix*, was published in the UK in 2011 and his third, *Because We Must*, is forthcoming.